CLAY PEOPLE

ALSO BY THE SAME AUTHOR

The Simian Curve

Execution Only

CLAY PEOPLE

MARK LALBEHARRY

CHAPTER 1

Ray Maynard was fifty-two years old and homeless. He had been homeless since his early forties, following the breakdown of his marriage and the loss of his job. Those things were distant memories now, memories which came back to him vividly sometimes, when he didn't have alcohol to blur his senses.

Finding food wasn't a problem. He had been on the streets for so long he knew where all the soup kitchens and canteens were. In winter he knew the best places to find shelter, but now that the weather was becoming warmer he had decided to look for somewhere new to stay.

He knew about the old hospital in Acton. It was still owned by the local trust, but it had stood disused for more than a year before the demolition crew had moved in. They had closed off the area, erecting high wooden fencing before demolishing the buildings.

Not all the buildings had been pulled down however. Several at the rear of the site had been left intact, much to Maynard's surprise. He had watched as the wrecking crew packed up and left, sealing off the area with a padlock and chain across the main gates.

The gates were nearly eight feet high – too high for Maynard to scale, but he knew that there was another way on to the land. The back of the nine-acre site bordered on to woods which were frequently used as a dumping ground. Here the wooden fencing was replaced with wire-mesh, and Maynard knew of a break, allowing access.

It was late on Monday evening when he crept on to the site. He had with him a small rucksack containing food, whisky and a tightly rolled-up sleeping bag. He was planning to stay in one of the remaining buildings. He wasn't sure how long he'd be able to stay for. In any case he'd have the place to himself, if only for a short while. He wouldn't have to worry about sharing his space. It wouldn't be like living in the shelter – the coughing, the shouting, the disagreements over alcohol or drugs. He'd have peace and quiet.

The ground was covered with footprints and tyre marks. Streetlights in the distance illuminated the yard. Maynard knew his way around, having seen it in daylight. There were large piles of rubble where buildings once stood. Everything was neatly ordered, with piles of bricks squared off.

He made for the ground floor of the largest remaining building. The door had been secured with a padlock, but a window to one side was smashed. Maynard carefully climbed through. Once inside, he took out a torch and turned it on. He was in a room next to the main corridor. It looked like an office. He didn't linger, and made his way along the corridor. There were numerous small rooms. One looked like a laboratory. He decided to go up to the second floor, and that was when he heard noise.

In the distance he could hear a dragging sound. He stopped. Something was definitely being moved. Maynard felt curiosity and then fear. The only light came from his torch, and he thought about turning it off.

The dragging was coming from close by. The corridor was L-shaped, and he suspected it was coming from the next wing.

He lowered the torch and slowly moved towards the bend. He paused, debating what to do and listened.

Something was *definitely* moving.

Maynard thought he could hear breathing. Should he leave? No, he didn't want to do that. This was his place. He intended to stay for as long as he could.

He decided to confront whoever was there. He steadied himself. He rounded the corner and saw a large figure in the distance. It was pulling something. Maynard lowered the torch and saw plastic sheeting. He was filled with fear as he saw pale flesh wrapped up inside. He saw arms and legs, and then a head.

.   .   .

Seconds passed and Maynard remained still. He turned and ran. He dropped his rucksack as he looked for the way out.

All the offices had windows, but he had to find an open one.

He was aware of someone behind him. The person he had disturbed was following. Maynard felt fear and shock. He turned to his right and went into an office. He saw a window on the far wall but it was shut.

Panic seized Maynard. He turned back and slammed the door. He turned the catch, and seconds later there was a thud.

He held the door and tried to focus. He shone his torch along the base of the window and saw a latch. He made for it and pushed the window up. The drop below was less than six feet. Maynard felt relief and forced himself through.

He hit the ground and could see the sweep of the yard. Behind him he could hear a splintering sound.

Maynard ran towards the break in the perimeter fence. He found the damaged section and ducked down. The top of his coat caught on something and he was pulled to a halt. Seconds passed, and he bent low, trying to release himself. That was when he felt a hand on his back.

Fear spiked. Maynard could hear breathing and a ripping sound.

Frantic with terror, he bent to the ground, and there was another ripping sound as he broke free. He struggled forward, moving through undergrowth until he could see the main road.

The road was less than twenty yards away, and cars were moving at speed. He glanced back and saw a person.

Without thinking, Maynard ran into the road. A horn sounded, and a car swerved.

Ray Maynard was hit and thrown across the carriageway.

CHAPTER
2

At Homicide West headquarters, in central London, the incident room was quiet. Detective Chief Inspector Tony Lane was seated at his desk. Several lever-arch files were open, and he was filing case notes. Every so often he took out a document that was super-fluous, screwed it up and aimed for the waste bin. More often than not he missed, and there was a collection of scrunched-up paper on the floor.

Lane was in his mid-fifties, a large, heavy-set man, with an expansive face which frequently displayed a dour look. He wasn't like that however. Those who knew him well said that he was more cheerful underneath, and that he simply hid the fact as he enjoyed complaining and seeming discontent.

At a desk opposite sat a younger man, Detective Inspector Steven Perez. Perez was taller and slimmer than Lane, and al-together more optimistic. He had been working with Lane for several years, and had surprised fellow officers by getting on well with him.

Perez was attaching a rectangular, grey box to his computer. They had closed their last case two days before, and had spent the previous day completing paperwork and tying up loose ends. Both men were looking forward to another busy week.

Lane stopped what he was doing and looked at Perez. "What is that thing you're fiddling with?" His face looked sour. "It looks like a damn toaster."

"It's called a network-attached storage device. I'm linking it to my computer." Perez continued with what he was doing. He felt comfortable around Lane, and knew when his criticism was heartfelt and when it was not.

Lane stopped to study the device and decided that it looked ugly. "They could have made it look better. It really does look like a toaster."

Perez was connecting cables. "When I'm finished here, I'll be able to access this via my PDA."

Lane looked at Perez, and knew that he had potential. Within a few years he'd be a chief inspector, and would make a good one. "You should speak to IT about that. They'll just complain when they find out what you've done."

"I'll take my chances," said Perez to himself.

Lane shook his head, screwed up another piece of paper and aimed for the bin.

He missed.

"You wait till Chief Superintendent Travers comes in. He'll take one look at that and complain."

"He won't even notice it's here," said Perez. "You're too harsh on Travers, although I agree he can be difficult."

Lane felt that his junior still had things to learn. It was something that he saw in many young officers. "People aren't always promoted because of how good they are – Travers being a case in point. He's a caricature – he's what people expect the top brass to be like. That's why he got the job." Lane considered that as the phone on his desk rang. He let it ring several times before leaning across.

"*Lane,*" he said quickly. He listened and then stopped, and Perez realized something was up.

"OK," said Lane, "we'll be there." His face changed as he put down the receiver. "Come on … we're needed."

. . .

St. Swithun's Hospital, near Chiswick, looked new and efficient. Too new and efficient, in DCI Lane's mind. He parked his car in a disabled parking bay, and walked with Perez into the accident & emergency unit. He ignored the people at reception, and looked about until he saw DI Len Newman.

Newman was a small man, of a similar age to Lane, with grey hair and worn features. He looked as if the job was getting to him, but he had a smile for Lane.

"Tony. How's it going?"

Lane shook his hand. "Not too bad, Len. I was having a quiet morning till I got your call." He felt curious. "So what's the story here?"

Newman led him up the stairs to the trauma unit. They stopped outside a door with a window in it. Beyond was a small room with one bed. A late-middle-aged man was lying on it. He was unconscious, and attached to him were a number of wires and tubes, several of which led to a machine that was periodically flashing.

"His name's Ray Maynard," said Newman. He looked towards the glass, but didn't look directly at Maynard, as if doing so was uncomfortable. "He was brought in last night, with multiple injuries after being struck by a car." Newman held up a medical report. "Compound fracture of the right leg, two broken arms, as well as swelling on the brain. They've sedated him. They're trying to bring the swelling down."

Lane looked at the hospital staff and felt there was a distinct lack of urgency. "Was it attempted murder?"

"He's homeless," said Newman. "He wasn't struck deliberately. It looks like an accident. The driver was unable to avoid him – he ran into the road."

"Understood." Lane waited patiently, not something he did for everyone.

"Maynard was conscious at the scene. The driver who struck him got out and called for help – thank heavens there're still some decent people. Maynard was muttering something. He spoke about a man and a murder, and being chased. He said there was a body." Newman consulted his notes. "Yes, he said he'd seen *a dead body*."

Lane looked at Perez, who was growing interested.

"The thing is," said Newman, "we might have discounted his story, had it not been for the driver who struck him. The driver is adamant that he saw another man chasing Maynard, seconds before the impact."

"What happened to this other man?" said Perez.

"No one's sure. After Maynard was hit, things became confused. The driver who struck him stopped, and two cars collided. We think Maynard was running from an abandoned building. I've got the area sealed off. As crime-scene coordinator, I'm about to send over a forensic unit. I also thought you might want to see the site for yourself."

Lane wanted to know more. "This is a lot of effort to go to for a homeless person – someone who may well have been drinking." Newman was holding something back, and Lane sensed it. Newman spoke.

"The driver who struck him – he works in the mayor's office as a special advisor. They've taken an interest – hence the call to you."

Lane disliked politics. The powers that be were often influenced by external factors, and tended to move officers around at will.

"Great."

"If you want to head over, I'll tell Forensics you're on the way."

Lane made to leave and paused. "Any idea when Maynard will regain consciousness?"

Newman looked doubtful. "He's been heavily sedated. They're not sure when he'll come round, or what condition he'll be in. It's the swelling they're worried about."

Lane looked down the corridor. "Put an officer outside his door."

Perez was surprised, as was Newman.

"Just in case." said Lane.

CHAPTER 3

Merl & Grey Construction had a sign at the entrance to their demolition site. It was 11 A.M., and DCI Lane was at the site in Acton, close to where Ray Maynard had been found.

Excellence through labour. Lane looked at the logo of Merl & Grey and frowned. "Sounds like something from a Russian gulag."

Perez smiled. He liked Lane's dry sense of humour. "I was thinking the same thing."

The gates of the site were open, showing a large space, with rubble and masonry gathered into piles. At the back of the site were three buildings that had been left intact. They were connected at ground level, and had a dated look.

"Very 1960s," said Lane.

Lane had been a police officer for nearly thirty years. He had seen many crime scenes, and became more alert than normal when faced with a new one. Perez watched Lane, trying to learn from him. He was coming to realize that there were certain things that just couldn't be taught in a classroom.

Lane walked across the site, noting the earth on the ground. A walkway had been laid down, and forensic officers were already inspecting the area, checking for footprints. Lane knew he was disliked by many of the forensic technicians. In truth, it was a situation of his own making. Many of the younger technicians would not take criticism from officers who appeared ungrateful, or expected information too quickly, or reached conclusions that didn't agree with the science.

Lane noted one technician who particularly disliked him.

"It might be best if you speak to the SOCO people."

Perez nodded. He was keen to avoid conflict. "Perhaps if you didn't rub them up the wrong way …"

"Yeah, but then I wouldn't be me, would I?"

"You like being a miserable sod, don't you?" Perez smiled to himself.

"Talking to them is like taking a pee in a tumble dryer: pointless."

Perez wished Lane was more cheerful. He felt life could be made easier with a few simple changes. "You're too impatient."

"And rude, and disrespectful," said Lane. "You forgot to mention those."

"True enough. Anyway, I'll go and have a talk with them." Perez stopped as he saw someone walking on to the site. There was a flash from a camera.

"I don't believe it," said Lane. He had caught sight of the stranger too. Lane's lips became thin and his cheeks reddened. Standing thirty yards away was a middle-aged man in a brown suit. He had fair hair and a pale face, with a pointed nose. The man lowered his camera.

"What the hell's he doing here?" Lane knew the journalist.

"That guy has no respect for a crime scene," said Perez. His face mirrored Lane's.

"I'm not going to stand for this." Lane left Perez and marched towards his target.

•   •   •

Perez walked into a building at the rear of the site. Were it not for the medical charts and notes on the walls, it could have been an old company office.

Forensic technicians had laid down a walkway, and Perez looked down the main corridor towards Maddy Webb. Maddy was in her early twenties, of small build, with long, dark hair which was tied up. She had on white overalls, and was inspecting the floor.

She saw Perez and was pleased. "Steve, good to see you," she said with a smile. She stood up and looked behind him. "Where's the big guy?"

"Outside, hassling a journalist."

Maddy had a knowing look. "It's what he does best."

Perez wasn't going to apologize. He liked Maddy, but didn't feel like siding with her. He felt a strong sense of loyalty towards Lane, in spite of any faults he might have.

"So what's the story here?"

"We've found signs of disturbance and damage to a window." Maddy pointed along the corridor. "I'm tempted to say more than one person broke in."

"That would agree with the information we received."

"A man's been hospitalised, right?"

Perez nodded. "He'll probably be unconscious for some time, assuming he survives his injuries. The more you can tell us, the better."

"I'll give it a go." Maddy breathed in and tried to look confident. She was comparatively new to the job, and wanted to impress Perez.

"There're a number of tyre marks outside, some fresher than others. One or more vehicles could conceivably have driven up to the building. Aside from the break-in, there are also signs of a confrontation. And beyond that bend in the corridor, it looks as if something was dragged." She led Perez towards the spot. He could see linoleum floor – black and white checks, with streaks across them. Something had been dragged along the passage, and he saw a door at the end that was shut.

"I was thinking the same thing," said Maddy. She walked up to the door. When she opened it, Perez could see a dozen steps leading down to the basement.

Maddy made a face. "The room down there was used for the disposal of clinical waste. When the hospital ran, it used to take in medical waste and burn it. Dr Croft is going through it now. Hopefully he'll be able to tell us more soon."

•　　　•　　　•

Lane and Perez were returning to Homicide West. It was an hour later, and they were in Lane's car, with Perez driving. Lunchtime traffic was heavy, and Lane had delegated driving duties.

"You look pleased," said Perez.

"I feel pleased," said Lane. There was a smirk on his face. "I enjoyed hassling that journalist. He should have known better – some people really make the case for population control."

There was something about Lane's comments that Perez liked. "If you said that in public, you'd be in trouble."

"Tell me about it …" Lane felt police officers were overwhelmed by rules and political correctness. It had been so different when he had first started out.

"So what did you make of the hospital?" said Perez.

"We'll have to wait and see what Doctor Croft has to say." Lane was calm and rather matter-of-fact. Perez felt more concerned.

"This could escalate. If that homeless man was correct, in what he said about a body –"

"Then that could explain what someone was doing there." Lane was a practical man, and tried to think logically. "Doctor Croft is examining the scene. Hopefully he'll have something for us soon."

Perez slowed the car as they reached traffic lights. "I don't know, it all seems rather gruesome …"

"You and your feelings." Lane was speaking absentmindedly, and thinking ahead. "Have you got your PDA with you?"

Perez reached into his jacket and took it out. It was a small, black device, rectangular, and about four inches long. He handed it to Lane, who slid it open. He began typing on the keyboard, his large fingers having difficulty with the keys.

"*Oh, crap.*"

"What're you doing?"

"Sending a message to Len Newman. He said that Ray Maynard was chased – that he was chased from the hospital to the road."

"And?"

"I want to know what other people saw. I'm getting details of the driver who struck him. We can speak to him and get his version of events."

CHAPTER 4

Daniel Riley was having family problems. He would never admit it, but sitting at the table, watching his family eating lunch, he thought about what he should do.

Riley was in his early forties, a well-built man, with long dark hair, which was swept back. He was dressed in an expensive suit, and had a confident look that bordered on the arrogant.

His wife, Erin, was at the worktop, preparing something for herself. Daniel looked at her and felt resentment. It hadn't always been like that. Something had changed, and he was wondering what the future held.

One of his children looked up. "Daddy, what's wrong?" Fran was only six, but she was good at studying people and reading emotions.

Daniel looked down. "Nothing, honey. I was just thinking about work." Erin sat next to him, bringing a bowl of fruit with her.

"How long will you be gone for?" She asked the question in casual way, but Riley knew what she wanted. She didn't want him to be out late, celebrating.

"There're a couple of things I have to go over with the other directors. I know we sold up, but the handover has to be done properly. The buyers expect it."

Erin looked away. She was disappointed by the fact that business was coming first. She was still hopeful, however, that things would change. Daniel had sold the company he worked for, and his stake from the sale would be enough for them to have a good life – no, a great life. He wouldn't have to work again, and she was looking forward to that.

Riley finished eating and put his plate in the sink. "It's OK," said Erin. "I'll take care of that before we go out."

Fran looked at her mother, and thought about the prospect of shopping. She didn't like it. Alex, her younger brother, was sitting quietly, playing with a toy car. Alex was often in a world of his own, seemingly oblivious to those around him.

Riley was wondering what he should do after the sale. He'd have the resources to do whatever he wanted. He'd been married before, and had a child from his first marriage. He knew about the fallout which went with divorce, and that made him think carefully.

He left his wife and children and went to the hall. He checked the time and picked up his case. After this was all over he'd be able to think more clearly.

The weather outside was overcast but it wasn't raining. He would drive to work, getting there just before one. He would meet his partners and prepare for the handover. Then all he would have to do was sign.

Riley's mood lifted as he thought about the deal. He checked his appearance in the mirror, turned back and said bye to Erin and the children.

"Hopefully we'll wrap things up quickly."

Erin was pleased. She wanted adult company, and didn't fancy spending the rest of the day alone with the children.

Riley picked up his keys, stepped out and pulled the door shut. It was warmer than he was expecting and that made him uncomfortable. There were cars on the street, and that made him uncomfortable too. Riley wondered why. It wasn't rational.

He marched to the pavement and looked up and down. Something wasn't right.

He couldn't see anyone looking at him, but he couldn't shake off the feeling. Riley knew he couldn't stand there indefinitely. He had to get to work.

•   •   •

Most people don't realize they are being followed, not until it's too late, except this guy. He senses something, and I can feel it. Cautious or neurotic people always cause problems. This guy could put up a fight, and I have to be careful. I do like a challenge, and he will be one, so best to be fully prepared.

•   •   •

The lobby at Homicide West could be an interesting place. Some days it was quiet but other days suspects, who had been arrested, and who were intoxicated or unwilling to come quietly, would fight with officers. Lane secretly liked it when such things happened. It livened up his day.

The detectives arrived at Homicide West a little before one. Lane was disappointed to see that the lobby was quiet. Max Denning, the duty sergeant, saw him. "Tony," he said, "I've got a couple of messages for you. Your wife rang – asked if you could call her back. Also, Chief Superintendent Travers asked if he could see you."

"What did my wife want?" said Lane.

"She didn't say. Said she couldn't reach you on your mobile."

Lane looked unmoved. "It's probably about the present I need to get. Don't tell Travers you saw me … If he asks, you don't know where I am."

Denning suppressed a grin. "Understood."

The detectives took the stairs to the mezzanine floor and walked towards the incident room. Inside there was a quiet hum of activity. A number of civilian staff were consulting computers or organizing records. The two desks in the centre of the room belonged to Lane and Perez. Perez's desk was clear of paperwork, and everything was neatly ordered. Lane's desk was swamped, and the wooden surface wasn't visible.

Close by sat Malcolm Brown, a civilian assistant who doubled as a PA for both detectives. Perez liked Brown because of his efficiency, but Lane thought he was an odd character. Brown, who was young and sloppily dressed, was slightly eccentric. He often spent time talking to himself, doodling and staring into space. He was however efficient and reliable, and that was the reason Lane kept him on.

Brown kept photographs on his desk, which frequently changed. Today there were four pictures, showing tourist sites in the capital.

"Detectives," said Brown, "I've got a couple of messages for you." He turned to Lane. "Your wife rang. She asked if you could call her back. Also, Chief Superintendent Travers asked if he could see you."

"I know," said Lane tersely. "If Travers comes by, you haven't seen me … I'll call the wife when I run out of other things to do."

Brown took a moment to process the information.

Lane sat down, nudged the mouse by his computer and the screen flickered to life.

"Ah, good. Newman's replied." Lane clicked on the message.

"What did he say?" said Perez.

"He sent the name and address of the driver who hit Ray Maynard. I'm going to call this guy – see if I can go and speak to him – convince the mayor's office that we're value for money." He thought about the mayor, who he had met once before. So far there was no death, no body and limited forensics. Were it anyone else, he would be telling them how stretched police resources were.

"What do you want me to do in the meantime?" said Perez.

"See if you can get in touch with Merl & Grey. They're the construction company who cleared the site. I'd like to know how many people had access, and if anyone had keys to the buildings."

CHAPTER
5

DCI Lane called Glenn Barber, explaining that he wished to speak to him about the man he had struck. Barber had a hoarse voice, and instantly sounded tense.

"How is he? ... they told me he was in hospital ... that he was critical."

Lane could sense his unease. Lane asked if he could come to see him, and reluctantly Barber agreed.

Glenn Barber lived in Epping. Lane arrived in good time, pulling up outside a semi-detached house on a well-looked-after street. At the door he was greeted by a woman in her early fifties, who introduced herself as Angela. There was worry on her face. "Glenn's inside. This has all come as a bit of a shock ..."

Lane nodded as if he understood, and Angela Barber let him in.

In the living room, Glenn Barber sat facing the window. The room had a dated feel. There was a cup of tea on the table and the TV was on, although the sound was muted. For someone who worked in the mayor's office, Barber was older than Lane had been expecting – in his early sixties. Perhaps he had been appointed because of his experience, thought Lane. Barber had a long face, with lines on it, and wore wire-framed glasses and a black cardigan. Lane found himself thinking of a retired schoolteacher.

"Mr Barber? My name's DCI Lane. May I sit down?"

Barber gestured to the sofa.

Lane took out his notebook and Angela Barber offered him a cup of tea.

"Thank you." Lane looked as if he was distracted for a moment, and waited for her to leave. "As I mentioned earlier, I wanted to speak to you about Ray Maynard – the man you hit."

Barber looked alarmed. His eyes were red, and Lane wondered if he had been crying.

"I didn't hit him, well … I did, but he ran into the road. He ran into the path of my car."

"We understand," said Lane slowly. He went over in his mind what Len Newman had told him.

"As we understand it, Ray Maynard may not have been alone. Could you tell me about that?"

Barber nodded. "There was more than one person – someone else behind – I told that to the inspector at the scene. I didn't see Mr Maynard's expression, but I got the sense that he was fleeing."

"And he ran into the path of your car?"

"Yes …" Barber looked shocked as he recalled the event. He reached for the cup of tea on the table. "Traffic stopped. There was the sound of screeching, horns – two cars collided behind me. It was chaos."

Lane nodded, trying to look sympathetic. Empathy wasn't something he was good at. Perez was much better at dealing with people, and right now Lane wished he was there.

"What happened after you struck Mr Maynard?"

"I got out to check on him. I had to do that – it was the right thing to do." Barber looked at Lane for reassurance. "He was conscious, but he was drifting away."

"Did he say anything to you?"

Barber thought for a long moment. "I don't know. It was garbled …"

"But you thought you heard something?" There was hope in Lane's voice.

"I may have done. I think – I think he may have mentioned a body. I think he may have said there was a body, but it didn't make sense."

Lane made a note. "What happened next?"

"I called for help. I had a mobile, and I used it. Other drivers got out. The ambulance arrived soon after, then the police."

"Nothing like this has ever happened to us before." Angela had returned, and Lane accepted the cup of tea. He didn't often drink tea or coffee, but was trying hard to be accepted.

"And were you in the car with your husband?"

"I was in the passenger seat. We were on the way back from my sister's. She hasn't been well, and … this was the last thing we were expecting."

The couple reminded Lane of someone or something, but he couldn't quite make the connection.

"Mr Barber, you said you thought Ray Maynard was being chased. What happened to the man who was chasing him?"

Barber seemed lost. "After the accident everything happened so quickly. I can't remember seeing the man. We were all focused on Maynard."

"Can you give me a description of the man who was following him?"

"I'd be guessing," said Barber. "It was dark – he was some distance off. If anything, I only got the briefest of glances."

Lane looked to Angela Barber, but she shrugged. She seemed like a determined person, and Lane hoped she would step in.

"I didn't see him," she said. "But if my husband said he was there, then he must have been."

Barber was keen to be helpful.

"I think he was large. He moved with speed. He may have been dressed in dark clothes, but I didn't see a face. Look, I don't want to give you details that border on guesswork."

Lane appreciated the frankness, but sat back and felt frustrated.

·   ·   ·

Daniel Riley came out of his office for a cigarette. His company was based in Cheapside, in central London. The main road wasn't busy, and Riley paced up and down, smoking and thinking about the meeting he had been in.

Things were going well. The Korean buyers were happy and were checking over final changes. Soon signatures would be applied. The company he had helped set up would be sold, and he would be wealthy.

Riley thought about calling his wife but decided not to. She wouldn't share his enthusiasm. She didn't think about money in the same way that he did. She seemed to measure the quality of her life in different ways, and that frustrated him. He wished she was more focused – more driven. And the more time he spent around her, the less tolerant he became.

Riley looked up and down the road but failed to notice the dark van thirty yards away. Its engine was idling, and it slowly moved down the road towards him. It came to within twenty yards, and then ten and then stopped.

A security guard had come into view. He had come out of the building to join Riley, and the two men chatted to one another as they smoked.

The van lingered for a moment then pulled away, moving quietly and slowly.

·   ·   ·

Merl & Grey Construction had offices in southeast London. DI Perez arrived at their site and took note of the Portakabins stacked on one side. He had rung ahead, to be told that the person he needed to speak to was Alex Grey.

He walked across a wooden walkway and looked at supplies of building equipment that were stacked in the yard. Alongside was an excavator and several cement mixers. A sign on one of the Portakabins said *Management,* and there was an arrow pointing upwards.

Perez climbed the wooden stairs using the banister which wobbled as he held on to it. He reached a landing with a door at the far end. On it was the word *Grey.* Perez knocked on the door and a voice said, "Come in."

The room was laid out as an office – well organized, with filing cabinets on one side, and several desks on the other. At one of the desks sat a woman, looking over a number of files. She was in her early forties and dressed in a black suit, with dark hair tied into a ponytail. She had on minimal makeup, but looked quite elegant.

"Excuse me," said Perez.

The woman looked up.

"I'm looking for the site manager, Alex Grey. I was told I could find him here."

The woman smiled a little. "You've found him." She stood up and held out her hand.

Perez looked bashful as he shook it.

"Sorry –"

"You're not the first to have made the mistake." Alex Grey sat down and gestured to a chair. "My secretary said someone would be calling – a police inspector?"

"That's right. I'm with Homicide West. I was hoping I could speak to you about the construction site you've been working on in Acton."

"The hospital trust," said Grey. Her eyes widened. "I understand you have officers there. One of your inspectors … a Len Newman, contacted my secretary. He wanted keys – something about a crime scene?"

"That's correct." Perez seemed surprised by how much Grey knew. "A man was involved in an accident close by. We think he may have been running from the site, and I was wondering if you could tell me what's been going on there."

"Well, I haven't been working there – not every day." Grey reached for a schedule behind her. She flicked through it in a relaxed manner, and sat back. "This lists work we've been carrying out. The local trust hired us to clear the site. They're looking to build a new facility – a research one, as well as a new complex for the disposal of clinical waste."

"Is that why some buildings have been left standing?" said Perez.

Grey nodded. "Those are to be refurbished. The waste disposal facility will be upgraded. The North West Trust has plans. They'll be providing waste management for other hospitals: there's money to be made there." Grey sounded pleased at the thought.

Perez studied Grey, and thought it odd she was doing the job that she did. "I wanted to speak to you about people who've had access to the site." He tried to sound casual. "We think someone may have been using one of the buildings. I was wondering if you could tell me who has access."

"I guess if you want to see our records, I should be asking for a warrant."

Perez looked disappointed and wondered if his thoughts betrayed him.

"Don't worry, Detective." Grey smiled. "I've got nothing to hide."

She stood up and walked to a filing cabinet on the opposite side of the room. She knew exactly what she was looking for, and after several moments returned with some thin, blue files.

"These are the people who've been working on site. We've had a team of twenty there, but the place has been closed for several days now. We've levelled most of it, and we're waiting for the hospital to get back to us."

Perez studied the files. He saw names and pictures.

"Do you know what you're looking for?" said Grey. Perez was thinking the same thing. He wasn't sure exactly what he hoped to find, but something suddenly made him stop. He felt a shot of excitement. He saw the name *Frederick Stoltz*, and a picture next to it. Early thirties, brown hair, blue eyes.

He knew him. He had arrested him before, and his name wasn't Frederick Stoltz.

CHAPTER 6

Perez left the offices of Merl & Grey and turned on his phone. He had five new messages. He was about to listen to the first one, when the phone rang.

"Christ – where've you been?" said Lane.

Perez felt indifferent, and found it hard to match Lane's level of concern. "I was talking to a rather nice woman about a construction company."

"Merl & Grey?"

"Yes. I've learnt a couple of things. There's a man we need to speak to –"

"Good. It can wait." Lane was impatient and sounded out of breath. "Doctor Croft has been on the phone. He wants to see us as soon as possible."

"Is something up?"

"I think so. Can you meet me at the Acton site, in an hour?"

Perez checked the time. "I can probably do better than that."

"Good." Lane hung up, in keeping with his abrupt style.

· · ·

DI Perez arrived at the hospital site, in Acton, to find an empty space in the car park at the front. He was pleased. Spaces were hard to come by, even if the car park was a temporary one.

He showed his ID to a uniformed officer, and made his way through the cordon to the building he had visited previously. He walked past rubble and masonry, and the three buildings at the back which had been left intact.

At the rear of the third building was a police presence. Forensic technicians were examining the ground. Soil had been removed, along with sheets of metal. They looked like corrugated steel. Perez was cautious. He felt something had been discovered, but wasn't sure what exactly to expect.

"Glad you could join us," said Lane. He was standing next to Croft and a technician, and was more interested in what was in the ground.

"… got here as quickly as I could," said Perez.

Lane gave a nod and returned to what he was examining. A technician was standing in a hole that had been made. It was nearly two metres square and almost a metre deep. The technician was handing up transparent evidence bags. They appeared to contain grey soot and ash.

"The good doctor has found something," said Lane. He knew Croft would like the way he had been described.

Perez studied the evidence bags, wondering how much he could ascertain by sight alone.

Doctor Croft was an elderly man. His hair was thinning and had receded, and he wore large glasses. He was past retirement but stayed on because of his experience. Some days he appeared tired, but today he was alert, his eyes darting back and forth.

"Someone dug this hole and covered it over with metal sheeting," said Croft. "They then put another layer of soil on top. It took us a while to uncover it." Croft spoke slowly, holding up more evidence bags so that Lane and Perez could see the contents.

"We've only had an hour or two to examine this, but I thought you'd want to know what we've found."

"We could do with some good news," Perez replied. He was curious, and wondered what direction their investigation was headed in. Best not jump to conclusions.

"Whether it's good news depends on your point of view. The furnace in the basement contains no soot or ash. I'm fairly sure it hasn't been used recently. This hole on the other hand – someone has been busy here." Croft offered an evidence bag to Lane, who held it up to the light. The contents looked like pieces of dried clay.

"What am I looking at?"

"That's the superior ramus of the pelvis."

"Pelvic bone?"

"Correct." Croft pointed to the evidence bag Perez had taken. "That contains fragments of a femur. And this one contains fragments of a scapula."

"A rib?" said Perez. "Are these remains human?"

"Absolutely. We recovered them along with other fragments, most of which have yet to be catalogued. My people will be sorting out material for days."

Perez felt the hairs on the back of his neck rising. "What does it all mean?"

"It means someone has been using this site to dispose of a body. I checked with the hospital, which owns the site. They confirmed it was shut down more than twelve months ago – that the building has been locked up ever since."

"Well that clearly wasn't the case," said Lane. He felt that people's idea of security varied considerably. People needed to invest in proper security.

Lane put down the evidence bag and walked around the hole. A metal grating had been put down to form a walkway, stopping people sinking into the earth. He was trying to consider things logically.

"Do you have any idea when the remains were buried?"

"I'd say within the last two to three months. I can't be more specific at the moment. Someone appears to have used chemicals to accelerate decomposition. That's why the bones have a clay-like quality."

"Do you know who these bones belong to?"

Croft paused. "Not at the moment."

"But you suspect something." Lane had known Croft for a number of years, and felt he could read him well.

"If I had to hazard a guess, I'd say the bone fragments were male – the shape of the pelvic fragments suggest that. Judging by size and density, I'd say they were probably from a male in his thirties or early forties."

"We need a name," said Lane.

"Some would say you're asking the impossible," Croft replied. "That won't be easy."

Perez was standing quietly. He was often like this when a body was found.

"If a body was put into the ground, what effect would normal decomposition have?"

"Not this," said Croft. "Chemicals have been used, and that means my technicians have to work more carefully."

"And these chemicals would break down everything?"

"Given enough time, yes. We got to them first. That sheeting was used to cover the hole." Croft pointed to the corrugated metal. "Someone did this in a hurry."

"Or did it because they were planning to come back," said Lane quietly.

"Perhaps they wanted to check on the decomposition," said Croft.

"Paranoid, eh?"

"There's something else you need to know," said Croft. He put on a solemn face. "We found sufficient remains to suggest two bodies."

CHAPTER
7

OK. So my secret's out. To be honest, I hadn't been expecting the police to find the remains. At least not so quickly. You see I planned ahead. That's something I always try to do. I was careful as well. It's best to be discrete, and I usually am.

It's the homeless man I blame. If he hadn't been there, I wouldn't have attracted attention. I should have dealt with him properly, and I realize that now. I keep going over it in my mind, thinking about what should have been. But that won't do any good, and it's best to focus on the present.

The fact of the matter is the police are on site, in Acton. My style's been cramped. I haven't been compromised – not yet – but it means I have to make changes.

It's such hard work. It's always hard work. Keep calm and roll with it. That's my mantra.

．　　　．　　　．

DCI Lane spoke with Croft for several minutes. When he left the site, he found Perez by the car.

"He's moving as quickly as he can," Lane explained. "They'll check the basement too and then move up through the rest of the building. I'm hoping they'll find ID – something relating to the remains. We need more to go on, that's for sure."

Perez could see the look on Lane's face. It was one of concern mixed with determination. "We need to move fast," said Lane. "Our good chief superintendent is going to be interested."

"He's always interested in a major investigation," said Perez. "He thinks he can help us."

"That guy supports me like a rope supports a hanged man." Lane remembered something. "You said you had a lead? A construction worker at Merl & Grey?"

Perez took out a piece of paper. "I've arrested him before. His name's Frederick Stoltz, except that's not his real name."

"Well let's get going."

·　　　·　　　·

The meeting had gone well. The papers had been signed, and ownership of the company had been transferred. Daniel Riley was wealthy.

He took the lift to the basement of the building and stepped out into the car park. Riley felt elated. He thought about the money that had just been transferred to him; he had never thought the moment would come. He had been meaning to call Erin, but he decided she could wait. She would understand. He hoped she would.

In his briefcase, Riley had details of the bank transfer that had been made. He wanted to take out the papers and look at them again. He walked through the underground car park and pressed the fob that unlocked his car. The lights around the Audi flashed, and Riley put his briefcase into the boot. His colleagues were waiting for him upstairs. They were going out to celebrate. Then he would call Erin.

As Riley locked the car, he heard a clanking. It reverberated in the enclosed space, and he looked to the corner of the car park where a man was loading a van. The man had a trolley with wheels, and was loading boxes. He was struggling – one of his arms was bandaged.

Riley took note of the way the man moved. He shouldn't have been working. Someone else should have been doing his job.

There was a loud noise as a box fell, and the man stopped. He didn't shout or curse. He just looked down, wondering how best to proceed.

Riley looked about. There was no one else in the car park.

"Do you want a hand?"

Ordinarily, Daniel Riley wouldn't have volunteered. He was selfish, but today he was in a good mood. Today would be different.

The man was wearing a baseball cap, which obscured part of his face. "If you wouldn't mind, sir …"

Riley walked over and bent down, picking up the box with both hands. He was surprised how light it was. The man didn't join him. Instead he struck Riley over the head, and watched as he slumped down.

·   ·   ·

There was nothing. Then Riley felt pain. His head was throbbing, and when he moved the pain worsened. He tried to open his eyes but realized he couldn't: there was something covering them.

He tried to reach up but it was impossible. His hands were tied behind him and that made him anxious. Anxiety filled his chest.

The car park, his car – the van.

Riley tried to free his arms but they were tightly bound, and his shoulders were beginning to ache. He could smell something – acrid, pungent. It was familiar, but he couldn't quite place it. Fear was overtaking rational thought. The throbbing in his head came back, as he was jerked to one side – he was moving.

Riley tried to sit up, and his fingertips made contact with metal. He was being jostled, and he realized he was in the back of the van.

·   ·   ·

The Wallder estate, in south London, was well looked after. Lane and Perez arrived a little before five o'clock, pulling up in a space in the main courtyard. There was still a lot of daylight, and Lane looked at the papers in his hand, ignoring the strong smell of pollen in the air. "So who exactly is this guy?"

"His name's Frederick Stoltz – at least that's the name he gave to Merl & Grey."

"And he's not in the construction business?"

"No he isn't," said Perez, with annoyance. "He's a serial offender. I arrested him four years ago. He was responsible for a string of burglaries. He often targeted homes when people were in, and was involved in a number of assaults. He hospitalized several pensioners – in spite of the fact that they posed no threat."

Lane felt anger. "What sentence did he get?"

"Seven years. He was out in four though."

The anger remained. "It's all about criminals' rights nowadays." Lane wanted to go on, but Perez had heard the speech before.

"When I arrested him, Stoltz was going by the name of Frank Sterling. It's not the name he was born with though. He changed it. The guy's a career criminal – a habitual liar."

"And this is where he lives?"

"According to his parole officer." Perez took out the report and passed it across.

"Flat thirty-five," said Lane. "OK, let's pay him a visit." Lane got out and looked around. There was some lawn and flowerbeds, which were well maintained.

"Nice to see our council tax being spent on pointless things."

"I think it's paid for by their service charge," said Perez.

"And they probably get housing benefit to cover it."

"You're too cynical."

"It has been said."

Several children were playing in the distance. They stopped and stared at the detectives. "I think they know who we are," said Perez, as he tried to judge their ages. He found it difficult to relate to young people.

"As long as they leave the car alone." Lane locked it and looked towards the flats. The building was a long, low construction, no more than four storeys high. There were landings running along the front, and green doors with numbers painted on. There were scores of flowerboxes – too many in Lane's mind.

"Flat thirty-five is on the second floor."

Lane turned back and caught sight of something out of the corner of his eye. A grey saloon had pulled up in the distance. It lingered for a moment and then pulled away.

"He's here," said Perez quietly. "Stoltz is by the door of his flat."

Lane turned back and looked across the yard. He looked at flat thirty-five and could make out a figure close by.

Lane walked towards the block, and looked back to check on the grey car. It was gone. There was a set of stairs to one side of the building. Lane took the steps in double strides and Perez followed, dropping back.

Once he reached the landing, Lane looked along its length. He was surprised to see that Stoltz was still there. He was standing with his back to him, close to the door of number thirty-five. Lane wondered what he was up to.

Lane nodded to Perez to remain by the stairs, and began walking towards Stoltz. He remembered Stoltz's reputation for violence, and wondered how he'd react.

As he approached, Lane realized something was wrong. The build wasn't right, and the hair colour was different. He took note of the man's clothes, and then the man turned around.

It wasn't Stoltz. The man took a step away and reached for the door of number thirty-six. He put a key into the lock and Lane studied him as he disappeared inside. Lane looked at Stoltz's flat and lingered for a moment before rapping on the door. He rapped again.

Nothing.

There was a small window to the left of the front door. Lane tried looking through, but netting and a lack of light made it difficult. He glanced back at Perez and shook his head.

The detectives returned to Lane's car and resumed their vigil. There was little conversation, and Lane soon began feeling frustrated.

"I'm going to knock on the neighbour's door and speak to him. You should go home: your wife will wonder where you are."

Perez was keen to stay. "What are you going to do about Stoltz?"

"He doesn't know we're on to him. He has to turn up at some point. I'll get a plain-clothed unit to keep an eye."

Perez winced. "When the powers that be find out, they'll complain about the hit to the budget."

"That's true enough."

"How about your wife?" said Perez. "Did you ever call her back?"

"No need." Lane found himself thinking about Irene. "I know what she wanted. It's her sister's birthday this week. They're having a party, and I need to do something."

Lane took out his phone and put through a call for the surveillance unit. He covered the mouthpiece. "We'll tell them to hold back if Stoltz turns up. I want to be here when we get him."

CHAPTER 8

Steve Perez arrived early at Homicide West on Tuesday morning, and was surprised to find the incident room already busy. Lane was at his desk, carefully going through paperwork, and Malcolm Brown and other civilian staff were assisting.

Perez knew Lane could be rough around the edges, but he was also efficient, methodical and got results. He was able to filter things out and press ahead. Perez wasn't sure if it was due to experience or innate ability. He suspected it was the latter, and he felt slightly envious.

"There you are," said Lane. "Glad you could make it."

Perez sat at his desk. "What's happening?"

"Malcolm and co. are helping me chase up leads on the paperwork you produced."

"Paperwork?"

"From Merl & Grey – from that good-looking woman, who you said helped?"

Perez felt embarrassed. "I didn't put it quite like that."

"Save it for the wife. Anyway, according to the personnel details she gave, there were twelve workers on site in Acton. One of them was Frederick Stoltz."

"And how is our Mr Stoltz?"

"So far there's been no sign of him." If Lane was disappointed, it didn't show. "The obo. unit is still there. They've got orders to ring the moment he returns."

"And he's our prime suspect?"

"Absolutely. Of the other eleven workers, none have criminal records."

Malcolm Brown, who was standing behind Lane, nodded.

Perez glanced at the photographs on Brown's desk. They were showing scenes of riots and demonstrations, and Perez wondered what had prompted Brown to put them out. He never questioned him about the photographs on his desk, but was always interested to see what appeared.

"Just because Stoltz is a criminal, it doesn't mean he's a murderer."

Lane considered that. "But his convictions for violence got me wondering. In my book, people like him deserve a little extra attention. Perhaps he'll have an alibi, and perhaps we can rule him out, but in any case we need to speak to him."

"The other thing," said Lane, "is that we need to get in touch with the NHS trust, which owns the site. We're going to need to speak to hospital staff."

"You reckon the person who disposed of the bodies could have been an employee?"

"It's something we have to consider." Lane stopped as his phone vibrated. He checked it.

"It's the obo. unit. Stoltz has just returned to his flat."

•   •   •

It took Lane and Perez nearly thirty minutes to reach the Wallder estate. Traffic was heavy, thanks to the rush hour, and Lane was frustrated. He checked in with the observation unit several times.

When they arrived, the estate was quiet. The two-man sur-veillance team was parked where it should be, facing the block in which Stoltz lived.

Lane got out and scanned the area. The strong smell of pollen was still present, and it irritated him. He headed towards the two plain-clothed officers. They were young, and had worked for Lane several times before. They were seeking promotion, but in Lane's mind their success had been variable, and so far he had been reluctant to sanction any advancement.

"Where is he?"

The younger officer looked out of the driver's window. "Still in his flat, sir. He got back about an hour ago – parked his van on the opposite side of the road."

Lane looked at the old van, which was clean and looked as if it had been washed.

"Was he alone?"

"Yes, sir. He had a box of tools with him – at least that was what it looked like."

"Any visitors?"

"None so far."

"Good." Lane tapped the roof of the car, his only real form of praise, and began turning away. "My inspector and I will pay him a visit … if shots are fired, call for backup."

The two officers looked at each other, wondering if Lane was joking.

In his car, Lane relayed to Perez what he had heard. "He's up there. It looks as if he's by himself."

"How do you want to play this?" Perez felt on edge. He knew Frederick Stoltz, and that only increased the tension. He wondered how Stoltz would react to seeing him again. Would he be angry? Would he refuse to come quietly?

"Don't look so apprehensive," said Lane. "This guy'd be out of his depth in a fishpond."

"I'll bear that in mind."

"Go to the back of the building and see if there's an exit. If there's a fire escape, block it."

Perez nodded. Lane looked up at number thirty-five, got out and walked towards the block. He met no one on the stairs, and found himself thinking that the building was surprisingly clean. It was obviously cleaned regularly. He felt that an ex-con like Stoltz didn't deserve to live there.

When he reached the front door, he looked through the window to the left. There was something flashing inside. A TV?

Lane listened for voices then rapped loudly.

"… who is it?" The voice was male – wary – some distance off.

"*Police.*" Lane reached for his warrant card.

There was no response and Lane felt annoyed. He stepped back. He heard tumbling, and the sound of a window going up, and realized what was happening.

·　　　·　　　·

At the back of the building, Perez saw the window opening. A man with light-brown hair was climbing out. He seemed anxious, and glanced back before climbing over the window ledge and looking down.

Perez recognized Stoltz. He stared, wondering where Stoltz would go. There was no balcony below, only a flat roof. The drop was nearly fifteen feet, and Perez wondered if Stoltz would make it.

"*Don't!*"

Stoltz hesitated and looked in Perez's direction. He turned his attention to the flat roof and jumped. He rolled as he hit it, and rose quickly.

Perez was no more than thirty yards away. He watched anxiously, as Stoltz crossed the roof and crouched down, trying to open a skylight. Perez looked at the building. He ran to the front and saw that it was a café that backed on to the flats. It looked empty, as it was being redecorated, and he pushed open the door and went in.

There was a strong smell of paint, and the man and the woman inside looked startled. "We're not –" the man began.

Perez took out his warrant card. "There's a guy on your roof. He's trying to get in. Can you show me where the skylight is?"

The middle-aged man thought for a moment. He nodded, and showed Perez towards the room at the rear.

Perez pushed his way through a beaded curtain and saw a large storeroom. Daylight was coming from above, and climbing through the skylight was Frederick Stoltz.

"Stop!" shouted Perez.

Stoltz looked down and let go, dropping in. He reached for a wooden pole, propped against the wall, and swung out. Perez lurched back, and the café owner fell over as he dodged the swing. Stoltz lunged forward and struck him across the head before turning to Perez.

"*Back up!*"

Perez could feel his heart beating.

"Away from the door," said Stoltz, lowering the pole to chest height. He looked older than Perez remembered him – the eyes, the face – he was desperate, and Perez wondered what had made him that way.

Stoltz cut through the beaded curtain. Outside a woman screamed and Perez dashed forward. He saw Stoltz leaving through the front door. The woman was cowering behind the counter.

Perez thought about calling Lane, but realized he didn't have time. He ran out and saw Stoltz in the distance. He was at least twenty yards away, and moving fast.

Perez had never been good at chases, and doubted he'd be able to catch up. People stopped and stared, and an elderly man quickly got out of the way.

Stoltz moved on to a residential road, dodging traffic. There were parked cars on either side. In the distance Perez could see a car pulling up. It reversed into a space and stopped. Stoltz passed the car and a door swung open. It struck Stoltz in the chest and he fell back on to the pavement. Lane stepped out of the car.

"Good to finally meet you, Mr Stoltz."

CHAPTER 9

Daniel Riley woke up and felt pain. It wasn't from his head, although there was still a dull ache; it was coming from his throat. He tried to reach up and touch it, but his hands were bound behind him.

Riley was lying down, his face pressed again a cold surface. Was he still in the van? He was no longer blindfolded, and there was no noise and no movement. This couldn't be the van. He was stationary, and had to be somewhere else.

There was bitumen black darkness all around. He managed to sit up and put his head against a wall. He knew time had elapsed. He couldn't be sure how much: he no longer had a watch.

Riley didn't panic. His legs were free, and he struggled to get up, pushing his shoulders against the wall for support. He wondered how long it would take for his eyes to get used to the darkness. He wanted to gain information – information that could help him escape.

Riley couldn't hear or see anything, and he decided to use his sense of touch. He was pleased that he was thinking logically. He congratulated himself on remaining calm, and used his shoulder as a guide.

Walking next to the wall, he rubbed his shoulder against the rough surface. He came to a halt as he met another wall. He followed it along, and abruptly came to a halt again.

The space he was in was small and rectangular, no more than seven feet by ten. A disused storage room perhaps? He couldn't find a door, but he knew there had to be an opening somewhere.

The walls he was moving against were dry and uneven. He turned around and used his hands to feel the surfaces. He didn't find a door or a handle. Instead his fingers touched a metal grate. The edges were sharp, and feeling excited, he realized he could use it to cut the rope that bound him.

·   ·   ·

On the Wallder estate there was tension in the air. Frederick Stoltz had been taken in a police van to Homicide West headquarters. Lane had ignored him after arresting him, instead mentioning the damage to his car door.

Lane turned to Perez. "Why are you looking so dejected? We got him, didn't we?"

"Yeah … but I nearly lost him." Perez felt bad, and a sense of inadequacy passed over him. "If you hadn't been there, he'd have gotten away."

"But he didn't," said Lane, "and that's the main thing. You live and learn in this game." He thumped Perez on the back, and walked with him to the courtyard, in the centre of the estate. Forensic officers had arrived, and were securing Stoltz's flat. Residents had come out to see what was happening, and Perez could feel many eyes on them.

Lane walked with Perez up to the flat. The landing outside had been sealed off with police tape. The front door was open. The lock had been forced, and Lane allowed himself a brief smile.

Chris Nolan, who was in charge of Forensics, was standing in the hall. He was a tall, middle-aged man, with greying hair and a calm manner.

"Thought you'd be over at the hospital site, in Acton," said Lane.

"Division of labour," said Nolan. "Croft is there, along with my assistant. It looks as if they'll be there a while."

Lane wondered what else Croft had found.

"Have they found anything new?" said Perez, reading Lane's thoughts.

"They've recovered more bone fragments, but so far it's still at two bodies."

"Thank God for that." Lane didn't welcome the prospect of Croft finding anything more.

"So who does this place belong to?" said Nolan, gesturing to the flat.

"His name's Frederick Stoltz," said Lane. "At least that's one of his names. He had access to the Acton site – he was working there as a labourer – and so far he's our only suspect." Lane wondered why Stoltz had run. It wasn't a good sign, and it was something that needed examining.

"We'll do a full sweep of the flat," said Nolan, "… see if we can find anything to tie him to the crime scene, in Acton."

Lane took a pair of latex gloves from his jacket. Stoltz's flat was cramped and poorly lit. The air was musty, and Lane made a face as he walked in.

"This place needs fumigating." Lane made his way to the front room, and what he found took him by surprise.

•   •   •

At Homicide West, the atmosphere in the incident room was energized. It was an hour and a half later, and civilian staff were aware that something had happened. A suspect was in custody, and Lane wanted as much background information as possible.

Lane turned to Malcolm Brown, who was sitting at his desk. "Stoltz has changed his name a couple of times. Bear that in mind when you do the checks."

"Understood." Working with Brown was a young woman from the HOLMES support unit. HOLMES was a major enquiry system that held a large amount of case information, often useful in murder enquiries. Lane glanced at the woman, and thought she bore a passing resemblance to Brown. They both wore the same style of glasses, and he found himself thinking that they would make a good couple.

"This is Stoltz's probation report," said Perez.

Lane took it and flicked through. "He's been arrested enough times. Some people really make the case for population control." Lane sat down and read the document more carefully. "When I interview him, I want you there."

Perez was pleased.

Stoltz was being held in the custody suite. He had complained about back pain but Lane had ignored him, murmuring he'd have more pain if he didn't cooperate.

Lane considered Stoltz's innocence or guilt. Then there was fact that he had tried to run. "How about the photos of his flat? Are they ready?"

"I'm printing off a set now." Perez turned to a small printer under his desk. He had installed it himself, allowing him to print high-quality, crime scene photos without having to go to Forensics.

Lane checked his watch: it wasn't yet midday. *Good.* He looked at Perez and felt determined. "Things are going our way."

"Wait till we interview him," said Perez cautiously. "He's good at being evasive – you'll see that for yourself."

•   •   •

Frederick Stoltz was sitting in interview-room two. Lane said nothing as he entered.

Stoltz was in his early forties. He had light-brown hair and blue eyes, with a placid look on his face. His expression gave little away, but there was a look of intelligence behind the eyes. He could think quickly: Lane was sure of that.

Perez joined Lane, sitting next to him at the interview-room table. Stoltz seemed more interested in Perez and studied him.

"You've aged, Sergeant." Stoltz's voice had a low tone.

"It's Inspector now," Perez replied.

Stoltz nodded. "Last time you arrested me you seemed out of your depth. Now you seem more – confident."

Perez didn't like the fact that Stoltz was focusing on him. He wanted to get on with the interview.

At times, Lane wished Perez was more forceful. Being subtle was OK, but forceful was better. Lane knew that there were a number of ways to get the right result, but still …

He turned on the tape deck next to the wall, and pushed a stack of documents to the middle of the table.

"You've had quite an eventful life, Mr Stoltz. Or perhaps I should call you Sterling, or Strathmore, or Swain. You've had enough aliases over the years."

Stoltz remained calm, but there was growing tension between the two of them.

"You've been doing your homework, Chief Inspector. I must admit though, I don't know much about you."

"We're not here to talk about me," said Lane tersely. He disliked Stoltz, and the feeling increased the longer he sat in front of him.

"What exactly is it that I'm being charged with?"

"I haven't formally levelled charges," said Lane, "but they'll be coming."

"Let me guess." Stoltz seemed amused. "Assaulting an officer, resisting arrest –"

"Actually it was a café owner that you assaulted."

"What can I say? He was in the way."

Lane was keen to move things on. He took several photographs from the stack of documents. "I want to talk to you about these."

The photographs showed the inside of Stoltz's flat. In the living room all the furniture had been removed. In its place were drums of copper and fibre-optic cable, along with boxes of mobile phones and walkie-talkies.

"You've been busy," said Lane, "hoarding like a pack rat."

Stoltz didn't like the way he had been described.

"You've turned your flat into a warehouse. 140 metres of copper cable; ninety metres of fibre-optic cable; thirty boxes of mobile phones, and two dozen walkie-talkies. Brand new. Where did you get all of this?"

Stoltz shrugged. "I buy and sell. What can I say?"

"Like hell," said Lane. He hit the table, in a move that startled Stoltz.

"I've been checking serial numbers. All these things were stolen from your employer. You've been stealing from Merl & Grey since day one."

Stoltz stared at Lane, and Perez cut in.

"There's something else we want to talk to you about." Perez selected a picture and pushed it over. "This is Ray Maynard. He's a homeless man, who was staying at the construction site in Acton. Do you know him?"

Stoltz glanced briefly at the photo and Lane studied his reaction carefully.

"I've never seen him before."

"Where were you on Sunday night," said Perez, "between nine and midnight?"

"I'd rather not say." Stoltz smiled a little, and Lane felt anger rising.

"You have a history of violence," said Lane. "Between 2002 and 2005 you attacked six people in their homes. You used an excessive level of force in the crimes you committed."

Stoltz looked indifferent. Lane had seen similar behaviour before, and wondered if he had a conscience at all.

"You were working for Merl & Grey," said Lane. "We'd like to know if you were there on Sunday night – and if you encountered Ray Maynard."

Stoltz wanted to ask a question but stopped.

"There's a furnace on site," said Lane. "Have you ever been into the building where it's housed?"

Stoltz didn't reply.

Lane was suddenly finding it difficult to read him.

"As part of your job, you were given keys to the site. Did you ever give the keys to anyone else?"

Stoltz remained silent.

Lane was becoming annoyed, and Perez could feel the tension reaching a peak.

"No comment?" said Lane angrily. "Is that the best you can do? Let's face it, that's the last refuge of the *truly* screwed."

CHAPTER
10

At the hospital site in Acton, forensic services were examining the hole in the yard. Doctor Croft had recovered more bone fragments, and was carefully cataloguing them as he placed them into transparent bags.

Assisting him was Maddy Webb, a junior member of the forensic services team. She was in her early twenties – nearly forty years younger than Croft – and thought he was slow and meandering, as he regaled her with stories of his career.

"The things I've seen in my time," he said. He shook his head. "You couldn't make it up. The things people will do to one another – whether it's spur of the moment anger, or premeditation – it makes you think about human nature."

Maddy wasn't taking in all that Croft was saying. She had been working in the forensics department for less than twelve months, and had yet to decide if the work suited her. Doctor Croft talked a lot. Maddy wouldn't have minded listening to music, but that wasn't something Croft allowed.

"Do you reckon it's only two bodies?" said Maddy.

"*Only two?*" said Croft with surprise. "My dear, two is a worrying number. It makes one think what could be next." Croft looked into the hole. "All things considered, two will provide us with enough work for the time being."

Maddy studied the bone fragments. Back at the laboratory they would be examined more closely. The chance of finding trace evidence was slim. Chemicals used in the decomposition could have destroyed all fibres, as well as DNA, and if they were going to find out who had been killed they would have to employ different techniques.

"We're going to need to do another sweep of the buildings," said Croft. "There're plenty of nooks and crannies … plenty of hiding places. We're going to need power tools to undo fittings and fixtures."

"Do you reckon we'll find what we're looking for in there?"

"There're many places to hide things," said Croft. He straightened himself up and looked tired. "People slip up … you never know. If you could put through a request for the personnel and equipment, I'd be grateful."

Maddy nodded. She took out her phone and walked away to see if she could get a signal. It was nice to get away from the hole. It was unsettling, and knowing what had happened there didn't help.

•　　　•　　　•

At homicide West headquarters, Lane and Perez left Frederick Stoltz in the interview room.

"What do you think of him?" said Perez.

Lane felt cross. "He's too confident. And smart, cocky and just too damn calm."

"Do you reckon he knows about the burial site in Acton?"

"He had access to the site and he has a history of violence." Lane hesitated. At the end of the corridor, he saw Chief Superintendent Travers and turned away.

"We've got to keep things under wraps. If the press gets wind of this, it'll make our lives harder. We'll have them camped out in Acton. They'll be following us around … we could even make the local TV."

"Press interest can be a good thing," said Perez thoughtfully.

Lane wasn't sure he agreed with that. He thought about the journalists he knew. He wondered how they'd react when they found out what he was investigating. Was there some sort of school they came from, which gave them all the same weaselly characteristics? It was as if they came off a production line.

"What do you want to do with Stoltz?" said Perez.

"Let's hold him. We've got twenty-four hours, so let's use it. We need to speak to our forensics people – see if there's anything that ties him to the crime scene in Acton."

"Resources are spread pretty thinly," Perez replied. "Going through the hospital site will take them several days, and then there's Stoltz's flat to consider."

Lane eyes flickered at the mention of the flat. "If he did kill two people, if he did try to dispose of their bodies, he may have kept personal effects – wallets, jewellery, that kind of thing."

"I'll get on to it."

Lane turned to go. "There's something about Stoltz. He has the kind of face you would never tire of –" Lane saw Travers walking towards him and stopped.

"Ah, sir, I was just about to come and see you." Lane put on his best smile.

Travers was a similar age to Lane, of average height and build, and almost bald. He had a red, slightly worn face. He was a decorated officer, with several commendations for bravery, and that often made Lane pause and think.

Travers led him down the hall, towards the kitchen at the far end. It was a small space, intended for making tea and coffee. The officers inside saw them approaching and quickly left. Lane saw the looks on their faces: they seemed to be wishing him good luck.

"To be honest, Tony, I was hoping you'd have taken the opportunity to speak to me." Travers spoke softly, and with a smile. The smile was disingenuous. Lane was sure of that.

He didn't know much about Travers. He knew that he was married and had children, but he didn't know their names or ages. And then of course there were the commendations for bravery.

Travers was almost the same age as him, and had risen to the rank of chief superintendent by following orders, being obsequious, and making enemies when required. Those were the things he did well, in Lane's mind.

"I'm sorry I didn't get back to you, sir. There's been quite a lot on."

"The Acton case?" Richard Travers was keen to know more. "I understand the mayor's office has taken an interest."

Lane explained what had been discovered in Acton. Travers listened without reacting.

"And you have a suspect in custody?"

"Yes, sir." Lane didn't want to go into detail about the lack of evidence. The mere fact that someone was in custody was enough to make his superior happy. Travers wanted things to look good on paper. Lane was the opposite. He didn't care about paperwork or crime stats. He thought of himself as more flexible.

"You know, Tony, sometimes this job takes a lot out of you." Travers looked down and his face sagged.

Lane wondered what he was referring to, and felt a spike of curiosity.

"I have a lot to deal with, juggling staffing numbers – trying to achieve more than I really can. Sometimes you feel as if you're taking things home with you."

Lane felt awkward. Did he want to talk? Lane knew how difficult Travers could be. If Perez had been there, he would have said something diplomatic, easing the situation with a deferential reply. Lane wasn't like that.

"I should get going, sir – things to do." He held Travers's eye and then left.

CHAPTER
11

Daniel Riley had been working for over half an hour. That was how long it had taken him to cut the rope that bound him. The edges of the metal grate were sharp, and he had carefully manoeuvred his wrists back and forth, cutting the rope.

When the final thread of rope snapped, Riley felt relief. The enclosed space was oppressive. No noise. No light. On more than one occasion he had wondered if he was underground. This place couldn't be purpose built. It was secluded, but where was he?

With his arms free, he rubbed his wrists and felt his shoulders aching. He spent several minutes regaining feeling, slowly rotating his arms, and then began checking the room.

The walls had rough surfaces. There were no doorframes and no signs of a way out. This place, wherever it was, seemed isolated. In the darkness, Riley dropped to his hands and knees. There was nothing on the ground. No signs of a trapdoor or a hatch. He rose, wondering if the opening was in the ceiling. He wondered how high the room was. All he could see above him was blackness, and looking up made him uneasy. He wondered if he was in a lift shaft of some sort.

He checked his jacket and trouser pockets, but could find no sign of his wallet or phone. Even the change that he had had was gone.

A knot of tension was growing in his stomach. He wondered if he would be able to escape. He tried to think about all those that he had wronged. No, best not go there.

Riley wasn't brave. He was normally a selfish man. And deep down he knew there were many other failings.

He felt the urge to urinate, and did so in a corner of the room, feeling self-conscious and embarrassed. He wondered how long he would be there. He needed food and water. Would anyone come back, or was the plan to simply starve him?

Another thought came to mind, and he went over to the metal grate. He undid the belt from his trousers, lifted the metal hook and began running it around the edge of the grate.

•   •   •

Steve Perez hadn't always wanted to be a police officer. He had studied for a degree in history, and after leaving university had thought that joining the police force would be an interesting choice of career. He hadn't been disappointed in that regard. The job was neither mundane nor routine, and he never dreaded the prospect of going to work.

He wasn't sure why he had been teamed up with Lane. It wasn't something he had requested, but they had been working together for several years, and the partnership worked well: the powers that be had known what they were doing.

Perez was married, but had no children. He and his wife had discussed it, and the feeling was that in a few years perhaps they would consider it. Lane had told him that his life would change forever. Perez knew that Lane had two children, in their early twenties. They had left home, and Lane didn't mention them often.

Perez arrived at the Wallder estate, in south London, a little after half-past one. He parked in the same spot he and Lane had used earlier that day. He looked up at the block of flats where Stoltz lived. Crime scene officers were still present. Perez could see white overalls, moving up and down the landing. Local children, who should have been in school, were watching, as were people in neighbouring flats. They seemed both tolerant and curious.

Perez showed his warrant card to the officer outside Stoltz's flat. The officer gave him a nod, and Perez went inside to see Chris Nolan, the crime scene manager, looking up from his work.

"Ah, Steve, glad you could make it."

"How're things going?" said Perez. He looked at the other forensic technicians, who were checking the living room.

"Swings and roundabouts. That's the best way of putting it."

Perez liked Nolan. He was a solid, dependable character, at least ten years older than him, who never complained and got the job done. Most of the younger forensic technicians were not like that. They were more forthright – more likely to answer back, particularly if they felt police officers were asking too much.

"We've found one set of prints so far," said Nolan. "They belong to Stoltz. We found a small amount of cash – about £400 – and of course the stolen goods."

"From his employer?" said Perez.

"Exactly," said Nolan. "Do you think this guy's linked to the remains we found in Acton?"

"He is a suspect," Perez conceded. He thought about Stoltz's propensity for violence. "Lane and I were wondering if you found any personal effects – wallets, cash-machine cards and so on – things that don't belong."

Nolan sighed. "Nothing so far. There is the money, but it's not a huge amount."

Perez felt disappointed.

"There is one thing though. We found women's clothes in the wardrobe – several dresses, some underwear – a pair of jeans."

"So Stoltz may have a girlfriend?"

Nolan paused and smirked. "Either that or he likes to cross-dress."

•　　•　　•

Perez spoke to Stoltz's next-door neighbour. He was the man Lane had mistaken for Stoltz the previous day. His name was Len Worthing, a tall man, with fair hair, in his early forties.

"So what did he do?" Worthing asked Perez, as he leant against the door.

"Right now he's just helping us with our enquiries." Perez hated using the phrase. It was insincere and evasive in his mind. "Does he have many visitors?"

Worthing shook his head and seemed impatient. "I explained all of this to your boss. I've never seen regular visitors. I must admit, he comes and goes at odd hours. I often hear that door going – it's damn annoying. I guess he must be a shift worker or something."

Perez knew that Stoltz worked regular hours.

"How long has he lived here?"

"Over a year … probably more like two. It's not a bad neighbourhood, all in all."

"How about a girlfriend or a partner? Does anyone like that ever come over?"

Worthing shook his head. "Not that I've seen. I see him carrying equipment sometimes. I guess he must work in construction or something."

Perez was curious. "Go on …"

"Bulky stuff – wrapped in canvas."

Perez thought about the copper cable that had been found in Stoltz's flat. It hadn't been wrapped, and there had been no sign of any canvas.

"There is one other thing," said Worthing. "He had an argument once. A man turned up at his door … I think he was uninvited. They were arguing about keys. In the end, Stoltz just slammed the door."

"Did you overhear anything else?"

"The guy may have been called Tanner or Banner – something like that."

Perez made a note and stopped as his phone rang. Caller ID said it was Lane.

"Thanks for your time," said Perez, turning away. The man shut his door and Perez answered the phone.

"How's it going?" said Lane at the other end.

"So, so," said Perez. He felt his energy waning. He explained what he had found, and Lane listened patiently.

"Let Nolan and his people complete their search."

"Will do."

"Doctor Croft has found something at the Acton site. Can you meet me there?"

Perez checked the time, hoping for more information. "Sure."

"Good." Lane hung up and Perez smiled as he thought about Lane's abrupt style.

CHAPTER 12

Perez arrived in Acton to find Lane parked outside the construction site. He was examining the dent in his car door, and looked unhappy.

"I should charge Stoltz for this, you know."

"Take it to the police garage," said Perez. "I know a guy there called Renni Law – he's good with panel work."

Lane looked as if he was considering it.

"So what has Doctor Croft found?" said Perez.

"He said it would be best if we saw for ourselves – that he could answer our questions there and then."

"A regular man of mystery," Perez murmured.

He and Lane walked across the site, towards the three buildings at the rear. There was something eerie about the large, open space. There were few people about – less than half-a-dozen forensic officers, and they were dwarfed by the piles of rubble and masonry scattered around. As they walked, Perez looked at the red masonry which covered the ground. It felt as if they were walking on the surface of an alien planet.

"So there's nothing in Stoltz's flat to tie him to the bodies?" said Lane.

"Not so far. Nolan is still searching though. It looks as if Stoltz may have had a girlfriend. It may be worth trying to track her down, as well as the stranger he argued with."

"Absolutely," said Lane. He paused for a beat. "My wife is having a get-together tomorrow evening for her sister. It's her fiftieth."

"I guess that's who you were present-shopping for the other day," said Perez.

"Yes … and it wasn't easy, believe me. Irene said you're invited, by the way."

Perez smiled. He suspected it was Lane who was inviting him, and he knew why: Lane didn't like being outnumbered by his wife's friends and family.

"Will I know anyone there?"

"Len Newman said he'd call by, as well as old Croft. We'll be heavily outnumbered though. My sister-in-law likes to socialize – has more friends than she knows what to do with."

Perez had met Lane's wife before, although he had never met her sister. He thought Irene was very different to Lane, lacking his rough and ready nature. Perhaps it was a case of opposites attracting.

"I'll be there," said Perez. It was short notice, but he suspected he'd be able to make it.

"Cheers."

They made their way to the hole in the yard, at the rear of the site. Both men were surprised to see that the space had been cleared. Maddy Webb and several other forensic officers had brought in lifting equipment and extracted more soil. Samples had been carefully catalogued as they were removed, and Lane watched as forensic officers took pictures of the pale earth.

Maddy Webb stood up and brushed herself down. "Chief Inspector …"

"How are things going?" said Lane. He wanted to seem upbeat and positive. "I heard you guys found something."

Maddy pointed behind her to Doctor Croft. He was placing transparent polythene bags into trays, ready to take them back to the lab.

"Ah, Chief Inspector. Impeccable timing."

"Progress isn't made by content people," said Lane. "So what have you found out?"

"I thought we'd have no luck, but it looks as if I may've been wrong." Croft held up an evidence bag. Inside was a chip from a mobile phone. Lane leant forward to study it and felt a flicker of excitement.

"Where did you find this?"

"Inside the hole," said Croft, pointing to the left-hand corner. Lane could see outlines in the earth where tools had been used. He looked at the spot in relation to the buildings.

"Someone who placed the bodies here could potentially have dropped it."

"Or it could have fallen from the pocket of a victim," said Croft.

Lane considered that. "Can we find out what's on it?"

Croft and Maddy looked pleased. Maddy produced a small, grey reader. It was barely bigger than a paperback, and had a slot for a SIM card. Putting on latex gloves, she took the SIM card from the polythene bag and slotted it into the machine. Lane looked at the display. "Is this telling us about the chip?"

"Yes. We can read what's on it. Not everything though. Certain parts of it are partitioned and password protected, but this gives us basic information – who the network provider is, the phone number assigned and when the chip was made." She held up the reader and Lane studied it.

"The chip was manufactured by Telcor," said Maddy. "You can see the phone number there. You can also see that it was made four months ago and only recently came into use. Hospital staff haven't worked on site for more than a year, so we can eliminate them."

Lane was impressed. "Can you read the address book?"

Maddy shook her head. "For that we'd need the network provider to unlock it. We can take this information to them, and get them to grant us access."

Lane took out his notebook and began jotting down the information from the reader.

"I'll do it," he said. He felt a buzz as he realized that it was a good lead. A thought flashed through his mind, and he wondered if the chip could tie Frederick Stoltz to the crime scene. He knew he shouldn't get ahead of himself. "OK … good work."

Maddy appreciated the praise. She removed the chip and put it back into the bag.

"I'll get in touch with the phone company," said Lane. "I'll let you know what I find."

"We'll be working here a while longer," said Croft. Something flickered at the edge of his mind, and he returned to his work.

Lane and Perez made to leave and headed for the entrance. "The thing I'm wondering is why Stoltz would suddenly turn to murder," said Perez.

"He has a history of violence," said Lane. "The burglaries and assaults – multiple assaults. With these things there tends to be a pattern of escalating behaviour."

"I'll head over to Merl & Grey. Let them know about their trusted employee, Frederick Stoltz."

"Don't tell them everything," said Lane. His tone was cautionary.

"Do you really think he's responsible for this?"

"Honestly?" Lane's face reshaped into something hard. "I can't be sure. He's smart and evasive, and too damn confident. See if Merl & Grey can tell you anything about friends or acquaintances. It would be good to build up a picture of his life."

Perez nodded. "I'll see you back at the incident room." And with that they split up.

•   •   •

Perez arrived at the offices of Merl & Grey a little after three o'clock, and noted all the construction equipment standing in the yard. He looked at the Portakabins to his right, and mounted the stairs, walking slowly. He was tired. It had been a long day and it wasn't over yet.

As he reached the Portakabin on the second floor, he took note of how few people were about. He could see how Frederick Stoltz had managed to steal supplies. He knocked on Alex Grey's door and waited until a voice said, *"Come in."*

Perez pushed open the door. Grey was sitting at her desk, studying paperwork. She was dressed in a black trouser suit, with her hair firmly tied back into a ponytail. She had on a small amount of make-up, and the bright red lipstick she wore contrasted with her pale features. Perez found himself thinking that she looked quite striking.

"Ah, Inspector. I got your message." Grey smiled and gestured to a chair opposite.

Perez glanced about. It looked as if no one else worked in the office.

"I heard you arrested one of my employees." Grey spoke casually, as if the news didn't surprise her. Her eyes ran up and down, appraising Perez.

"Mr Stoltz is in custody." Perez sounded apologetic. "He's helping us with our enquiries, but there're a few things that you should perhaps know."

Grey sat back and appeared relaxed. At that moment, Perez could see why she was in charge. Perhaps leadership was not something that could be taught.

"It looks as if Stoltz has been stealing construction supplies." Perez took out his PDA, scrolling through it, listing off the items that had been recovered from Stoltz's flat.

Grey listened. "And there I was thinking he was a reasonable man. He was reliable – took little time off. I thought I'd been lucky to hire him."

"Perhaps that's the impression he was trying to convey. I understand Mr Stoltz had keys to the site in Acton?"

"He was a key holder for a while. He also had keys for the yard here. Will I get back the supplies that he stole?"

"In due course," said Perez. "At the moment they're with our forensic officers. One of the reasons I came to see you was that I wanted to ask about Stoltz. How long had he been working here?"

Grey thought. "About two years? He came through a recruitment agency. He had some experience working in construction, and I took him on."

"And he was a good employee?"

"Apparently not," said Grey calmly. "What I mean is, on the surface everything seemed OK. He was reliable, he got the job done and he was easy to get on with. My foreman certainly didn't complain."

"Did you know much about Stoltz's life outside of work?"

"It seems as if I didn't know enough." Alex Grey tilted her head, as if accepting that she had made mistakes.

"One thing you should be aware of," said Perez, "is that his name isn't Stoltz. He's changed it several times over the years, and he has a lengthy record."

Grey's face fell slightly, as Perez continued. "Do you know if Stoltz has an acquaintance by the name of Banner or Tanner?"

Grey shook her head. "I never socialized with him. I think Stoltz has friends among the men he worked with. The person you need to speak to is Adrian Norton. He was the site foreman in Acton. The two of them seemed to get on well enough."

She wrote something down on a sheet of paper. "This is his number. He's currently working on a job in north London."

Perez gave a nod and folded the page. "OK … thank you."

"Not at all," said Grey. There was something disquieting about her smile. Perez remembered thinking that as he left.

CHAPTER
13

Daniel Riley had been working for some time. He had taken breaks as the work was tiring, but he felt that he was making progress.

The metal grate on the wall was a foot wide and less than a foot high. He could barely see what he was doing, and he had to use his fingers to feel his way around.

He ran the metal hook of the belt along the top of the grate. The brickwork there was tough, and he quickly realized it was not the best way to go about it.

He put down his belt and felt around the edges of the grate, noting the four screws that held it in place. That was where he should focus. He used the hook on the belt to loosen the screws. It was slow, painstaking work, and it would have been easier if there had been more light.

One screw came away from the wall and the grate loosened. Riley put his fingers around the edge and slowly tugged at it. It didn't move. He worked on the next screw, and eventually it came away. Now the grate was entirely loose on one side.

He was able to slip a hand behind. With all his strength, he pulled the grate away from the wall. It hinged on its two remaining screws, and there was a *pinging* sound, as the screws gave way.

Riley felt hope. Quickly, he lowered the grate and looked into the opening. It was pitch black and cold to the touch. The air duct was made of metal and extended into the distance. He was sure he could fit in.

He put on his belt, thought for a moment, and crouched down, climbing into the opening. He climbed in feet first and tried to slide along. The space was small and cold, but claustrophobia had never been a problem for him.

As he moved, he wondered where he was. Was he in the roof of a building? No, that didn't make sense. He had to be underground – somewhere disused. But what kind of building?

He squeezed himself through the duct. His legs made contact with rivets, joining one section to another. He eased himself over the join and carried on. There was another set of rivets and another join.

After a while, Riley felt hope giving way to concern. How long was the duct? Would he be trapped?

His feet touched something: another grate. Cold air was blowing through, and water was dripping on to his legs, but through the grate Riley could see that he had reached another room.

·   ·   ·

Perez returned to the incident room, at Homicide West, to find DCI Lane shouting. He was on the phone, and his face was red, as he concentrated and stared ahead.

"Yes, that's right … name, address *and* an itemized bill. In fact I want *all* the bills – sooner rather than later. Look … are you trying to be obstructive? … A homicide enquiry … Do you understand? … No, I don't care: that's not my problem!" Lane's face became even redder. Other people in the room were doing a poor job of pretending not to listen.

"I don't give a damn! Listen, I've got your address. If you keep this up, I'll come round and shove my boot up your …! No, I don't want to speak to your supervisor! You've got our email address. I want it before the end of the day … No! I'm not going to pay for it!" Lane slammed down the phone. Perez tried to conceal a smile.

"Is that to do with the SIM card?"

"Yes." Lane reached for his coffee and tried to calm himself down. "They must employ complete fools over there." He rolled his eyes. "How's it going at your end?"

"I saw Alex Grey."

"The good-looking one?"

"The very same." Perez felt a little embarrassed. "I told her about Stoltz – well, the edited version. She gave me the name of her site foreman. She said that he and Stoltz were friends – that he might know something about his day-to-day life."

"Good." Lane reached for a stack of papers. "I've got some background information. It turns out Frederick Stoltz was born in Shrewsbury. Came from a single parent family. His father left home before he was born, but there is an elder sister. His mother died recently – about the time he started becoming more violent.

"Stoltz seems to have drifted about. He held down a couple of jobs. It looks as if he tried legitimate work for a while." Lane seemed surprised. "He seems to be fairly well educated. He stayed at school and did A-Levels – even went to university. He started a maths degree but didn't stay. He dropped out in his first year."

"A man of hidden depths," said Perez, as he considered the matter.

"I wouldn't go that far. I think we should speak to him again. There're some questions I want answered." Lane rose and picked up the stack of papers from his desk.

.   .   .

Frederick Stoltz was sitting at the interview-room table. He looked impassive and sat upright, staring ahead. As Lane came into the room, the officer who was keeping watch left. Perez followed Lane and shut the door.

Stoltz seemed more interested in Perez, and his eyes followed him as he sat down.

"Your boss really does like taking charge, doesn't he?"

"That's the nature of the job," Lane interrupted. "You commit crime, and I arrest you: such is life."

Stoltz looked amused. "What can I do for you, Chief Inspector?"

"You know what's interesting?" said Lane. "I'm surprised you haven't asked why we're holding you. If this was a simple case of theft, you'd be bailed by now."

"I'm sure you have your reasons," said Stoltz. He spoke slowly and calmly, and it irritated Lane. He wanted Stoltz to react and display anger. Lane was usually good at provoking people.

"There're a couple of questions I have for you." Lane flicked through the papers in front of him. "Could you tell me if you own a mobile phone?"

"If you didn't find one at my flat, then I don't have one."

"A suitably evasive answer."

Stoltz turned to Perez. "Don't you have anything to ask me?"

"Just answer the question," said Perez. He disliked Stoltz's manner. He was worried that Stoltz could read him too well.

"I don't own a mobile," said Stoltz.

"And I don't believe you," Lane replied.

The room felt uncomfortably warm.

"When your people are finished at my place, I'd be grateful if you tidied up."

"You'll be lucky," said Lane. "I mentioned to you before that a man, by the name of Ray Maynard, had been chased into a road and struck by a car. It happened on Sunday night. Can you tell me where you were on Sunday?"

"No comment."

"And why's that?"

Stoltz remained silent, his lips pursed.

"Do you have any family, Mr Stoltz – any brothers or sisters?"

"I'm an only child."

"How about parents?"

Stoltz didn't answer, and Lane studied his face.

"When you worked on the hospital site in Acton, did you enter any of the buildings?"

Stoltz shook his head. "Our job was to clear the yard. Our foreman might have gone in; I can't be sure."

"You had keys for the site, didn't you?" said Perez.

Stoltz seemed pleased that Perez had spoken. "People trust me."

"And that explains why you were able to steal so much," said Lane.

Stoltz didn't react. "What's your point, Chief Inspector?"

"When you were a key holder at Merl & Grey, did you pass on your keys to anyone else?"

"No."

Lane studied his expression.

"We're going to hold you until we get some answers."

"There's a limit to how long you can hold me, Chief Inspector. Twenty-four hours, if memory serves."

"We can get an extension. But you know what concerns me? I have trouble believing anything you say." Lane was growing increasingly frustrated and made to leave. "Bloody oxygen thief."

·   ·   ·

"That guy annoys the hell out of me."

"Everyone annoys you," said Perez quietly. The detectives were walking back to the incident room.

"You know in the old days we would have locked him in a room, and hit him with a phone book."

"Don't say that too loudly," said Perez. He looked about, a sliver of concern rising up inside.

"OK. Perhaps threaten him. In any case, we weren't overwhelmed with rules or political correctness."

"Your interview technique is hardly laid back."

"He's hiding something," said Lane.

"I agree," said Perez, "but we need more evidence. We have no prints, no eyewitnesses – no one that's conscious anyway – and we certainly don't have a motive."

"Duly noted." Lane was pensive. "We can't hold him on the stolen goods charge. Without anything else to bring before a judge, he'll get bail."

Lane polished the silver plaque outside the incident room. Inside, Malcolm Brown was looking excited. He had papers fanned out in front of him, and couldn't wait to tell Lane what he had found.

"Phone records have come through, sir. They've sent most of what you asked for. The SIM card you found belongs to a James Stein. He's got an address in Epping. We've got itemized bills going back to when the phone came into use."

Lane studied the bills. "The phone provider said the SIM card was new. Is it true?"

"Yes, sir. It was first activated three months ago. What's interesting is that the calls stopped suddenly. They stopped roughly a month ago. Since then there's been nothing."

"About the time the bodies were disposed of," said Lane to himself.

"You think the SIM card belongs to one of our victims?" said Perez.

"It's a possibility," said Lane. "How much do we know about this James Stein?"

"Not much," Brown admitted. "He has no criminal record, but he does appear on one database."

"Which one?"

"Missing Persons."

CHAPTER 14

Lane and Perez travelled through rush-hour traffic. It took them nearly an hour to reach Epping, and Lane grew frustrated in spite of the fact he wasn't driving.

Malcolm Brown emailed Perez details of the missing persons report on James Stein. Perez was unable to read while driving, so Lane took his phone and scrolled through it.

"It looks as if Stein was reported missing by his business partner. He failed to attend several meetings, and his partner grew worried."

"Does Stein have family?" said Perez.

"It doesn't say. I'm guessing he didn't live with anyone, otherwise they'd have reported him missing too." They had rung Stein's house but no one had answered, and that had left the detectives none the wiser.

They reached Epping a little after 6.30, and continued towards the outskirts, where there were a number of residential streets with large, detached properties. House numbers weren't readily visible, and Perez drove slowly, noting numbers on gates. It was growing dark, and that only made the task more difficult.

"There it is," he said, "Millford Lodge." The house had a long drive, with open gates. Perez turned on to the gravel drive and drove slowly, checking left and right.

"The place looks deserted."

"It's a large place for one person," said Lane, scanning the garden.

Millford Lodge was more modern than the detectives had been expecting. It was an art-deco building, well maintained, with lawn and tall conifer trees all around.

"I hate those things," said Perez, glancing at the trees. He shivered inwardly. "There's something about them … their skeletal shape …"

"No accounting for taste," murmured Lane. He noted that there were no lights on inside the house. He had been hoping to see some signs of activity.

"Do we split up?" said Perez.

"No … let's stick together."

Perez parked and they walked around the house, checking the windows. There was a door at the rear. Lane ignored it, and continued his lap, while glancing at the trees and undergrowth. He heard the sound of crunching gravel as they walked, and realized that they were advertising their presence. He suddenly felt vulnerable.

When they returned to the front of the house, Lane waited a moment and pressed the bell.

Nothing.

He pressed the bell again, and there was a faint chiming sound from inside.

No one answered. Lane did something Perez didn't think of: he tried the handle of the front door. It turned. The pair looked at one another, and Lane led the way, stepping inside.

"Something isn't right," Perez whispered. There wasn't much light, and neither Lane nor Perez called out. Perez noted a wooden staircase, directly ahead. It was a broad affair, planted in the centre of the house. There was a length of taut rope, coming from the floor above. One end was tied to the banister, at the base of the stairs. Perez was curious and stepped forward.

Before Lane could stop him, Perez touched the rope. The knot tethering it began to undo, and a body swung down and hit him.

•   •   •

Doctor Croft, the medical examiner, took his time.

Lane watched as Croft slowly worked his way around the body. Lane wondered how old Croft was. He had to be past retirement, but for reasons Lane wasn't entirely sure of, he continued to work.

The body had been removed from its hanging position. It was laid out flat on white tarpaulin, in the hallway of the house. Forensic officers were outside, along with Perez, who was feeling unwell.

"So what have you got?" said Lane.

Croft studied the corpse. "White male, aged somewhere between his mid-thirties and mid-forties. Height approximately five foot ten. Initial examination suggests C.O.D. was a broken neck. It looks as if there was a high level fracture: C2 or C3."

Lane wasn't put off by the sight. He wanted to know as much possible.

"How long has he been here?"

Croft paused. "Judging by signs of decomposition, as well as insect and larval stages, I'd say it hasn't been long. I can be more precise, but you will have to wait till we get back to the lab."

The body was dressed in a white top and blue tracksuit. There were socks but no shoes.

"Did you find anything in the pockets?"

Croft shook his head. "At the moment there's no way of being sure who he is. We'll find out though. We can go by prints or dental records. Visual identification may also be possible."

Lane looked around, wondering if there was any family. The house didn't feel like a family home.

"There's not much exterior lighting," said Croft. "Do you want Forensics to set up lights when they search the grounds?"

"That'd be useful," said Lane. "We'll need to be thorough – it's like a forest out there."

"It may be best to wait until daylight."

Lane felt that Croft had a point. "Were you very busy in Acton?"

"Afraid so." Croft knew the nature of the work. Things could and often did happen suddenly. He sometimes joked that dead bodies were like buses: he waited ages for one then several turned up at once. Lane was one of the few people who found the joke amusing.

"How's young Perez doing?" asked Croft.

"A bit shook up. Then again it's his own fault: he shouldn't have been so damn curious."

Croft felt young people were impetuous. But the same could be said of Lane, and he could hardly be described as young. "Do you reckon this is linked to the Acton site?"

"Possibly. That SIM card you found led us here."

At that moment Perez came in through the front door, looking pale. "You should go home," said Lane. "If I'd been struck by a corpse, I wouldn't feel too good."

Perez had tried to shrug it off, but he kept recalling what had happened. Part of him wanted to be there. He wanted to show that he could cope.

"I'll get one of the uniforms to drive you," said Lane.

Perez tried to stop him but Lane insisted. "Our crime scene will still be here in the morning. You've been on the go for what? – eleven hours?"

Perez appreciated what Lane was trying to say, and in the end relented. As he left, Lane looked at Croft.

"You should call it a day too," said Croft. "I'll coordinate with scenes of crime – get them to start processing the inside of the house."

Lane considered that. He looked reluctant to leave, and studied the scene once more.

CHAPTER
15

You have to admit it's funny. I didn't do it deliberately. I didn't leave that body to make a statement. It's just circumstances that resulted in that guy being hanged. I have to admit though that he was a pain in the arse. He deserved what he got, and that's what happens when you cross me.

The police have discovered another crime scene. It means it's somewhere I can't go back to. That annoys me a little, but I still have room to manoeuvre and I still have options. I'm certainly not done yet.

You know what would be interesting? – watching the police from a distance. I'll have to have a good think about Stein's house. It's in a good location. I could conceivably go back and watch. There's a lot of undergrowth, and I could observe them fumbling about. Would I get caught? Possibly, but there's nothing to tie me to the crime.

I have to admit it's fun to think about taking risks. I'm beginning to like living on the edge, which is one of the reasons I do this.

But I'm not going to explain more. Not yet.

.   .   .

Early on Wednesday morning, DCI Lane arrived at St. Swithun's Hospital, in Chiswick. He ignored the woman at reception and carried on up to the trauma unit. He showed the duty nurse his warrant card, and asked how Ray Maynard was doing.

"The homeless guy who was brought in?"

Lane nodded, looking around. He didn't mind hospitals, but he disliked mortuaries. For him they brought back too many memories.

The nurse checked her screen. "He's still in room twenty. One of your officers is posted outside."

"I know," said Lane, "I put him there."

The nurse gave him a look, as if to ask whether it was really necessary, and the stare Lane returned made her focus elsewhere.

"We're still concerned about head injuries." She didn't sound very positive. "The swelling's not going down as we'd have hoped. Perhaps it's his age, perhaps it's his general health, but it's by no means certain that he'll recover."

"He may never come round?" Lane sounded surprised.

"It's early days, Inspector. There're a number of things that we can do."

"I suppose questioning him is not going to be possible."

The nurse bristled. "Definitely not."

Lane walked down the corridor to room twenty and noted the uniformed officer, sitting on a chair outside Maynard's room. The young man rose hastily as he saw Lane.

"Sir … everything's quiet here. It's been quiet since I started my shift."

"No visitors?" Lane looked up and down the corridor. He thought about the mayor's office, and when they would call back.

"None so far."

Lane looked through the glass window, into Maynard's room. He was lying on a bed, with a tube coming out of his mouth and a machine helping him to breath. He was wearing a white gown, with rolled-up sleeves. He looked at peace.

Maynard was only a few years younger than Lane, but appeared older. That was what life on the streets did for you, Lane thought. He wasn't often moved, but there was something about Maynard's plight that made him think about mortality.

"If anyone does turn up, let me know. This guy's our only witness, and I don't want him coming to any harm."

The young officer looked nervous.

"Yes, sir."

Lane turned away and returned to the duty nurse. The waiting area was half empty, and Lane's eyes came to rest on a dishevelled man, who was standing by a vending machine close to the door. His hair was unkempt as were his clothes. Lane studied the man's shoes. They were second hand, possibly third hand. He was clearly homeless.

As Lane watched, the man slowly tilted the vending machine. A packet of sandwiches fell through the chute at the bottom. The man was pleased. He picked them up and made for the exit.

"Aren't you going to stop him?" said the nurse.

Lane looked at her with contempt.

"Live and let live." And with that he left.

•　　　•　　　•

Lane arrived at James Stein's house, in Epping, to find a police cordon across the drive. Several neighbours, who looked old enough to know better, were standing at the entrance, looking towards the house.

"Haven't you got jobs to go to?" Lane said. They turned towards him. They remained where they were, and looked at him in a questioning manner. He showed his warrant card to an officer at the cordon, and bent under it, walking down the drive.

At the front door of the house, Lane put protective guards on his shoes. He glanced at the tall trees all around. There was something foreboding about the place. It was the garden: it was dense and overgrown.

The house was teeming with forensic officers, and a uniformed constable was standing just inside.

"How's it going?" Lane asked.

The constable was alert, and knew Lane by reputation.

"It's been busy all morning, sir. DI Perez is here. He's with your crime scene manager now."

Lane nodded. He saw Chris Nolan and Perez in the distance. Forensic officers were dusting surfaces, and Maddy Webb was checking the stairs.

The body that had been laid out on the hallway floor, the previous evening, was gone. Perez and Nolan saw Lane, and walked towards him.

"It's all systems go," said Perez. He seemed upbeat, and Lane was glad he had regained his composure.

"Found anything of use?"

"A couple of interesting things. The deceased is at the mortuary. Doctor Croft says he'll perform the post-mortem later today. He'll send us the results."

"Good."

"Scenes of crime are still going through the house. They've already done the hall and the ground floor, but they want us to stay out of the other rooms."

"Any prints that might be of use?"

"None so far."

Lane felt disappointed. He wished he could tie someone to a crime scene. "Any idea about our vic?"

Nolan, the crime scene manager, had a look on his face. Lane could tell that he had found something.

"We believe his name is Nigel Warner. We found documents in the house belonging to him. We found a passport that was particularly useful."

"Have next-of-kin been informed?"

"We haven't been able to trace them. The owner of the house, James Stein, has an elderly mother. She lives in Dundee. We liaised with colleagues there, and they gave her the news this morning."

Lane felt confused. "How is James Stein related to this new guy, Warner?"

"Time of death suggests Warner died close to when Stein went missing."

"What's the link between the two of them?"

Nolan and Perez shared a glance. "They lived together," said Nolan. "They were married – well, a civil partnership."

"They were gay?" said Lane.

"It would seem so."

Lane processed the information. "Do you think Stein had anything to do with his partner's death?"

"We don't believe so," said Nolan. "If Stein's remains were among those found in Acton, someone else was involved."

"So whoever killed Stein had a hand in Warner's death?"

"That's a reasonable assumption."

"This is the last thing we need." Lane felt frustrated. "We now have three homicides, and that excludes the body Maynard saw."

"How do you want to proceed?" said Perez. At that moment he was glad Lane was in charge. Things were becoming complicated, and he wanted to see how Lane would react.

Lane paced up and down. "James Stein was reported missing. Who submitted the missing persons report?"

Perez took out his phone. "His business partner. Stein ran his own company."

"So let's go pay the business partner a visit."

•   •   •

The detectives were nearing central London. It was half an hour later and Lane was driving.

"You were really hoping to tie Stoltz to that crime scene, weren't you?" said Perez.

"Was I that obvious?"

Perez didn't reply to the question. "We've either got to charge him or let him go. And we haven't got much time left."

"I realize that. One o'clock today: that's our deadline. Either we come up with new evidence, we apply for an extension or we let him out."

"Do you reckon Travers will grant us the extension?"

"Our good chief superintendent help us? You must be joking." Lane thought about previous occasions when Travers had obstructed him. There must have been occasions when his presence had helped, but right then Lane could not remember them. "That guy was born to create problems."

"What are you going to say to Stein's business partner?" said Perez. "Do you think it could be a homophobic crime?"

Lane paused and considered it. "Let's look before we leap."

Perez was surprised, as he thought of Lane as naturally impulsive.

Lane seemed to sense his thoughts. "Bull in a china shop, eh?"

"Well …" Perez felt a little embarrassed and looked away.

"After I get angry, I pause and consider things. We're sitting here with nothing but crickets chirping. We have to find out more about our vics."

Perez agreed with that. "Stein's remains were put into the ground, but his partner, Warner, was hanged. What happened there?"

"I've been thinking about that. There's method and planning in all of this. We simply can't see the bigger picture."

They drove through Mile End and headed towards Liverpool Street.

"James Stein has offices near Goodge Street," said Lane. "We need find to out what his business does, and if it has any link to his death. It's time we became more focused."

CHAPTER 16

Stein Engineering had offices in an old Victorian building. Lane parked on a side street, and saw a traffic warden slowly working his way down the road. Lane got out and walked up to the man, showing him his warrant card.

"Keep an eye on the car, will you?"

The middle-aged man looked at Lane, slowly comprehending what he was saying.

"6-1-2-6," Lane said, reading the number on the warden's lapel. "Just in case." He walked away, smiling to himself.

"What was that about?" said Perez.

"Just avoiding any future problems."

Lane pressed the intercom at the front of the building, and waited while someone answered. He was let in and showed his warrant card to the woman at reception.

"DCI Lane … DI Perez. We rang earlier. We were told to ask for a Stan O'Mara?"

The woman hesitated, and looked towards the main office behind her. A youngish man was looking through the glass doors. "That's Mr O'Mara," said the woman in a whisper. "It looks as if he's expecting you."

"Excellent," said Lane, although he didn't look as if he meant it.

He and Perez made their way towards the office, and O'Mara opened the door to greet them. The detectives introduced themselves and O'Mara led them towards a side office.

Stein Engineering occupied a modern, clinical-looking space. The floor was the colour of pine, and the desks and chairs looked as if they had been made to match. White, slim computers sat on almost every table, and around them were piles of paper, being scrutinized by young employees. Everything looked perfect. Too perfect, in Lane's mind.

O'Mara sat down in his own office and appeared nervous. He was in his mid-forties, with a boyish face and thin, wire-framed glasses. They were elliptical, and he reminded Lane of a schoolboy who hadn't quite grown up.

"I understand you have news, gentlemen … about James?"

"Indeed." Lane looked at Perez, as if trying to exchange information by thought alone. "As you may be aware, we're from Homicide West. We have reason to believe Mr Stein may have been murdered."

O'Mara's eyes widened. He was anxious. "… I thought he was just missing. I reported him missing several weeks ago … I spoke to one of your colleagues."

"I understand," said Lane calmly. He opened his notebook. "You spoke to a Sergeant Haimes, I believe?"

"From Missing Persons … yes. James didn't turn up for work." O'Mara's face was rigid. "We were worried. We rang him at home, but no one answered. When he didn't turn up for the rest of the week, we tried to get in touch with his partner. We couldn't reach him. It was at that point that I decided to call the police."

"And you spoke to Sergeant Haimes?" said Lane.

"Yes." O'Mara was breathing faster. "He said he visited James's home but no one was there. He said he'd be in touch, but we never heard back."

Lane seemed interested to hear that.

"This is not good." O'Mara looked through the glass door of his office to the employees outside. "How could this be? What am I going to do?"

"You said Stein has been missing for several weeks?"

"I've been running things in his absence." O'Mara was thinking about other matters.

"Do you know if anyone would've wanted to harm your boss?" said Perez.

O'Mara turned to him. "No. James is, was, a businessman. A good man."

"And what exactly is it that your company does?"

"We're an engineering firm." O'Mara studied the paperwork on his desk. "This office deals with oil and gas – we design off-shore installations. Stein Engineering has a number of divisions. That was how James built up the firm. We also do aviation and marine work, and we have defence contracts."

Lane made a note and looked out to the main office. "How many people does the company employ?"

"We have three offices in the southeast," said O'Mara, "as well as two engineering sites. There are also overseas offices. James grew the company by taking over other firms." O'Mara was tense. He wasn't interested in discussing company history. "I can't believe this … How about his partner, Nigel? Have you contacted him?"

"That won't be possible," said Lane. "Mr Warner is also deceased."

O'Mara face sank. "What? … How?"

Lane didn't want to divulge too much, and was coming to the conclusion that he didn't like O'Mara. He wondered what exactly made him think that. "We were wondering if you could tell us more about Mr Stein."

"I'm not sure what I can tell you. He was my boss. He ran the firm … it was his brain child really."

"And how long have you been here?"

"Nearly eight years." O'Mara looked pale. "Are you saying someone killed both James *and* Nigel?"

"We're at an early stage of our enquiries," said Lane. "We're trying to get as much background information as possible, and to that end we'd be grateful if you could help us … Did Mr Stein have any enemies?"

O'Mara thought. "… I don't think so. There were difficulties, problems from time to time, but that comes with running any business."

"Is the company successful?"

"Very much so." O'Mara seemed confident for a moment. "James grew the company aggressively, taking over a number of other firms."

"We're aware that Mr Stein was gay," said Lane. "Do you know if he had any problems in his personal life?"

O'Mara looked awkward. "I don't think so. I've met his partner, Nigel. He didn't work for the firm. I think he worked in the voluntary sector. They were happily married – well – a civil partnership."

Lane nodded.

"Does the name Frederick Stoltz mean anything to you?"

O'Mara shook his head.

"You've had no dealings with anyone of that name?"

"I don't think so …"

"We're trying to build up a clearer picture of James Stein's life. Could you show us around his office?"

O'Mara hesitated. "Sure." He rose and led the detectives to the adjoining room.

•　　　•　　　•

The room Daniel Riley was in was large, and he was surprised at the amount of space. It was rectangular, approximately ten metres long and five metres wide. There was little light. A dim glow came from the ceiling, and Riley looked up to see florescent tubes. He wondered how they came on. Was it a timer?

He walked across the tiled floor and he felt the coldness. He couldn't make out all the features of the room and decided to walk along its length. There seemed to be heaps of rubbish – masonry, planks of wood, wooden panels, all swept into piles. Building work had begun, but there had been a temporary or permanent halt – it was difficult to tell which.

Riley looked for a door. He reached the far end and saw a metal wall. It stretched from ceiling to floor, and when he looked down he thought he could see a runner. He reached out with his fingers, trying to find a groove.

Nothing.

He reached up, looking for a door handle, and hope quickly turned to frustration. Riley thought for a minute then pressed his palms against the metal door and pushed.

It wouldn't move. There was nothing to hold on to, nothing to pull back.

He banged the door and the sound reverberated. He knew he was drawing attention, but he became bolder. Perhaps no one would come. Perhaps he had been abandoned, in which case his survival depended on escape.

Riley had never been a brave man, and he was aware of his shortcomings. He wanted to get out, and promised himself that if he did he would put things right: he would treat people better.

He checked the other walls. They were covered in white tiles. The tiles were dirty, as if the room had been neglected for some time. Where was he?

Riley thought he was underground. The coldness and still-ness made him think so.

As he moved to a corner, his knee touched some-thing – curved, hard. He lifted up a sheet of tarpaulin to see a toilet bowl. Next to it was a sink. He turned on one of the taps. There was spluttering, before a jet of water came out.

Riley was reluctant to drink the water. He looked up, and in the far corner of the room saw a tiny red glow, and a camera lens.

He realized he was being watched.

CHAPTER 17

As Lane left Stein Engineering, Perez could see that he was annoyed. Lane said little, but his face was etched with anger. He got into the driver's seat, and waited impatiently as Perez closed the car door.

"What's up?" said Perez, trying to calm things down.

"It's that Sergeant Haimes, from Missing Persons."

"The one who looked into Stein's disappearance?"

"The very same. If he went to Stein's house, how did he not discover the body?" Lane was trying to think the situation through. He started the car, and rather than head back to Homicide West drove towards Fenchurch Street.

"Where are we going?" said Perez.

"Fenchurch East. That's where Haimes is based."

When they reached Fenchurch Street police station, Lane pulled up outside, stopping the car in the middle of the road. He left the engine running, and Perez knew that he was expected to park it. After he did so, he walked into the station, and nodded to the desk sergeant who he vaguely recognized.

From somewhere in the distance, Perez could hear shouting.

"What *the hell* are you playing at? You're supposed to be running a Missing Persons Department for God's sake!"

Perez walked along the corridor, towards the incident room. There were only four officers in there, all in their mid-thirties. One of them was Sergeant Bill Haimes, a well-built man, with a round face and dark hair. He was sitting at his desk, looking down, his lips pursed. Lane was standing over him.

"What sort of operation are you running? How busy are you really?"

"It's not about numbers," Haimes began, "but –"

"I don't want to know. The guy you were supposed to find – Stein – he's dead. Someone murdered him, as well as his partner. It's part of a homicide enquiry *I'm* having to deal with." Lane looked about, his face scarlet.

The other officers in the room were looking on discretely, but had decided to stay out of the argument.

"This guy, O'Mara, was relying on you to find Stein. What did you find when you got to Stein's house?"

There was a pause. Haimes looked at the paperwork in front of him but remained silent.

"You didn't go, did you? In spite of the fact he was reported missing, in spite of the fact that no one could reach his partner, you didn't go."

Haimes didn't reply.

"You told them you'd gone, but you didn't."

"Most missing people turn up in the end," said Haimes. As the words came out, he realized that it was a poor defence.

"And you lied. You said you'd checked on him, but you did nothing. Perhaps Stein and his partner were alive. Perhaps you might have been able to do something!"

Lane realized that that was highly unlikely, but he wanted to say it anyway.

"Are you going to report this?" said Haimes quietly. His mask was slipping.

Lane looked about, but there was no sign of Haimes's commanding officer.

"Unbelievable!"

Lane left, knocking over a pile of papers. Perez looked at Haimes for several seconds, and followed Lane out.

•   •   •

The drive back to Homicide West was subdued. Lane stared out of the window as Perez drove.

"So do you feel any better?"

Lane grunted. "I hate it when coppers don't do their job."

Perez knew Lane's views, although he hadn't seen him this angry in a while. It was probably best to change the subject. "At one o'clock we have to apply for an extension to hold Stoltz."

"Yes … the clock is ticking. I'm not sure which way that one will go."

They drove in silence for several minutes until Perez remembered something. "Is your wife's do still going ahead this evening?"

"Yeah. You will be there, won't you?"

"Of course." Perez had only been to Lane's home once before and thought it would be interesting to see it again.

"Len Newman said he'd be there, as well as old Croft, so it shouldn't be too bad."

"And it's for your sister-in-law?" said Perez.

"It's her fiftieth."

"I should really bring something – a gift of some sort."

Lane thought. "She drinks a lot. A bottle of wine would go down well."

"Wine it is."

When they reached Homicide West, Perez parked the car. Lane left quickly, heading for the holding area to arrange an interview with Frederick Stoltz.

•   •   •

Stoltz was sitting at the interview-room table. He was shivering slightly, but sat upright and looked directly at Lane.

The room was small and cramped. It had no air conditioning, and there were problems with the radiators: it was always too hot or too cold. Stoltz was feeling the effects, and Lane was pleased.

Perez's phone vibrated and he checked it. It was a message from Chris Nolan.

We've found something interesting at Stein's house. Give me a call.

Stoltz noticed Perez's interest in the phone. He liked goading Perez, and felt he could get away with it.

"I must say, I was expecting more of you, Inspector. I was expecting you to be more … assertive. You weren't like this in the past. Now you're very much DCI Lane's man."

Perez was distracted by the message.

"We're not interested in your views," said Lane curtly. He didn't want Stoltz dictating the course of events. Stoltz seemed too self-assured, and criminals never deserved to feel that way. "Do you know what I *really* dislike? Your attitude."

"I'm innocent, Chief Inspector. How else should I behave?" Stoltz tried to look blameless.

"I very much doubt your innocence. You've already been charged with theft. You're out of a job, and you're probably going to jail."

"But there are other things, aren't there?" said Stoltz. He felt playful, and wondered if Lane would take the bait. "What is it that you really want to know, Chief Inspector?"

Lane opened a folder. "Does the name James Stein mean anything to you?"

Stoltz looked blank and Lane held his gaze. "How about Nigel Warner?"

"I can't say I know either of them."

Lane tried to read Stoltz. He appeared to be holding something back.

"Stein Engineering. Have you ever worked for them?"

"I'm not an engineer," said Stoltz with a grin.

"James Stein went missing four weeks ago," said Lane. "Could you tell us where you were at the time?"

Stoltz looked amused. "I can't remember where I was *a week ago*. How am I supposed to remember that?"

"You have a history of violence," Lane said. "Have you ever been involved in any homophobic crimes?"

Stoltz looked puzzled. "I'm fairly sure I haven't beaten up any gay men, if that's what you mean." He checked the time on the wall clock. "You have to let me go, Chief Inspector. Either that or …"

Lane didn't appreciate being given advice. Stoltz wasn't nervous. He seemed almost too calm.

"You've refused to say what you were doing over the weekend. On Sunday evening, a man by the name of Ray Maynard was chased into traffic, in south London. He was struck by a car."

"I don't know anything about that."

"What were you doing at the time?"

"That's none of your business."

Lane saw stress on Stoltz's face, and the sense of superiority seemed to diminish.

"You've gone by many aliases, had many jobs – some of them less legit than others. You have little in the way of family or friends."

"And your point?" said Stoltz. He stood up. "If you want to hold me, you're going to need that extension. I suggest you get it."

Lane wanted to react but left the room, leaving Perez to accompany Stoltz back to his cell.

# CHAPTER 18

Lane and Perez met in the incident room and found it busy. Civilian workers were collating information, preparing reports and making phone calls.

"Things aren't going our way," said Lane. He glanced at the photographs on Malcolm Brown's desk. They had changed, and were now showing scenes of London in summer. Brown looked flustered.

"Quite a lot's been happening, sir. I've been looking into the background of Stoltz. It turns out his parents died several years ago. He has a sister however, and she lives in West Sussex. I'm not sure if she and Stoltz have kept in touch over the years."

Lane was interested. "We need background information. There's missing time we have to account for. Leave the details on my desk."

Perez sat at his own desk and dialled the number of Nolan, the crime scene manager. He waited while the phone rang and glanced at his computer.

"What happened to the NAS unit?"

"The what?" said Lane.

"The network-attached storage device – the thing I installed."

"Oh," Malcolm murmured. "IT came along. They said they didn't like you attaching things without permission. They took it."

Perez seemed concerned.

"Hello?" said a voice at the other end. Perez raised the phone.

"Chris, it's me. I got your message. What did you find?"

The connection was weak. Nolan was on his mobile and appeared to be moving about.

"We found some prints on a computer in one of the bedrooms, here at Stein's home. They don't belong."

"Did you get a match?"

"That's where it gets interesting. We ran them through the system. We got a hit on a Michael Kern – he has a lengthy record."

Perez wasn't sure whether to be pleased or not.

"Does the name mean anything to you?" said Nolan.

"No …"

"I'll email you the details and you can look at his previous."

"Thanks. Did you find the prints anywhere else?"

"They were mostly on Stein's computer – a desktop system – and on some files in the room. They were also on the banister of the stairs, close to where Warner was hanged."

Perez listened more keenly.

"Nothing seems to have been taken or damaged however, and the computer itself is password protected."

"Can you bring it in?"

"We're one step ahead of you. We're packing it up, to bring it back to the lab."

"Excellent."

"I'll send Kern's information over and we can speak later." With that Nolan hung up.

Perez held on to the phone, thinking.

"I've got to go and see the chief superintendent," said Lane, "regarding the extension for Stoltz."

Brown looked at the file he was compiling. "You can take this, sir. It may be of use, but there're also a couple of other things."

"Mmm?" Lane was studying the file that Brown had passed over.

"A Darren Thorn rang. He's the chief executive of the Acton Hospital Trust – the one that owns the Acton site."

"What was he after?"

"He was worried. He wanted to know what our officers were doing – when they'd be leaving."

"They'll be leaving when I'm satisfied," said Lane.

Brown felt unsettled. "Mr Thorn asked for your number. I gave it to him … I hope that was OK."

"Not a problem, Malcolm. If he calls, I'll speak to him. I guess I better go and see Travers." Lane was having to juggle a number of things, and paused for a moment to clear his mind.

·   ·   ·

Maddy Webb was watching the forensic officers as they worked. She was in the grounds of James Stein's house, in Epping. She had arrived earlier that morning, and had parked at the end of the street and watched as other forensic officers arrived.

The house had grounds all around. The trees and undergrowth provided cover, and once on site she had skirted around the outside of the property to gain her bearings.

She knew what had been discovered. Other forensic officers had been assigned to go through the property. Her job was to concentrate on the outside, and she moved across the garden at the rear.

Maddy recognized a tall man with greying hair – Nolan, the crime scene manager. Nolan gave directions to his officers as they checked the outside of the house. Maddy wondered how the house could be connected to the place in Acton. Given the number of personnel, they should be able to find something. Of that she was certain.

Junior forensic officers were combing the lawn and the drive. Maddy moved across the back garden, and continued for another forty yards. A search grid had been established, and her job was to check the trees and the undergrowth beyond.

She moved almost silently, humming to herself as she checked the vegetation. The garden was a strange mix. The lawn immediately behind the house had been tended, but someone had given up after fifty yards, and undergrowth was encroaching on to the trimmed grass. Maddy moved into the undergrowth but could see no signs of disturbance – no broken branches or trampled vegetation. There was woodland beyond, but she was sure there were no wild animals – no deer, nothing like that.

She felt prickling on the back of her neck and turned around. In the distance she could see the rear of the house. She had gone further than she thought. Perhaps she should think about heading back. She wanted to get to the woods. Then she knew she would have done a thorough job. She felt the prickling again: there was something foreboding about the place. Maddy wondered how many people had lived in the house. This wouldn't be a nice place to live – not by yourself.

Suddenly there was a snapping sound. Maddy turned and looked about. It had been loud – something large, cracking a branch.

There were no animals, no wildlife large enough to make that sound. Instinct made Maddy stand still. She wondered if she was being watched. Branches snapped again and she paused. She held her breath. Was someone there?

There was rustling – something was coming towards her. Without thinking, Maddy straightened up and ran. Common sense was pushed aside, and it was only several seconds later that she fully appreciated her situation.

She ran through the thick undergrowth, pushing branches away. Something tore at her jacket, and she was aware of someone getting closer.

Maddy thought she could hear a voice. Low-hanging branches obscured her view. Undergrowth was thick, but not impassable, and she tried to avoid creepers and vines at ground level. She felt her heart beating. She should have stayed put – she realized that now, and a sense of nervous exhaustion passed over her.

Maddy was almost out of breath. She hoped the trees would thin out, and she found it hard to gain her bearings. She had moved away from the house. She jumped over a branch and glanced back.

Suddenly the ground disappeared and she lost her balance. She pitched forward, and put her hands out to protect her face. The drop was more than six feet, and she struck the ground hard. Something was lying next to her and she pushed it aside and glanced up.

Maddy was aware of earth and the mouth of a hole. She sensed that something was wrong, and realized that she was in a grave.

CHAPTER
19

DCI Lane was livid. He returned to the incident room and slammed the door. Perez had been putting his IT equipment into a box, and looked up.

"What's happened?"

"Travers didn't grant us the extension on Stoltz." Lane felt anger rising as he recalled the conversation. "He asked about evidence … wanted to know about trace and fibre … if there was anything linking Stoltz to the crime scene in Acton."

"And?"

"I had to tell him the truth – *no*. I told him about the thefts from Merl & Grey, but he said that they weren't related."

"I suppose he has a point. So what happens now?"

Lane didn't like thinking about it, and wished he could do as he wanted. "Stoltz will walk. He'll be charged with theft, but he'll probably make bail. He'll be free." Lane sank into his chair, trying to calm down.

"Travers is more of a bureaucrat than a police officer," Perez said.

Lane knew Perez was quite different to him. He tried to smooth things out, and see arguments from other people's points of view. He was young, and would go further than him, all the way to borough commander or higher.

"Travers is like a fish out of water," said Lane, "and he isn't getting any closer to the bowl."

"Don't be too hard on him. He has a lot on his plate."

"So you keep reminding me. Well, go on then: tell me what problems Travers has to deal with."

Perez paused. "You know he has two children?"

"A boy and a girl?"

"Two boys. They're teenagers – fourteen and sixteen. He thought they were gifted, and sent them to private schools. However things went wrong. One of them started dealing drugs – apparently he became the school drug dealer. He was found out and expelled. Now Travers isn't sure what to do. He thinks his children are going down the wrong path."

Lane had grown-up children, although they had never got into that sort of trouble. He had difficulty seeing Travers as a father. Now it turned out he might not be a good one. Lane wasn't sure if sympathy was warranted.

"There is this Michael Kern," said Perez, and Lane came back to the matter in hand. He listened as Perez explained the situation. "He is a suspect we have to consider."

"Bring up his details on the PNC. Let's have a look at the printout."

Perez set to work and Lane continued. "I still want to know more about Stoltz." Lane looked at the file Brown had prepared. "There's something there."

"Are you sure that's the right direction to go in?"

"Stoltz is concealing something." Lane felt anger as he saw Stoltz's face in his mind. Lane knew how criminals behaved.

He thought for a minute, then picked up the phone and dialled an officer he used for surveillance. Perez listened as Lane explained that he wanted Stoltz followed. When he put down the receiver, Perez gave a disapproving look.

"That'll affect the overtime budget. *And* Travers will find out."

"Not for some time." Lane began feeling more satisfied. "If it gets us somewhere, well …" He stopped as the phone rang. He picked it up and listened, and his eyes widened.

"*Unbelievable.* Yeah, we'll be there." He hung up. "We're needed. Bring that printout on Kern with you."

·   ·   ·

Digging that grave had to be done. It wasn't easy; I won't lie about it. Bloody hard work, but Stein had a large garden and it made sense to use it. I would have liked to spend more time there. He had a nice home. I wouldn't say the same about the person he lived with, but that's a different matter.

I could have made much more use of Stein's land. I could have made more use of all of his resources. He was so fortunate, and he never realized it. That's the thing with rich people: they become arrogant and divorced from reality, totally unappreciative of what they have. I wouldn't make those mistakes.

I should have taken more from Stein, but my timetable has changed. That discovery in Acton has forced me to move. That damn homeless guy. Don't make me go there again. But I'm a realist.

I'll watch the police stumble for a while. After all it's amusing. Then I'll move on. There's a lot to do and little time, and I still have some distance to cover.

·   ·   ·

Lane and Perez made their way to James Stein's house in Epping. As they arrived, Lane looked out of the window. A news crew had set up a van on the opposite side of the road, a short way from Stein's home. Lane looked at the dish on top the van, and the two reporters standing outside. They were talking animatedly to one another.

"Christ on a bike … that's the last thing we need."

"We couldn't keep it quiet forever." Perez glanced at the journalists.

"I wonder if our suspects have anything to do with this," said Lane.

"We'll find out soon enough." Perez stopped at the police cordon, showed his warrant card through the window, and drove on.

They parked in front of Stein's house and got out. There were a number of forensic officers searching the grounds, and Lane caught sight of Chris Nolan. He walked over to him.

"News travels fast," said Nolan.

"Where exactly is it?" said Lane gruffly.

Nolan didn't react to Lane's manner. He had known him long enough not to take offence. "This way." They moved through conifer trees towards the undergrowth. The sky was overcast, and little light was reaching the ground. There was a musty smell of vegetation all around.

"The garden extends for quite a way," Nolan explained. "All of this belonged to Stein, but it doesn't look as if he maintained it."

Perez noted a walkway which had been laid down. "It's best if we stick to this," said Nolan. "Less chance of contamination."

They passed a broken fence, which marked the end of Stein's land, and continued into the woods. The walkway, which was made of tarpaulin, crunched as they moved over it. In the distance Lane could see a young forensic technician, Maddy Webb.

"It was Maddy who found it," said Nolan. Maddy looked shaken. Her clothes were dirty, her jacket torn, and she bent her head as Lane approached.

The ground dipped sharply, and Lane and Perez peered over. They could see soil and branches. Two forensic officers were in the hole that had been dug, removing soil with small brushes. Perez felt uncomfortable and pulled back.

"It's quite large for a grave," said Nolan. "It's fairly recent and was quite well hidden. We've found no body, but we have found some clothes and a rucksack. Do you want to go down and take a look?"

Lane nodded. With Nolan's help, he made his way down on the ladder that had been set up, swearing as he attempted to maintain his balance. Forensic officers stepped aside.

Lane studied the rucksack that had been uncovered. It was dark brown, and looked as if it had recently been buried.

"Is there anything inside?"

"Some clothes and a watch," said Nolan. "No ID though." He pointed to a shirt and a pair of trousers, which had been transferred to an evidence bag. Both were dark brown, and looked as if they formed part of a uniform.

"Any labels or company logos?"

"No logos. The labels have all been removed."

Lane felt curious and tried to make sense of the information, wondering how it fitted in with what he already knew. "There's a lot of land here. We're going to have to search the whole area."

Nolan understood that it had to be done.

"Do the best you can," said Lane. "I know resources are stretched thinly." He made for the ladder.

Maddy was standing where Lane had left her, and looked uneasy. Lane caught her eye and tried to appear understanding. "There's something I need to check. Then you can explain to me exactly what happened."

CHAPTER
20

Daniel Riley could hear noise. The large room, in which he was standing, was beginning to feel cold. He had nothing warm to wrap around him and looked about. All he could see were small pieces of masonry and wood.

He looked up to the corner of the room, where he could see the red light. It flickered occasionally – a small sphere of red, blinking at him. He couldn't make out the camera. It appeared to be concealed in a dome.

He turned his attention to the noise, which was dim and distant. He couldn't be sure where it was coming from, but he thought he could hear a door opening and then footsteps. Riley wanted to call out. He wanted to ask for help but hesitated. For him silence was becoming a friend.

He closed his eyes to concentrate, listening for more movement. He was beginning to wonder if he had imagined it, when there was a noise nearby. There was the sound of a key going into a lock, and the metal door began to slide back.

Fear rose through Riley's body.

The room remained dimly lit. He had been expecting light, but none flooded in. The door stopped moving and a figured appeared. Its face was shrouded, but Riley realized that it was a man.

Riley tried to back away but stumbled. The man reached for him, hauling him up, and punched him in the stomach. Riley felt pain surging through his body. The man was strong. He spun Riley around and threw him down.

Violence wasn't something Daniel Riley was good at dealing with. He didn't know how to respond, and felt shame. He was struck on the back and collapsed on to his stomach.

"Learn your place!"

The voice was low, and filled with anger. The man struck him again and paused for breath.

• • •

Lane made his way up the stairs of James Stein's home. Nolan walked ahead of him and Perez followed.

"Show me the room where the computer was," said Lane.

Nolan led him to a bedroom off the main landing. It was a small room that had been converted into a study. Wooden bookcases lined two walls, neatly packed with hardback titles. Lane glanced quickly at them and saw technical manuals, engineering texts and several on maths.

In the far corner of the room was a small table. Lane could see where a computer had once stood. Dust marked the position of the keyboard and monitor.

"As I explained on the phone," said Nolan, "the machine is partitioned and password protected. "We'll pass it over to the e-crime team. It may take them a while, but they should be able to gain access."

"Stein did work for the government, didn't he?" said Lane. He looked perturbed.

"Defence work," said Perez, "some of it classified."

"And you said you found fingerprints on the machine?"

Nolan looked up. "We got a match for a Michael Kern. The lack of additional prints and smudges, particularly on the keyboard, suggests he was the last person to use it."

Lane looked out of the window, to the gravel at the front of the house. He turned to Perez. "How much do we know about this Mr Michael Kern?"

Perez unfolded the PNC report. "He's forty-six years old and has a criminal record going all the way back. He was born in Glasgow – one of seven children. By the age of ten he was sent to a reform school. A minor conviction landed him in a young offenders' institute.

"Upon his release he returned to crime, and in his early twenties served sentences for burglary and forgery. In his early thirties he moved to London and lived with a girlfriend for a while. They were engaged to be married but they split up. She accused him of violence and threatening behaviour.

"Kern seems to have drifted from job to job. He stayed in the south however. In his late thirties he served another prison term for burglary. He was accused of rape by another girlfriend, but it never came to court. He left London when he was thirty-eight."

Perez paused. "This is surprising …" Lane looked up and Perez continued.

"He spent two years with a religious sect, in the West Midlands. He was there under a false name. He then returned to London at the age of forty. He hasn't been arrested since."

Lane considered all that he had heard, and looked at the picture of Kern. He was older than his years, with short, greyish hair and a round face. He might have once been good looking, but he now seemed worn down. Lane turned to Nolan. "You said Kern's prints were found in one or two other places?"

"I found prints on the bookshelves and on the door." Nolan pointed to the door of the study. "There were also prints on the banister, close to where Nigel Warner was hanged."

"How about the rope that was used to hang Warner? Did you find anything there?"

"It's difficult to lift prints from a surface like that." Nolan had experienced problems like this before. "The same is true for the clothes Warner was wearing. We'll do what we can back at the lab though."

Lane appreciated Nolan's efforts. He made for the stairs and headed down.

·   ·   ·

Maddy Webb looked sheepish. She was standing at the base of the stairs, waiting. She was smaller than Lane remembered, as well as younger. He knew that she didn't particularly like him, but then again a lot of the forensic technicians didn't like him: that was life, and as far as he was concerned you just had to get on with it.

"I guess you want to know what happened," said Maddy.

"It would be useful," Lane replied. "I understand someone chased you?"

"That's what it seemed like." Maddy explained how she had been searching the undergrowth at the back. "I had a sense I was being watched." She looked up and to her right, trying to recall the incident. "I was by myself. The other techs were some distance off."

"So no one saw anything. Did people hear anything?"

"… I don't think so."

Nolan, who had joined Lane, interrupted. "I got several people to search the undergrowth. We went all the way into the woods but we didn't find anything."

"How about signs of someone?" said Lane. "Broken branches, trampled vegetation …"

Nolan hesitated, and Lane could sense that he had something.

"There were signs of a trail, but it looks to be an old one."

"So someone may have been in the woods at some point, possibly watching?" Lane seemed thoughtful and stared at Perez.

"People do like to come back to the scene of the crime," said Lane, "– watch and gloat as the police search for evidence."

"I don't think this guy was interested in gloating," said Maddy, "assuming it was a guy." She felt confused. "I *think* it was a man. I *think* it was someone large. They moved quickly – nearly caught up with me."

"Until you fell into that hole," said Nolan.

"What happened then?" said Lane.

"I don't know. Nothing. Whoever was pursuing me – *if* someone was pursing me – they stopped. I began shouting. Some of my colleagues heard. They set up the ladder and got me out."

"Do you want us to do another search?" said Nolan. He could sense what Lane was thinking.

"I would appreciate it. Look beyond the woods. I'll get some uniformed officers to help. You guys have enough on your plate."

Nolan was grateful that Lane understood the pressures he faced.

"If someone was here, they're probably long gone." Lane thought about Stoltz, who was due to be released. This wasn't him; this couldn't be him.

CHAPTER 21

There was a buzz of activity in the lobby at Homicide West. Lane saw the custody sergeant and gave him a knowing look: they both knew how frantic things could get. In the incident room, Malcolm Brown was pleased Lane had returned.

"I've got a couple of messages, sir. Darren Thorn, the chief executive of the Acton Hospital Trust, rang. He seemed keen to speak to you." Brown wondered if Lane could be persuaded to return the call.

"It can wait." Lane checked his messages. There was only one of importance. Doctor Croft had said he would be carrying out an autopsy on Nigel Warner, that afternoon. He'd invited Lane to join him, and it was something that Lane was keen to do.

"Where do we go from here?" asked Perez.

Lane sat down and loosened his tie. "The trench in the woods complicates matters. We have the remains of two people, found in Acton, and we have Nigel Warner, found in his home. Was that hole in the woods going to be used?"

"Perhaps it was meant for the body Ray Maynard saw being dragged at the hospital."

"Transport would have been needed," said Lane. He thought about the logistics. "What do all of our victims have in common?"

"We know that at least two of them were gay," said Perez, "Stein and Warner."

"And you think that the other one may also have been?"

"It's worth considering."

"We have yet to ID everyone," said Lane. "That's what we need to focus on."

Perez knew it would be hard to ID the remains of the second body, found in Acton. They had got lucky with James Stein.

"We have to go with what we've got," Lane said. "I'm going to find out more about Stein and try and track down this Michael Kern. In the meantime I want you to look into Stoltz. He's a man who's more lucky than he deserves to be." Lane felt angry. "He's been keeping something back, and I want to know what it is."

"I've got something related to that." Perez searched the top of a stack of documents on his desk. "Here: the woman at Merl & Grey Construction. She gave me the name of Stoltz's foreman – said they worked together on a number of jobs. It looks as if they worked together for nearly a year. Stoltz may have talked to him."

Lane liked Perez's thinking. "Follow it up."

Perez checked the number of the foreman and made the call. Lane remembered the custody sergeant downstairs. He picked up his phone, dialled an extension, and the sergeant answered almost immediately.

"Tony. I got the sense you wanted to speak to me."

"I have a guy that's due for release – a suspect."

"Stoltz?"

"That's the one. He's a viable suspect in my case."

"He'll probably make bail soon," the sergeant replied. "Are you looking for an administrative error? His paperwork could go missing."

"It's tempting, but there was something else I wanted to ask. Has he had any visitors while he's been here?"

The sergeant paused and Lane sensed that he was checking.

"Nothing. No one on my watch; no one since he was brought in."

"How about phone calls? Anyone wanting to speak to him?"

The sergeant checked again. "No. I have to say there seems to be quite a lot of interest in your case."

Lane felt a wave of concern. "How so?"

"The press. We've had journalists coming to the desk, asking to speak to you."

"Sometimes I wonder how information leaks," Lane murmured.

"You and me both," the sergeant replied. "I'll keep you posted if anything breaks."

"Cheers." And with that Lane hung up.

Daniel Riley felt pain. He was buckled over, lying on the floor in the disused room. The man who had attacked him had left, pulling the door shut behind him.

Riley looked up and tried to ignore the pain. In the dim light he checked the door. Nothing. It was firmly shut.

He wondered why the man had beaten him, and why he had stopped. This couldn't be happening. It was unreal, and he knew his situation would only worsen.

Riley thought about what his life had been like before. Then a new thought filled his mind: he was losing track of time. He didn't know how long he had been held. Had it been twenty-four hours? Forty-eight?

He thought about his wife and children, his home and job. He'd been successful; he'd been someone. He tried to think about why it had all happened. Was it a mistake? It had to be. He hadn't seen the face of the man who had attacked him, but he had noted his height and build. He tried to make the connections.

Riley hadn't had any arguments, hadn't wronged anyone. It *had* to be a mistake. He wondered if he'd die in this place. Erin must have raised the alarm, but how would anyone find him?

He thought about his location. Up to now he had assumed he was still in England. There was something lurking at the back of his mind however. What if he'd been smuggled out of the country?

How would he ever be found? He felt hope slipping away, and as time passed he knew it would become worse.

He'd drunk from the basin in the corner, but he was beginning to feel hungry. Was that how he'd die? Through starvation?

Riley heard a metallic sound and looked towards the large metal door. He felt worried, as he realized his attacker was returning.

In the dim light Riley focused on the door. It didn't slide open. Instead there was movement near the base. A hatch opened and Riley was surprised, as a small tray was pushed through.

. . .

DI Perez arrived at the construction site run by Merl & Grey. He checked the details on his phone, to make sure he had the right address. He kept a sat-nav system in the car, and frequently used it when Lane wasn't with him.

The construction site was in north London, a short distance from Finsbury Park. Perez stopped on the main road, left his police ID on the dashboard, and walked towards the entrance.

There was a small wooden hut, with a window cut into it, and a sign on the front saying, *No hat, no boots, no job.*

"Can I help you?" said the man inside.

"I'm looking for Adrian Norton," said Perez. "He said I should meet him here."

There was immediate recognition on the old man's face. "Mr Norton's our site foreman. Hold on … I'll call him up."

The workman reached for a radio splashed with paint and cement. He said something inaudible and there was a crackling sound. Eventually a voice replied.

"You might as well stay put," said the man. He looked at Perez's shoes and suit, and Perez understood what he meant. He took a step back to survey the site, and looked at the building that was being renovated. It was large, six storeys high, and at least thirty metres long. White tarpaulin covered it from top to bottom, and Perez could see little of what was going on behind. He looked at the sign at the front of the site, and saw the name of the local NHS trust.

Presently, Norton appeared. He was a tall man, at least six foot three, and appeared even taller with the hardhat he was wearing. He had on a florescent jacket that was splashed with cement, and brown trousers and heavy boots. He could hardly be described as good looking, but he broke into a smile as he saw Perez.

"Inspector?"

Perez put out a hand. "Thanks for taking the time to see me."

"Not a problem, Inspector." Norton tucked his hardhat under his arm, and walked with Perez towards the main road. They stopped by a low wall and Norton leant against it.

"So what is it that I can do for you?"

"I got your name from Alex Grey."

There was a nod from Norton. "Our much-loved boss."

Perez thought for a moment about the way he said it. There was more going on than he was aware of. "I'm looking into the background of a man by the name of Frederick Stoltz. Ms Grey explained that he worked with you."

Norton nodded again. "We worked together for more than a year. We did a number of jobs in and around London."

"Stoltz has been assisting us with our enquiries," said Perez.

Norton didn't seem surprised and waited as Perez continued. "I'm wondering if you could tell me more about him. We're trying to build up a better picture of his life, in particular his movements over the last two months."

"I'm not sure how much I can help. Freddy and I weren't close. Acquaintances I'd say, though we got on well enough."

"And you were his boss?"

"I was the foreman on all the jobs he worked. He was a good employee – solid, reliable – turned up on time. Put in the effort too." Norton sounded pleased.

"Did you know he was an ex-con?"

Norton was unmoved. "To be honest, I've worked with a number of people who are. This business attracts more than its fair share."

Perez appreciated his frankness.

"Stoltz was fired," said Norton. "That was what Grey told me."

"He stole a large quantity of supplies," said Perez.

"I was surprised when I found out about that. All I can say is, he was good at concealing things."

"Did Stoltz tell you much about his life?"

"Not really. He explained that he'd been inside. He didn't say what for. I got the feeling it was something serious though."

Perez was reluctant to divulge too much. "How about friends and family? Did he talk about them?"

"As far as I'm aware, he has no parents. I think he may have been brought up in foster care. He mentioned it once. He had a girlfriend, but I never met her."

Perez was surprised. "We don't have any details of a girlfriend. Do you know her name?"

"I can't help you there. He did mention her though. I got the impression things were going OK – it was a fairly new relationship."

"How long had they been seeing each other?"

"Six months? – possibly a bit more?"

"And did he mention how he met her?"

Norton thought. "No. He did say that things were *complicated*." Norton hesitated. "Look, I don't like speaking ill of people, but I got the impression …"

"Go on."

"Well, I got the impression that she wasn't single."

"She was in a relationship with someone else?"

"I had that feeling. It may have been why he didn't say much. The way he spoke, it sounded tricky."

Perez made a mental note to write down the information later. "How about other things? Did he talk about his spare time?"

"Not really. We worked regular hours – 8.30 to 4.00. Outside of that, I don't know what he did. Look, he was an OK guy, a good employee, but …" For the first time Norton looked troubled. "There was something about him. He was smart – there was a lot going on behind those eyes. But I'm not sure how much I trusted him."

Perez studied Norton, and took in the tone of his voice. "There're a couple of names I want to run by you: *James Stein* and *Nigel Warner*. Do they mean anything to you?"

"Sorry …"

Perez took out his card. "If you should think of anything, or if Stoltz should get in touch, I'd be grateful if you called me."

"Spying, eh?" Norton accepted the card and gave a grin. "I'll think about it."

CHAPTER
23

DCI Lane arrived at the mortuary, near King's Cross, to find a free space in the staff car park. According to the sign, it belonged to a Doctor Hinkle. Lane was not one to let a good opportunity pass him by, and quickly parked in the spot.

He entered the building through the service entrance, and nodded to one or two technicians, who wondered who he was. He headed towards Doctor Croft's office, and saw that he was in the adjoining suite that was used for autopsies. Lane rapped on the glass and walked in.

There was something oppressive about the atmosphere in the room. It was neat, and tiled from ceiling to floor, but there was enough on view to make Lane pause. There was a body on the metal slab in the centre. It was covered with a white sheet, and standing next to it was Croft.

"Tony … glad you could make it." Croft had a smile for him.

"I got your message. I'm hoping it's good news."

"I'm not sure about that." Croft looked philosophical. "I thought you'd be interested to hear about the post-mortem on Nigel Warner."

"Stein's partner?"

"The very same."

Lane was pleased that Croft had conducted the post-mortem quickly. He had undoubtedly done it as a favour.

Croft folded down the sheet that was covering Warner's body. Warner's face was pale. His eyes were closed, and he seemed at peace. There were dark ligature marks around his neck, and Lane could see all the tell-tale signs of a hanging.

"C.O.D. was a cervical fracture, causing traumatic spinal cord injury." Croft spoke soberly, and pointed towards Warner's neck. "There was closure of the airways, as well as the jugular vein, however it was the cervical fracture that was critical.

"Warner seems to have been a healthy male, in his late thirties. Rate of decomposition was slow because of the air conditioning – you probably noticed it was turned up. Toxicology and stomach contents haven't revealed anything out of the ordinary, but there is one thing that I wanted to show you." Croft lifted up one of Warner's arms. Lane could see bruising on the outside of the forearm.

"He has bruising on both forearms. It represents typical defensive injuries."

"Are you saying someone attacked him?"

"He fended off blows. There *was* an altercation prior to death."

Lane nodded and thought. "We didn't see any signs of disturbance in the house."

"It could have happened outside," said Croft. "Plus all the rooms in the house are large. A fight could conceivably have taken place without much being disturbed."

Lane considered that. "We have two suspects: a Michael Kern and a Frederick Stoltz. Did you find anything that could rule them in or out?"

Croft was disappointed. "Stoltz's DNA and fingerprints are on record. Incidentally, I'm surprised how often he's changed his name."

"He's gone by a number of aliases over the years."

"It makes you wonder what he has to hide."

Lane liked Croft's thinking. It provided some reassurance, and he wished others thought like him.

"Anyhow," said Croft, "we checked the house for trace and prints. Kern's prints are also on record, and we found them several times on the stairs, and numerous times in the study. The same can't be said of Stoltz however. We're still carrying out DNA checks."

Croft raised the sheet, covering Warner's body. "All in all, it was a routine autopsy. What you see is what you get: death by hanging." He paused, no longer a medical examiner, but an old man, looking weary. "I take it you know why Warner's body was found in the stairwell."

"In a two-storey house it's the easiest place to hang someone," said Lane.

"Exactly. It's very difficult to hang a conscious person. They'll put up resistance – fight, struggle – particularly when they realize what's about to happen.

"You need a drop of four to six feet for hanging to be effective. If you can catch someone walking downstairs, well …"

"You can loop a rope around their neck …"

"Precisely. Warner was a well-built man. His assailant might have found it difficult to beat him in a straight fight, hence this …"

Lane sensed that there was something else Croft wanted to say.

"I've been continuing to go through the remains from the hospital site."

"Have you got an ID for the other body?" There was hope in Lane's voice.

"No such luck, I'm afraid. There is one thing that may be of interest." Croft took Lane to a bench on the far side of the room. He opened a plastic container and used tweezers to remove a large, metal pin.

"This is a surgical pin, used to hold bones in place after a compound fracture. This particular one is used for thigh bones. We found it in the hole in the yard.

"All these pins are coded so that they can be traced back to the manufacturer. I checked the medical records of James Stein.

He suffered a compound fracture in a skiing accident, four years ago. This pin was used in surgery."

"So Stein was definitely one of the victims, whose remains we found."

"Yes."

"We need to identify the other victim," said Lane.

"It's going to be difficult. We need more to go on."

"I'll expand the search of the surrounding area. I'll speak to SOCO."

"Sorry I couldn't be of more help."

"Don't worry." Lane liked Croft. He was someone who was solid and reliable, but who spoke his mind, and those were qualities that he valued.

.   .   .

Michael Kern lived in small block of flats in Mornington Crescent. That was what Lane had ascertained from social security records. He drove there, arriving shortly after two o'clock, and parked on the road opposite.

The building had been built in the 1970s, but had been renovated, and had orange and blue rendering. Lane wondered if it was a housing association property: it looked like it might be.

He crossed the road and studied the intercom at the front. There was a tradesman's button, and when he pressed it a clicking sound indicated that the main door had unlocked.

The lobby was clean. According to the details Lane had obtained, Kern lived on the third floor. He thought about Kern's reputation for violence, and wondered about calling for backup. That wasn't Lane's style however.

He took the stairs, rather than the lift, and on the third floor came to a small, rectangular landing, with two doors. He rapped on the door of flat six and waited.

Nothing.

He rapped again, and the sound of knocking echoed out towards the stairwell. Lane wondered if Kern was looking at him through the spyhole. The door behind Lane suddenly opened, and a face appeared.

"Are you a bailiff?" said a middle-aged woman. She had curlers in her blonde hair and was holding a paper.

"Not exactly," said Lane.

"He isn't there. People have been calling for him. He was kicked out."

"Kicked out?"

"A couple of weeks back. The housing people made him leave – he wasn't paying the rent."

Lane looked at the flat door, but there was no letterbox.

"Any idea where he moved to?"

"Sorry … but I'll say this: I'm glad he's gone." The woman gave a brisk smile and made to close the door.

Lane felt frustrated and decided to check the lobby for details of the housing association.

•   •   •

I didn't enjoy hanging that guy. Well actually that's a lie. I did. But I didn't do it for the reasons you think. He was arrogant and looked down on me. I could feel it. Him, can you believe that? And what did I do to him? He didn't even work for a living – some sort of house husband.

I have principles. I need to let you know that. And I didn't steal from him, although I should have done. I just took care of him, did what I needed to and left. He was gay, by the way. But I knew that beforehand.

•   •   •

When he returned to Homicide West, Lane gave a nod to the duty sergeant. The sergeant held his eye. "Tony. There're some people here to see you."

Lane stopped and saw the middle-aged couple, sitting on the bench. He saw the face of the man and his stomach clenched. The man bore an uncanny resemblance to Nigel Warner.

The stranger seemed to sense Lane's unease.

"Chief Inspector? My name's John Warner." He rose and gestured to the woman next to him. "This is my wife."

Lane made to shake their hands.

"We identified our son's body at the mortuary, this morning."

Lane wasn't sure how to reply. "I'm sorry about what happened."

"We understand you're conducting the investigation into his death." Warner bit his lip, as if he was having trouble putting things into words. "We were wondering if we could speak with you."

"Sure …" Lane looked around. The incident room wasn't the best place to go. It wasn't meant for the public, and in any case it held confidential information.

"Let's go to the interview suite." Lane led the way, wishing Perez was with him. He was so much better at dealing with the bereaved.

CHAPTER 24

DCI Lane led Mr and Mrs Warner to interview-room three. It was the best interview room, with comfortable chairs and air conditioning. Lane didn't use it often.

He offered them coffee, and went to get it from the percolator in the staff room. He returned with a sympathetic look, and placed the cups in front of them. He wasn't sure how to deal with the bereaved. He felt awkward at the best of times. He found himself thinking about all the other officers he could have called in.

John Warner looked solemn and his wife looked tearful. "I understand you're looking into our son's murder," said Warner. "Are you the officer who found his body?"

"Yes. I was there along with a colleague."

Warner didn't look as if he wanted to hear the news. Lane had seen the look before. Bereaved parents, searching for the right words, having difficulty taking in what had happened – that the world could be so cruel, and could deal such abrupt and unexpected blows. You weren't meant to outlive your children. Lane thought about that, and considered his own children, who were grown up.

"There're a lot of things you need to know," said Warner, "the least of which is that James Stein was a man who made enemies."

"Your son's partner?" Lane was curious.

"They'd been together for several years. They were looking to enter a partnership – a civil ceremony."

Lane nodded. "How did your son meet Stein?"

"He came to work for his company. That was about four years ago."

"Our son has – had – a background in engineering," said Mrs Warner. She seemed keen to talk about him. "He was good at what he did. He worked for one of the firms that James took over."

"I've heard that Stein was a successful businessman," said Lane.

Mr Warner made a face. "That's one way of putting it." Lane felt tension in the air.

"James was an aggressive man – ruthless. Like my son, he was an engineer, but he had a business mind, and he put it to use. He set up his own company and then grew it by taking over other firms."

"I assume you know what happened to Stein," said Lane.

"Doctor Croft explained. I think Stein's death may have had something to do with our son's."

Lane agreed with that, but didn't want to say more. "Do you feel your son may have been killed because of something Stein did?"

"Stein made enemies. He was aggressive, riding roughshod over promises he'd made."

Lane took out his notebook.

"Nigel wasn't anything like him," said Mrs Warner. "They were opposites, but perhaps that's why … why they were attracted to one another."

"Did anyone make specific threats to Stein?"

"There's a man you need to speak to," said Warner, "Myles Appleferd."

Lane made a note of the name.

"He was a businessman who Stein crossed. They parted on bad terms – very bad terms."

Mrs Warner nodded slowly.

"Do you have an address for this Mr Appleferd?"

"I've got a company address." Warner handed over a business card and Lane studied it.

M. A. Solutions was embossed at the top, in gold letters.

"Did your son ever say he was threatened by anyone?" said Lane.

Both Warners shook their heads. They looked old beyond their years, and Lane wondered if Nigel Warner had been their only child.

"Nigel was a meek man – mild mannered," said Mrs Warner. "James was the go-getter. He was the one who drew attention."

"We found your son at Stein's house," said Lane. "Did he have a place of his own?"

"No. The two of them lived together. They had done for several years." Mrs Warner didn't look as if she was comfortable with the arrangement. "Nigel had stopped working about a year ago. James was successful. Both of them didn't need to work. It was something they'd already discussed."

Mrs Warner took out a picture and handed it over. It showed her son with Stein. Stein was the more flamboyant of the two. He had a youthful face and long brown hair, with the beginnings of a beard. He looked like a man who didn't care – who was confident and had a plan.

"Please find out who did this." Mrs Warner looked anxious.

Lane didn't like making promises he couldn't keep, but underneath felt resolve.

·　　　·　　　·

When Lane returned to the incident room, it was quiet. It looked as if people were leaving. *Slackers*, Lane thought to himself.

He saw Perez and Malcolm Brown at their desks, and was pleased that they were still working. "Malcolm, this business card belongs to a guy called Myles Appleferd. Let me know what you can find out about him."

Brown nodded, looking both curious and nervous.

Lane sat down opposite Perez. "Any progress?"

"Swings and roundabouts." Perez looked up from the notes he was working on. "I spoke to the site foreman who used to work with Frederick Stoltz. It turns out Stoltz has a girlfriend. He's been seeing her for a while. There's also something else you need to know." Perez handed over a Post-It note. It was from the unit which had been observing Stoltz's flat. "After Stoltz was released on bail, he didn't return home."

Lane was mildly surprised. "Where did he go?"

"We're not sure. The obo. unit outside his flat says the place is quiet – has been for a while. In truth we don't know that he's guilty of anything. There's been no forensics to tie him to Stein's death, *or* that of Nigel Warner." Perez looked towards the incident-room door. "Obo. units just hurt our budget."

CHAPTER
25

Daniel Riley ate the food that had been left for him. Afterwards he felt tired. He picked up some plastic sheeting in one corner of the room, wrapped himself in it, and crouched down next to the wall.

He wasn't sure how long he slept. He slept soundly, dreaming of nothing, and when he awoke he was sure hours had passed.

The room was dimly lit. Little light came from the florescent strips above, and the metal door on the opposite side of the room remained shut.

Riley felt pain. Where he had been punched and kicked, his body ached. He knew bruises were coming up, but in the dim light it was difficult to see clearly.

He looked around and something made him feel nervous. The tray with the plate on it had gone. He looked about to make sure. It had definitely gone. His attacker had come into the room while he had been asleep.

Riley was fearful and wondered what else had been done. The room seemed unchanged. On one side there was the dirty sink and toilet, and in the middle of the room a small pile of masonry and tarpaulin. There was still a red light near the ceiling.

Riley wondered if anything was concealed under the tarpaulin, and felt a hollowness in his stomach as he thought about it. Slowly he rose, discarding the sheeting. He moved towards the tarpaulin, and bent down, lifting it up.

Nothing. Just piles of masonry and lengths of wood. He thought about the wood, and realized he could use it as a weapon. He picked up one piece that was more than a foot long. It looked as if it had been broken off from a doorframe. What had gone on here? Where exactly was he?

Riley felt fear give way to confusion. He was beginning to doubt whether anyone would ever find him. His wife, Erin, must have been worried. So must the children, but what could they do? Even if the alarm was raised, no one knew where to look.

He had to keep track of time. He had to do something to keep himself sane.

Riley crouched down in the corner of the room. He marked the brickwork with the edge of the wood. He would do so every time he thought a day had past. That way he would have a record.

Riley stopped suddenly, as he heard noise. There was the sound of a door opening and closing, and then footsteps. He looked towards the metal door, but nothing happened.

Not his door. Not his room, but somewhere nearby.

Riley concentrated, and thought he could hear the sound of something being dragged. There was a voice.

"No. Please …" The voice continued. "Why are you doing this?"

•　　　•　　　•

When Lane returned it was nearly six o'clock. Perez tried to read his mood, but couldn't see any signs of happiness or anger.

"That guy can cover his arse," said Lane. "If it was an Olympic sport, he'd win gold." Lane was his usual self. "You know what our good chief superintendent said? He offered the services of a press officer as well as a counselling officer."

"I don't think we need either," said Perez, confused.

"Exactly. A less charitable man would say he's gone completely out to lunch."

Lane dialled the number of the housing association that owned the block of flats Michael Kern had lived in. He was put through to a manager called John Barron, who spoke with a Yorkshire accent. When Lane mentioned Kern's name, Barron swore loudly.

"I wasn't expecting to hear about that *bastard* again."

"Sorry?"

"He threatened me. He threw a punch at me. We evicted him a few weeks back – non-payment of rent, plus antisocial behaviour. He wasn't an easy person to deal with."

"*We?*" said Lane.

"A couple of security guards and me. Our association uses them from time to time, when tenants are difficult." At the other end Barron sounded tense.

"Do you know much about Michael Kern's background?"

"I know he has a criminal record," Barron replied. "I guess I shouldn't be surprised to hear from you. You know what he said, after he threw a punch at me? He said he'd be getting lawyers on to me – that *he* had rights. Can you believe that?"

"I'm trying to track him down," said Lane. "Do you know where he might be?"

"No." Barron sounded as if he wanted to end the call, and there was noise in the background. "That man made my life hell. Some of our tenants can be difficult, but he was at the extreme end."

"Did he give any clues as to his plans?"

"I think he was going to stay with friends. Other than that, I can't help." There was more noise in the background. "Look, there's something I have to deal with. I should go, Inspector." With that he hung up.

Lane put down the phone. He checked the time and picked up his jacket. "I've got to go and help the missus prepare for her sister's do." He glanced at Perez. "You will be there, won't you?"

"7.30."

"Good man." And with that Lane left.

Steve Perez arrived at Lane's home a little before 7.30. Lane lived in north London, on a quiet residential road. He had lived there for over twenty years, in a Victorian house made of red brick.

The garden at the front was well tended, and as Perez walked towards the front door he wondered who did the work. He couldn't imagine Lane looking after flowers. No. The place had a woman's touch.

Perez pressed the bell and the door was opened a few moments later by Lane's wife. Irene Lane was tall and thin, smartly dressed in a long, floral skirt. Perez had met her twice before, but wasn't sure if she remembered him.

"Steve, good to see you again." Her face broke into a smile, as she welcomed him in.

At the end of the hall he could see a kitchen with people. It was full to overflowing and there was noise coming from the garden beyond. The overall atmosphere was formal, yet relaxed. People, mostly in their forties and fifties, chatting over wine, oblivious to Perez, all apparently known to one another. Outside there was the sound of pop music – seemingly at odds with the atmosphere inside.

"I brought this for your sister." Perez held up a bottle of wine.

"Oh she'll like that." Irene continued to smile and wrinkles appeared at the corners of her eyes. She led him towards the kitchen and then out into the garden, where there was a barbecue.

Perez hadn't been to Lane's home many times. He couldn't remember there being a patio. *Was it a new addition?* A large hi-fi was set up on a table, a device so old Perez knew it could only be Lane's. Two boys, in their early teens, were fiddling with it, unimpressed with Led Zeppelin's *Kashmir*, which was playing.

A woman who resembled Irene came up to Perez. She was younger and had bright-red lipstick, which contrasted with her tan.

"This is my sister, Fran," said Irene.

Fran smiled and kissed Perez on the cheek.

"You must be Tony's friend. Good to finally meet you."

Perez did his best to smile, feeling slightly overwhelmed, and held up the wine.

"For you."

Fran seemed pleased and took it, studying the label. A woman came up to speak to her, and after a moment Irene took the opportunity to lead Perez towards the barbecue. There he saw an overweight, middle-aged man, tending sausages and pieces of chicken.

"This is Ron – Fran's husband."

The man looked up and gave Perez a nod. It was a brisk gesture, without any real warmth. The man was sweating, and it looked as if tending the barbecue was too much for him. A guest approached with a plate and he put a sausage on to it.

"I'm not sure if that's done properly. You might want to be careful."

Perez smiled inwardly and turned away. Irene handed him a glass. "Tony is in the study. He and his friends are holding court there." There was something about it that she found amusing.

Perez often wondered if Lane got on with his wife. They seemed very different – Irene out going, attentive, with good social skills, and Lane the opposite. Perez knew they had been married for over twenty-five years, and had two grown-up children. Family was not something Lane talked about often however. Perez noticed that soon after they had been teamed up.

Irene handed him a plate with chicken from the barbecue. It seemed cooked, and he slowly turned it over. He picked up some bread and followed her, as she led him towards the study. There were a number of people standing and chatting in the hall, and they had to squeeze past. Irene opened the study door and Perez saw Lane, Newman and Nolan. He was glad to see familiar faces, and instantly felt more relaxed.

"There you are," said Lane. "Was wondering where you'd got to."

CHAPTER
27

On Thursday morning DCI Lane arrived late at Homicide West. It was nearly 9 A.M. by the time he reached the incident room. He felt awkward, like a junior officer creeping in, hoping no one would notice.

Perez was at his desk. Malcolm Brown was also there, along with most of the civilian staff.

"How are you feeling?" asked Perez.

Lane dipped his voice. "Hung over." There was a dull ache at the back of his head.

"You're not the only one," Perez replied. He looked none the worse for wear however, and Lane felt envious. He turned on his computer and looked at the messages on his desk.

Lane noticed a well-dressed young man coming into the incident room. He was tall and thin, with blond hair that was swept back and neatly combed into place. He had a clean-shaven face, and a slightly stiff look.

"Chief Inspector?"

"Yes?" Lane felt cautious and didn't like surprises. He felt he was about to be hit by one.

"My name is David Mear. I'm with press liaison. Chief Superintendent Travers asked me to speak to you. He thought that I might be able to help."

Lane glanced momentarily at Perez and felt like speaking his mind. Then he considered what Perez would say, and decided to try a different approach.

"Are you any good at observational work?"

"Sorry, sir?"

"Stakeouts?"

Mear hesitated and shook his head. "Not really, sir. I'm with press liaison … I deal with journalists."

"Well if I need your help, I'll let you know."

Mear seemed disappointed and hesitated. He decided to withdraw, and Lane wondered what Mear would say to Travers.

"By the way," said Perez, "when Stoltz made bail he left a note with the custody sergeant." Perez handed it over.

I'll get you back for this.

Lane grinned. "I guess he didn't appreciate his time in custody."

"You realize the most he'll get is a few months for handling stolen goods?"

"In that case we have to try harder." Lane thought about it and turned to Brown. "Have you got an address for this businessman who's supposed to have had rows with Stein?"

"Myles Appleferd?" Brown looked pleased, and Lane could sense that he had found something.

"Appleferd runs a company called M.A. Solutions. He has offices in the West End. He's an interesting character – he's on the PNC."

"He has a criminal record?" said Lane with surprise.

"He has a conviction for assault." Brown produced a printout. "It dates from nearly five years ago. He didn't serve time, but he was given a suspended sentence."

Lane read the report and saw a picture of Appleferd. He was a well-built man, with a large, expansive face. He looked like a boxer in Lane's mind, rather than a businessman.

"I think it's time I paid our Mr Appleferd a visit."

. . .

Michael Kern was feeling the strain. It was bad enough that he'd lost his home, but now he was staying at friend's flat – a friend who didn't really want him there. Then there was the attention from neighbours. An elderly man opposite had noticed him. He'd noticed him moving in. He'd made a complaint about noise, and Kern wondered how long he'd be able to stay.

Kern had tried to put things right, but it was all falling apart. He felt angry and wanted to blame someone, but wasn't sure who.

There was a knock at the front door. Kern moved to the door, looking through the peep hole. He removed the chain and turned the latch.

"How's it going?" he said to the stranger in the hall. The man was in his early twenties, of Middle-Eastern appearance, with short, black hair and stubble.

"I heard you'd moved."

"Yeah," said Kern, sourly. "Have you got it?"

"Sure." The man took out a small packet and handed it over, concealing it with the palm of his hand. Kern accepted it and handed over some rolled-up notes.

"If you need any more, you know where to reach me," the man said.

"Sure." Kern made to close the door and stopped. The elderly man opposite was staring.

"What are you looking at?" said Kern. "*Damn coffin dodger.*"

. . .

Lane arrived at the offices of M.A. Solutions a little after ten o'clock. Myles Appleferd's company was based in a mews, close to the legal chambers of Lincoln's Inn. Lane parked in the mews outside Appleferd's office, and took note of the whitewashed building. Several ground-floor windows were open, and he could hear shouting inside. The voice was deep – male.

From what was being said, Lane suspected he knew who it was. He tried to see through the windows, but they were tinted. A series of thoughts ran through his mind. In general, he enjoyed stepping into an argument, and wasn't afraid to confront people.

He walked into the reception and paused. There was no receptionist and he looked towards the office doors, which were etched with the words *M.A. Solutions*. Beyond them he could see an open space. A man in his early forties was standing up, shouting. He had dark hair and a heavy face, with extra weight around his cheeks and neck. He was livid. Around him staff were sitting at their desks, listening to Appleferd, with their heads lowered.

"I expect better from you! I pay you good money for God's sake!"

Lane stepped up to the door and the receptionist appeared from the other end of the room. "Excuse me, sir. Can I help you?"

"It's OK. I've seen who I want." Lane marched forward.

"Sir, you can't go in there. You need –"

"You're a bunch of *fucking* second-raters!" Appleferd's face was the colour of roast beef. "I show you how I want things to be done –" He looked up and saw Lane. "Who *the hell* are you?"

Lane held up his warrant card. "Do shut up."

CHAPTER
28

"So what can I do for you, Chief Inspector?"

Lane scanned the room. It was modern – minimalist. A large, white desk stood in the centre, and behind it Lane could see a picture of a small child. In front of it was a picture showing Appleferd receiving an award of some sort. Lane wondered what exactly it was.

"May I sit down?" Lane sat down without waiting for a reply.

Appleferd's frown did not improve his appearance. He sized Lane up, trying to work out the best way to deal with him. "What exactly is it that you want, Chief Inspector?"

"I work with Homicide West. I'm looking into the murder of James Stein."

There was recognition in Appleferd's eyes. Then he linked Stein's name to the word *murder* and felt tense. Lane had seen the reaction many times before.

"I know Stein … He's dead?"

"Very much so." Lane continued to look around. He noted the pictures on the walls. "What exactly is it that you do here?"

"I run a consultancy. We provide business services, advising our clients on a range of corporate matters."

"Sounds like a lot of hot air." Lane smiled, and his eyes came to rest on Appleferd.

"If you're trying to get a rise out of me, it won't work, Chief Inspector."

"Oh I don't know about that. You looked pretty het up a few minutes ago."

"That was just a … a misunderstanding." Appleferd was turning even redder, more in embarrassment than anger. "These things happen."

"Well, how about James Stein? Did you have a *misunderstanding* with him?" Lane was beginning to enjoy himself. He could spend a while here.

"I think someone has misled you."

"Really? Well how about you enlighten me? – tell me what's really going on."

"Stein was a client of mine – for a while." Appleferd spoke reluctantly. He wondered what his employees in the offices outside were thinking. "You could say that the two of us didn't get on."

"What did you do for him?"

"I provided him with advice. He runs – ran an engineering company. He wanted to expand – wanted to get finance, as well as find ways to raise his profile."

"And you helped him?"

"I tried. He is – he was a difficult man to get on with."

"How about you?" said Lane. "Are you a difficult man to get on with?"

Appleferd was trying not to be provoked. "I don't know what you've dug up, but I'm professional and I get results."

"By assaulting your staff? Yes, I know about that. It was someone who worked for you, wasn't it?"

"That was unfortunate, but it was a long time ago." Appleferd was out of his comfort zone and didn't know how to react.

"You were lucky to get a suspended sentence."

"I've learnt to control my anger. I have a company to run and I have an image to maintain."

"And some would say you aren't succeeding." Lane realized he should stop enjoying himself. He had to remember he was here for a reason, and had things to do.

"What exactly do you want, Chief Inspector?"

"Can you account for your whereabouts on Sunday evening?"

"I was at home on Sunday with my family. My wife can verify that."

"How about over the last four weeks? Where have you been?"

Appleferd thought. "Here at the office. I've been out occasionally – I had to go to Glasgow, but mostly I've been here. It's hard running your own firm."

"I'm sure it is," said Lane, unconvinced. "I read the report. You know you were lucky that it was your first offence."

"Things got out of hand," said Appleferd.

"But prison is a much-needed filter on the gene pool."

Appleferd was caught off-guard.

"How did you first come to meet Stein?" said Lane.

"He approached me. My company does advertise, but we've done work for other engineering firms. That was how he heard about me."

"And what caused the relationship to break down?"

"Let's just say we didn't see eye to eye. He said I wasn't delivering, and he was reluctant to pay me."

"And were you delivering?"

"I pride myself on what I do. I drive people hard and I get results."

Lane looked at the picture of Appleferd's family. "Do you have any written correspondence from your time with Stein?"

"Most of our old files are stored off site. There are probably some documents somewhere …"

"When did you have this falling out?"

"I don't know. Twelve months ago? Perhaps a little longer?"

"Did you threaten him?"

Appleferd looked insulted, at least that was Lane's reading. Then he wondered if it was something else.

"No." Appleferd checked his watch. "Chief Inspector, I do have things to do."

"I'm sure it's nothing that can't wait." Lane smiled and took out his notebook, slowly leafing through it.

CHAPTER
29

Daniel Riley could hear sobbing.

He was still locked in his cell. The air was becoming cold, and in the dim light he looked about. He was alone, he was sure of that, and he wondered where the sound could be coming from.

He hadn't heard footsteps for a while – his attacker had gone. His body still ached however, and when he twisted left or right he could feel pain in his ribs. He wondered if any were broken and thought about the consequences.

The crying made Riley focus. He moved to the far wall and listened. After several seconds he heard small, sharp gasps, and then a long sob. Someone was definitely nearby.

Riley thought about the camera near the ceiling. How should he deal with it? Should he ignore the noise?

Curiosity got the better of him and he put his ear to the wall, listening. The noise was coming from close by – possibly the next room. Riley felt excitement slowly building. He wasn't alone: there was hope.

He looked to the top of the wall and saw several small holes that formed a vent. The sound was coming through them. He stretched up. "Can you hear me?" he whispered.

After a moment the noise stopped. There was nothing for a while, and Riley felt tense. "I know you're there – I can hear you. You're not alone."

Finally someone spoke.

"Who are you?" It was a male voice, quiet, cautious.

"My name's Daniel. I'm in the room next door."

The man remained silent, as if considering what to say.

"We shouldn't talk. He can hear us."

Riley thought about the camera but decided not to mention it.

"What's your name?"

There was a lengthy pause.

"Will."

"How long have you been here, Will?"

"I don't know." The man sounded confused. He wasn't young. He was at least as old as Riley, judging by his voice. "I don't know where I am." There was a hint of desperation. "We shouldn't talk."

"Why?"

"It's safer that way."

"How long have you been here?"

There was a pause. "A while."

"Do you know why you're here?" said Riley. He thought that he could hear the stranger moving. Why hadn't he heard him before? How large was this place?

"It doesn't make sense. There were more of us …" Will stopped and Riley felt frustrated.

"Did you hear that?" said Will.

"Hear what?" Riley strained and listened. There was noise in the distance – the sound of doors opening and closing, and then footsteps.

"He's coming back," Will said quickly.

Riley looked towards the large, metal door. Someone was approaching. He braced himself, expecting the door to open suddenly. Instead a small hatch at the bottom opened, and a tray shot through.

•   •   •

DCI Lane was content and left Appleferd's office with a smile. He wanted to share his good mood with someone and dialled Perez.

"It's me … How it's going?"

"Little change so far." Perez sounded tired, and Lane could hear noise in the background.

"I've spoken to Myles Appleferd," said Lane. "In my considered opinion the guy's a bell end."

"Let me guess," said Perez, "you highlighted this fact for his benefit."

"Just doing a public service." Lane felt buoyant. "Appleferd did have a falling out with Stein. He said he had some business correspondence from his dealings with him. Said he'd get the paperwork shipped over. Once it appears, get Malcolm to go over it."

"Will do. On a different note, I've been looking into Michael Kern's earliest probation report," said Perez. "It mentions a grandmother he used to stay with. Unlike the rest of his family, she lives here, in the South East."

Lane thought about Kern.

"See if she's still around. If so, we should pay her a visit."

"Understood."

"I'll see you later." And with that Lane hung up.

He was about to put his phone away when he heard a bleeping sound. He looked at the screen and saw a message. Lane had never been comfortable with technology. He studied the keypad and pressed a button. The message appeared in full.

It was from the duty nurse at St. Swithun's Hospital. Ray Maynard was still unconscious, and no one had come to collect his belongings.

Lane realized he wasn't far from the hospital, and decided to pick up Maynard's effects.

·　　　·　　　·

It was a little after 11.30 A.M., and there was a new woman on the reception at St. Swithun's. She looked at Lane expectantly.

"Can I help you?"

"Only if you have a cure for a hangover."

The woman looked confused, and Lane showed her his warrant card and carried on up to the trauma wing, thinking how much he disliked hospitals. He recognized the duty nurse, who was a small, stern-looking woman he had met before. She raised her eyebrows.

"Chief Inspector. Glad you could make it."

"How's Ray Maynard doing?" Lane looked about, noting the orderlies moving along the corridor.

"His condition hasn't improved." The nurse consulted a chart behind her. "We've managed to relieve intra-cranial pressure, but with traumatic brain injury things are often unpredictable."

"I'd like him to regain consciousness."

"That goes without saying." The nurse pursed her lips. "In cases like this, the brain tries to protect itself by shutting down. We can only hope that when he comes round – *if* he comes round – he'll have retained most of his higher brain functions."

Lane felt disappointed and didn't want to continue the conversation. "You mentioned his personal effects?"

"Indeed. Mr Maynard's homeless." She checked her computer screen. "No relatives have come by or enquired after him. It might be best if I passed his things on to you."

Lane tried to look affable but the nurse continued looking stern. She led him down the corridor towards the trauma unit. Lane saw the police officer who he had put outside Maynard's room. He was unconscious and slumped down in his chair.

Lane's heart sped up. He looked through the window, into the room, and saw a man leaning over Maynard.

CHAPTER
30

Lane reached for the door and realized it was locked.

He turned the handle furiously and the man in the room looked around. He had on a ski mask, and Lane felt a tremor of fear. "Get a key," he hissed. The duty nurse checked her pockets and headed back to the reception.

Maynard was unconscious on the bed. The stranger looked at him and then made for the window.

Lane tried to force the door open. He put his weight against it and there was a splintering sound. He threw his weight against it once more and the wooden frame cracked. A third time and it gave way.

He tumbled in as the man climbed out. Lane grabbed his legs but was kicked away. The man made it through the window, on to the flat roof. Lane looked at the black felt, unsure if it would take his weight.

The nurse reappeared. "Keep an eye on him," Lane shouted, pointing to Maynard. He dashed into the corridor and pushed through a set of double doors. Large windows, on his left, showed the roof and the man who was running across it. There was a door in the corridor saying *Emergency Exit*, and Lane pushed it open.

An alarm sounded, but he ignored the noise and stepped on to the roof. Ahead of him was a grey walkway, narrow, with railings on either side.

"Stop!" Lane shouted.

The man flinched but carried on.

Lane ran down the walkway, as the man ahead zig-zagged across the roof. The man avoided skylights and air ducts, making his way towards the edge of the building.

Lane felt cold wind against his face, and it reminded him of how high up he was. The man reached the edge and stopped abruptly, putting his hands out for balance.

Lane stopped, as the walkway came to an end at the edge of the building. Grey railings prevented him from going any further. The drop was at least fifty feet and he could see cars and refuse bins, neatly arranged on the street below. There was noise coming from the air duct behind him.

The stranger turned around. Lane could see blue eyes darting back and forth, and then the man crouched, climbing over the edge.

Lane looked on in surprise as the man climbed down a drainpipe. He moved swiftly, using his legs to grip the pipe and his arms to support his upper body.

Lane craned his neck, wondering how he could reach him. Suddenly there was a cracking sound. The pipe began to separate from its brackets. It bowed outwards, and the man let go. He fell nearly twenty feet, landing on the roof of a parked car. Its windscreen shattered and the roof caved in. People in the street stopped and stared.

"Stop him!" Lane shouted.

Passers-by looked up at Lane, but did nothing.

The masked figure rolled off the car and slowly rose. Gripping his right arm tightly, he glanced up at Lane and turned to run.

CHAPTER
31

DI Perez managed to track down Michael Kern's grandmother. Kern's first probation report had listed contact details for next of kin, and when Perez called her, she didn't seem surprised to hear from him.

"I'm working," she explained, "but if you want to talk, we can do so at lunchtime." She gave him an address, and when he arrived it was a little before one.

Angela Morris was a school governor. When Perez arrived at St. Cuthbert's School, in Basildon, he could see children in the yard. It was a secure area, with high fencing all around. Two teachers were on duty, and after he spoke to them Perez parked in the staff car park.

He noticed a space reserved for a Mrs Morris, and a small Peugeot parked in it. He made his way to the staff room, and they directed him to an empty classroom.

As he walked, Perez thought back to his own time in school. He had been a nervous child, always fearful and anxious. For him, school had been an intimidating place. He liked to think that he had changed. Sometimes though he wondered if that was really the case.

He rapped on the door.

"Come in."

Perez entered and saw Angela Morris sitting at a desk, at the front of the room. Around her were piles of documents, and she had an exhausted look on her face.

Morris was a small woman, of slender build. She had brown hair, tied into a ponytail, and dark-brown eyes. She was dressed in a white blouse and dark-blue trouser suit, and looked younger than her years.

"You must be Inspector Perez," she said, standing up. She managed a smile and shook his hand.

"Thank you for taking the time to see me," said Perez.

"Not at all. Take a seat, Inspector."

Perez looked at the small chairs dotted around. Angela Morris smiled a little. She gestured to a larger chair at the back of the room, and Perez brought it over.

"So what is it that I can do for you?"

Perez took out his smartphone. "I've come to speak to you about your grandson, Michael Kern."

"Such is life …" Angela didn't seem fazed. Perez suspected she'd spoken to the police before.

"What exactly is it that he's done this time?"

"It's part of an ongoing enquiry," said Perez. "We can't divulge much at present, suffice to say he's a person of interest."

Angela held Perez's eye. "Mike – that's how I know him – he's never been an easy person to get on with."

"I understand he grew up in care?"

"That's right." Angela looked uneasy. "I tried to look after him. His mother, my daughter, died when he was young. His father, well, let's just say he didn't put in many appearances." Her face hardened at the thought of him.

"And what exactly happened to your grandson?"

"He was placed with an older couple in the end. They'd never been able to have children, and they fostered him. I tried to look after him initially, but there were problems, and I had problems of my own …" Angela looked far away.

"As he grew up, Mike was difficult to deal with – unruly, disrespectful – not just towards his foster family, but to others. He was expelled from several schools. Years later he told me that his foster parents hadn't been good. I never fully understood what he meant. I got the impression that they'd mistreated him." She carried on before Perez could ask a question.

"Contact with Mike was limited. We kept in touch for Christmases, birthdays and so on, but in truth we've never had much in common. I eventually moved down south to work. Mike had more ups and downs in his life. I understand he assaulted his foster parents."

Perez was surprised. That hadn't appeared in Kern's probation report.

"I don't know what it was," said Angela. "Perhaps it was their age; perhaps they weren't able to cope. In any case, Mike left them soon after. He started committing crime on a regular basis, and it set the tone for the rest of his life."

"I understand your grandson is well educated," said Perez.

"He was always bright. He eventually passed two A-Levels and had the option to go to university, to study IT. He did go for a year. He had an aptitude for the subject but in the end he dropped out. The drugs didn't help matters." She thought for a moment. "Is that what this is about? – drugs?"

Perez hesitated. "Not exactly. Have you had any recent contact with your grandson?"

Angela shook her head. "At Christmas we exchanged cards. He rang me." The memory made her smile. "I told him to come over – spend time with me and my family, but he didn't want to. In truth, I think he was embarrassed."

"How do you mean?"

"The fact that I've held it together – settled down and led a normal life. Somewhere along the line his life spun out of control. I think he knows he should have done better."

A sympathetic look briefly touched Perez's face. "Did your grandson mention what his plans were?"

"He said he was trying to go straight. I know he was looking for work, but I don't know what came of it."

"He did work at an IT company for a while. We're having difficulty tracing him now though. Has he been in touch? – texts, emails, anything at all?"

"I haven't heard from him since Christmas." Angela was disappointed and it showed. "I know about some of the crimes he's committed. Burglaries – assaults – it all fits together really. The burglaries were for money. The people, well, he's had difficulty trusting people since his experiences in care."

"If your grandson does try to get in touch, could you let me know?"

Angela looked at Perez. It was hard to read her thoughts.

"We just need to know where he is," Perez said.

"Do you intend to arrest him?"

"That depends …" Perez didn't feel that it was an adequate answer, but Angela Morris accepted it. Her face softened a little.

"I'll see what I can do."

•   •   •

In the yard at St. Swithun's DCI Lane looked cross. Hospital security was scouring the campus, and Lane had been joined by several crime scene officers, including Chris Nolan.

"He tried to slide down that pipe," said Lane. He pointed to the car the man had landed on. "The pipe gave way and well, you can work out the rest."

Nolan studied the shattered glass. "Did he actually land on the windscreen?"

"No. It was the roof; the glass shattered afterwards. He must have struck it with his boots. He rolled off the car and ran towards the main road." Lane pointed to the road in the distance.

Nolan noticed the cuts on Lane's jacket, and wondered how he had come by them. "You were lucky. This could have ended much worse. What did he look like?"

"He was bigger than me. His face was covered – some sort of balaclava."

"Do you know if he injured himself – any cuts on his hands or legs?"

"I didn't see any. If he left blood, it'd be a good way to trace him." Lane felt angry. "We need to search further out." He pointed to the road.

"Take it easy," said Nolan. He was mild mannered in comparison to Lane. "At least he didn't produce a weapon … How about that young officer who was guarding Maynard?"

"It's worth checking him for trace, I guess."

"That's not what I meant."

"Oh … He should pull through." Lane checked the time. "I'm going to put through a call for more uniforms – get them to check the main road."

Nolan studied the smashed car. "Was he wearing gloves?"

"Tight-fitting ones. He was basically covered from head to toe."

"A pity." Nolan looked around. "My team'll stay on site. If we find anything, I'll let you know."

"Thanks." Lane knew he should call Perez, but was putting it off. "I'm going to head out – do some searching myself. I'll let you know before I leave."

"One other thing," said Nolan. "Weren't you looking at a suspect?"

Lane thought about Stoltz. He wasn't sure if the man he had fought with was Stoltz. The height and build were right, but something was preying on his mind.

"I don't know … I can't be sure."

$$\cdot \qquad \cdot \qquad \cdot$$

Michael Kern needed something for the pain. He stumbled into the pharmacy, taking little note of the people around him. It was only a short distance away from where he was staying, in West Norwood, and at this time of day it wasn't busy.

He waited impatiently, as an elderly woman signed a prescription. In the end, he decided he couldn't wait any longer, and nudged her aside. The assistant, a young woman behind the counter, looked at him in surprise.

"Can I help you?"

Kern didn't look well. "I need something for pain."

"How do you mean, *pain*?"

"A headache. Something for headaches, muscle pain …"

"Ibuprofen?"

"That's it."

"Well, I'm actually dealing with someone right now."

Kern wasn't sure how to reply. In truth, he didn't really care about the elderly woman, but he knew he had to maintain appearances if he was going to get help.

"Give me a moment," the assistant said.

Kern waited, looking around the pharmacy as another shop worker at the back watched. Eventually the elderly woman moved away, and Kern had the counter to himself.

"Ibuprofen, pain killers – anything like that."

The woman nodded and looked into Kern's eyes. "Are you on any other medication?"

Kern thought about the drugs he took.

"No."

The assistant turned and selected a box from the shelf. Kern took out a ten-pound note. He waited for his change and left the pharmacy quickly.

The street was quiet, with little traffic. Kern rounded the corner and felt a hand grabbing him by the throat. Before he could move, he was slammed against a wall.

"Jesus Christ!" said Kern.

"Not quite," said Lane.

CHAPTER
32

There is such a thing as police brutality. They're not all fair and pro-fessional. I've seen enough in my time to know that. There's a public image – the one you see when cameras or the press are there – then there's the private one. I know what goes on in police stations and cells. I even know what goes on in prison, but that's another story.

I don't fear the law. It's an occupational hazard: that's the way I look at it. And while some coppers are smart, there are more than a few dumb ones.

You have to get up early in the morning to get one over on me. I'm professional and hard working. I have attention to detail and I have a plan – you need to know that, and I intend to stick to my plan. I won't be interrupted or stopped by the law. They're trying to move one step ahead of me but they won't. I can portray an image. I can act in a way that won't make people suspect.

There's much I have to do, but we'll meet again. I'm sure of that.

·   ·   ·

By the time DCI Lane returned to Homicide West, it was nearly three o'clock. There was a buzz of activity in the incident room, and Lane looked about and saw civilian staff at their desks. He saw Malcolm Brown and glanced at the photographs next to him.

"Malcolm?"

Brown looked up, startled and worried.

"I went to see that businessman, Myles Appleferd. He agreed to send over documents relating to the work he did for James Stein. I want you to go through them when they arrive, and see exactly what their arrangement was."

"Yes, sir," said Brown. "If it's technical, I can get help from Economic and Specialist Crime."

Lane didn't think much of them. In his mind they rambled on too much and were divorced from the real world. "A university degree doesn't make you smart or good. Just let me know if you find anything."

"Yes, sir."

Perez looked up. "How did it go with Michael Kern?"

"Could have been worse," said Lane. "He's cooling his heels in a cell. We'll speak to him shortly. I've got uniformed officers and forensics on scene at the hospital. I've also increased the guard on Maynard's room."

"You could always move Maynard to another ward," said Perez.

Lane smiled to himself.

"We've had the mayor's office on the phone, by the way," Perez added. He wondered if Lane could be persuaded to return the call, and allay any concerns the mayor might have.

"Say something creative. And before I forget, there's something you can help me with." Lane held up a digital cassette. "This has footage for the main entrance at St. Swithun's. We need to go over it, to see if there's an image of the man I chased."

Perez studied the cassette. "I don't have anything that'll play this. We need to speak to IT."

Lane's face sagged. "In that case you should handle it."

•   •   •

Michael Kern was transferred to interview-room two. As Lane and Perez entered, he looked at them impassively. To Lane, there was something about Kern that made him seem too relaxed. His eyes were sharp and intelligent, and he seemed too comfortable in a police station.

"So what can I do for you, Chief Inspector?" Kern looked at the tape deck on one side of the table. "Are you recording this?"

"Do I need to?"

Kern ignored the question. His weather-beaten face looked relaxed. "There's something I need to ask you first: how did you find me?"

Lane reached into his jacket and took out a small object wrapped in an evidence bag. It was a mobile phone. "Cell-site analysis," said Lane. "You carry this on you, and your probation officer had the number. It was simply a matter of talking to the network provider."

Kern felt annoyed and looked at Perez. He knew he should be more careful, and realized that he needed a new phone. "So what can I do for the two of you?"

"You're not exactly an easy man to find," said Lane, "almost as if you have something to hide."

"Blame my landlord," said Kern sourly. He looked aside, hoping to let the matter rest.

"Money problems?" said Perez.

Kern spoke reluctantly. "You could put it like that. I've been staying at a friend's. I'm sure your chief inspector knows this by now."

"We're conducting a multiple-homicide enquiry," said Lane. He looked down at the paperwork he had brought in. Kern glanced at it, a first glimmer of anxiety in his eyes.

"Does the name James Stein mean anything to you?"

Kern thought for a moment and Lane studied him. He wasn't easy to read.

"It sounds familiar."

"How about Nigel Warner? They live in Epping, or rather they *lived* in Epping. Both are now dead. I was wondering if you could tell me anything about that."

Kern folded his arms and leant back. "Is that what this is about, Chief Inspector? What makes you think that I was responsible?"

"You have a reputation for violence. Your fingerprints were found at their home, which is now a crime scene. They were mostly confined to one room – an upstairs study."

"Doesn't surprise me," said Kern. "I did work for them."

Lane was taken aback. "What sort of work?"

"IT work. They were having problems with a computer and I fixed it."

Perez felt he and Lane were being outmanoeuvred.

"And when was this?"

"A while ago – two months at least."

"Who sent you?" said Lane.

"The company I work for – *used* to work for."

"And does this company have a name?"

"CSM. Speak to the guy in charge – Chris Mann."

Lane was annoyed. "I'm going to check this out. An officer will return you to your cell. You're going to be staying with us a while longer."

CHAPTER
33

Perez made the phone call. Lane waited and watched, sitting on the edge of his desk as Perez called CSM. After speaking for several minutes, Perez hung up. From the look on his face, Lane could tell that it wasn't good news.

"Well the company does appear to exist, and it does provide IT services. The owner of the company, Mr Mann, confirmed that he hired Michael Kern. Apparently Kern studied for an HND in Information Technology, while he was inside. He was trying to turn his life around."

Lane was unconvinced.

"Kern worked for the company for over a year, but was sacked for poor time keeping," said Perez.

Lane thought. "He could have done it, you know. A job like that would have given him access to people's homes. He could have been tempted … Do a background check on this computer company. Also confirm that Kern really did get that qualification." Lane made to go.

"Where are you off to?" said Perez.

"There's something I need to check out."

·   ·   ·

Lane spent nearly twenty minutes in IT. An Australian technician, with dyed red hair, helped him. Lane found his accent grating and the hair off-putting, but tried to ignore both. He waited patiently, as he heard the young man talk about digital cassettes, and the future of data storage.

"Let's just see the footage," said Lane, gritting his teeth.

He watched as the technician reviewed the images on the screen. Lane checked the time stamp, and looked at people walking through the hospital entrance. None of them seemed to resemble the man he had chased. He looked for signs of Kern or Stoltz, but saw nothing.

"How much footage is there?" said Lane.

"Nearly six hours' worth."

Lane groaned inwardly. He had no intention of staying that long. He'd assign the task to a junior officer. He asked Kevin, the technician, to make a copy of the cassette, and headed back to the incident room.

Perez was standing up, looking at a large, freestanding board that had arrived. It resembled a whiteboard but was transparent.

"Ah, good, it's turned up," said Lane.

"What's it for?"

Malcolm Brown and several colleagues looked at the board, as Lane repositioned it in the middle of the room.

"It's to help us chart our progress." Lane looked through the transparent board, to the civilian staff on the other side.

"We need information readily available, where everyone can see it. We need to start making connections."

Lane took a slim folder from his desk that contained photographs. The first was a mortuary picture, showing James Stein's remains. Lane stuck the picture in the middle of the board, and wrote Stein's name underneath.

Next to it he placed a picture of Nigel Warner. Underneath he wrote Warner's name and then in brackets *Partner*.

To the left of Stein's picture, Lane used a marker pen to draw a large X. "That's for the remains of the other person in Acton, who we haven't yet identified."

Lane put the cap on the pen and stepped back. "At least three victims – two identified, one unidentified. All male, all murdered roughly within the last two months."

"And that's all the information we have," said Perez.

"Exactly," said Lane. "I want to start filling in gaps. Once we have all the identities, we can work out what our vics had in common. Then maybe we can find out who was targeting them."

Lane's phone rang and he reached for it. "Homicide West …"

"Chief Inspector Lane?" It was a deep voice, but not a male one.

"Yes? How can I help you?"

"My name's Diane Thorne – I'm in charge of the North West London Hospital Trust. I understand you've been conducting an investigation at one of our sites?"

Lane thought. He remembered the message he'd received, about someone who'd been trying to call.

"Yes. I'm not sure how long we'll need access to the site for. This is an ongoing enquiry –"

"That's not the reason I'm calling, Chief Inspector. I appreciate you have things to do, and I'm not one to stand in your way, but we do have an employee missing … a Paulo Raymus. He's been absent from work for nearly two weeks. Given your investigation, I thought I should let you know."

Lane felt the hairs on the back of his neck rising. He turned to the board. "This Mr Raymus … what does he look like?"

Thorne paused. "Mid-forties, Hispanic, average height …"

Lane thought about the uniform that had been found in the woods, behind Stein's home.

"Does he wear a dark-brown uniform?"

There was surprise in Thorne's voice. "How did you know?"

"I think perhaps we should meet."

·   ·   ·

The North West London Hospital Trust had an administration centre at St. Mark's Hospital, in Middlesex. Lane and Perez arrived just after five o'clock, and Lane took note of the large, grey building, towering in front of them.

"Sixties architecture at its best," he said to himself.

A number of ambulances were parked outside. Lane saw an elderly woman being removed from one. She seemed remarkably cheery, in spite of the fact she was being wheeled on a trolley.

At the reception, he asked for Diane Thorne, and presently a secretary came to collect them.

"Ms Thorne is on the ninth floor," she explained. "We can take the lift."

Lane and Perez followed, and waited as several patients got in ahead of them. It was a tight squeeze, and the lift slowly made its way up.

On the ninth floor, they were led to a corner office. On the door was the name *Diane C. Thorne*. The secretary knocked and then opened the door.

Thorne was standing at her desk. She was a tall, thin woman with dark hair, dressed in a checked skirt and white blouse. She was in her mid-fifties, and had a confident look, but Lane sensed that underneath she was nervous.

"Chief Inspector?" She held out a hand and Lane shook it.

"This is Inspector Perez," said Lane.

Thorne shook Perez's hand and gestured towards two chairs. "Can I get you anything to drink?"

"We'll be fine, thank you," said Lane. He sat down and took out a folded picture. "I'll get straight to the point, Ms Thorne."

Thorne smiled, as if she appreciated his business-like approach.

"This is a crime-scene photo," said Lane. "It shows clothes we uncovered in woodland, behind a property in north London. We were wondering if they belonged to your missing employee."

Thorne didn't flinch. She put on her glasses and studied the photo. She opened a folder on her desk. Lane glanced at it and saw details – names, addresses and a timesheet. On the left-hand corner of the page was a small, colour photograph.

Thorne held the crime scene picture next to the photo and compared the two. "They may well have belonged to him. I recognize the uniform: it is one of ours."

"May I take a look?" said Lane.

Thorne turned the file around. Lane held it against the crime scene photo, as Perez leant in.

"Paulo Raymus," said Lane. Raymus had a round face, with dark hair and thick eyebrows. He had a mole on his right cheek, and looked much younger than he was.

"Do you mind me asking, Chief Inspector, what exactly happened to him?"

"It forms part of an ongoing enquiry. We're unable to divulge specifics at present, but we'd be grateful if you could tell us what you know about Mr Raymus."

Thorne looked at Lane with frustration. "In truth, I don't really know him. He's a junior member of staff – we do employ a large number of people. His line manager was unable to contact him. When I heard about the investigation you were conducting in Acton, I became concerned."

"And why was this?" said Perez.

"Acton is one of the sites Raymus looks after. He's a caretaker. We have four main sites – Northwick Park, St. Mark's, Central Middlesex and Acton. We have a small team of caretakers, who between them look after all the facilities. One of the team members is Mr Raymus."

Thorne looked into the distance, as if she was somewhere else.

"When did he go missing?" asked Perez.

There was a strained paused. "His line manager reported him missing six days ago, but he hasn't turned up for work for more than two weeks."

"Has he been absent from work before?"

"Not for this long. And it's rare for employees to just disappear. If people want to leave, they can simply give notice." Thorne looked composed, but she was tapping her desk repeatedly with her right hand.

"Were you aware of Mr Raymus being threatened in any way?" said Lane.

Thorne shook her head. "No. It's something you'd need to take up with his manager."

"If you could give us some contact details, that would be helpful."

"Certainly. I'll give you a copy of this file before you leave." Thorne inhaled and then exhaled slowly. A missing employee was a problem, particularly if violence was involved.

Lane looked around the office. It was large, but simple and functional. He imagined running a hospital could be stressful, perhaps more so than being a police officer.

"Has the hospital received threats from former employees?" said Lane, "– people who claimed they were unfairly dismissed – who had grudges of one sort or another?"

"We've had employment tribunals – claims for unfair dismissal. I can't imagine this has anything to do with that." Thorne had a question that she wanted to ask.

"Do you think he's been murdered?"

Lane and Perez looked at one another.

"I wouldn't wish to speculate," Lane replied. "At the moment we're pursuing a number of lines of enquiry. Can you tell us about his next of kin?"

"We've already tried to contact them, but without success. I spoke to Paulo's manager. He said Paulo doesn't have a wife or a girlfriend – doesn't have any family here. I know he hasn't been in the country long. He's worked at the hospital for less than a year."

"A person few people would miss," said Lane to himself. "There're some names I'd like to run by you: *James Stein, Nigel Warner ...*" he paused, "and *Michael Kern*. Do any of these names mean anything to you?"

Thorne looked at her computer. "I don't recognize any of them, but I can access the network from here – see if we have records. With a workforce of our size, you never know. If you could give me a few minutes …"

"Sure," said Lane. "Go ahead."

CHAPTER
34

"So what did you make of that?" said Perez.

It was a little after five o'clock, and Lane and Perez were trying to drive out of St. Mark's Hospital.

Lane shrugged. "I think Diane Thorne's a capable woman. She knows we need a break like a dead man needs a coffin."

"That's not exactly what I meant …"

"I take your point."

They were sitting in Perez's car. Perez was driving, and he was having difficulty leaving the hospital car park. "I can't believe they have a rush hour," said Lane. His face turned sour as he saw ambulances blocking the road ahead. One ambulance driver honked at another. "She gave us some good information. Now we have another name to go on."

"Paulo Raymus," said Perez. The ambulance in front moved and he edged the car forward.

"We have to consider how this helps us," Lane muttered.

"I'm not sure the hospital is a common link," said Perez.

"You may be right. Neither James Stein nor Nigel Warner had a connection to it."

"Perhaps they all knew each other socially."

Lane looked doubtful. He wound down the window. "Get a move on!" he shouted to an ambulance. "How do you respond to emergencies, for God's sake?"

Lane wound up the window and took out the photograph of Raymus. "This guy is younger than both Stein and Warner, is of a different ethnic origin, was born overseas …"

"How about sexual orientation?" said Perez. "What if they were all gay?"

"We'll have to ask friends and colleagues about that. But the other thing is that Stein and Warner were well off. Raymus doesn't appear to have been." He noted the home address Raymus had given the hospital. It was in Bethnal Green. "We'll check out his place. Not today though – first thing tomorrow morning. We'll also speak to his supervisor."

Traffic began moving and they left the car park, making it to the main road.

"The traffic is just as bad here," said Perez.

"The real rush hour," Lane replied. "We should have organized things better." He felt disappointed. "I'm going to have to let Michael Kern go. We really don't have enough to hold him. I'll get the custody sergeant to do it this evening. There's no point heading back to the incident room. You might as well go home – surprise that good wife of yours. We can make an early start tomorrow."

Perez felt pleased, but also found himself thinking about Kern.

"There's a tube station up ahead," said Lane. "Can you drop me off? There's something I want to check out."

·   ·   ·

Lane arrived at the mortuary, near King's Cross, a little after six. He entered through the side entrance, and looked at two morose-looking technicians, as they left. That was what working here did for you, he thought.

He wasn't challenged by anyone, and he made a mental note that security needed to be improved. He found Doctor Croft's lab and knocked on the door.

"Come in!"

Lane stepped in and saw Croft at the examination table, in the centre of the room. He was sorting out medical instruments.

"Tony, this is a surprise." Croft was genuinely pleased to see him. "What can I do for you?"

"I was hoping to catch you before you left," said Lane. He looked about and saw that the examination room was otherwise empty. It was clean, and had a faint smell of disinfectant. Lane disliked the smell. Smells brought back vivid memories.

"I came to see you about our latest vic."

"I wasn't aware we had a *latest vic*," said Croft. "I thought all you found were clothes in the woods, behind Stein's home."

"We may have a name for the person who used to wear those clothes," said Lane. He explained to Croft about Paulo Raymus's disappearance. Croft listened intently, asking what work Raymus had done. Lane explained, adding that Raymus had only been in the country for a comparatively short period.

Croft winced. "Lack of details – lack of medical records. That'll make it harder to get a match, if and when we do find a body."

"I was thinking about that," said Lane. He walked around the room, looking at the equipment on the benches that ran along the walls. The set up reminded him of a chemistry lab. "I was wondering if Raymus could be our first vic – if his remains could be among those we found in Acton."

Croft sat down by a bench. "Male ... Hispanic ... late twenties ... it's possible. It would fit. But I have to stress that all we found were bone fragments. I'm not sure I'd be able to give you a conclusive answer: we got lucky with Stein."

Lane had to agree there. "I'll see if I can go about securing Raymus's medical records from abroad – the Dominican Republic."

"Good luck." Croft knew from experience that securing records across international boundaries was difficult and time consuming.

"There was something else I want to ask you," said Lane. "You used to work in the NHS, didn't you?"

Croft had mixed feelings about his time there. "I spent nearly eight years at the Chelsea & Westminster Trust. Why do you want to know?"

"Do you know anything about the North West London Hospital Trust? Have there been any rumours, any scandals?"

"Not that I'm aware of. I have colleagues who work there. It generally has a good reputation. From time to time there're complaints, but that's to be expected in any large organization. Disgruntled patients are a hazard of the job, I guess."

Lane thought about negligence, and whether work at the trust's hospitals could have led to what they were dealing with. What linked Paulo Raymus and James Stein?

"Stein worked in engineering. What would link a hospital to an engineering company?"

"Some hospitals have research contracts for drugs or surgical development. There are often relationships with private-sector firms."

"Stein worked in civil engineering," said Lane. "I don't think he had anything to do with surgical or medical work."

"This is out of my area of expertise," said Croft. His shoulders rose an inch and then fell. He thought he was of limited use, and knew he should stick to the areas he was good at. "I'm not a detective. That's how come I landed up here." He put a hand on Lane's shoulder and guided him towards his office.

"James Stein and the other unidentified remains were buried. Nigel Warner was hanged, and as for Paulo Raymus, he may still be alive: all you found were clothes."

Lane considered that. Croft led him to a seating area. "I'll make some tea and we can chat some more."

·   ·   ·

Daniel Riley woke up. He wasn't sure how long he'd been asleep, and he felt a chill run through his body as he remembered where he was.

The lights on the ceiling were barely glowing, and things were no longer quiet. In the distance he could hear noise – footsteps, and a door opening and closing – at least that was what it sounded like. Riley panicked. How much time had elapsed? How could he have fallen asleep?

He pushed the cardboard he was covering with aside and stood up. Noise was coming from next door – from Will's room. Riley put his ear to the wall and listened, then moved towards the ventilation grille and listened again. He decided to chance it.

"Are you there? Will … are you there?"

There was scuffling. Finally, a weak voice replied, "Yes."

It was one word, but Riley felt tense, and knew that something was wrong.

"What happened?"

There was a pause. "He took me. Something went wrong … he beat me." Will's voice trailed off.

"Are you OK?"

There was nothing.

"Will … are you OK?"

"I don't know. My ribs … I think something's broken."

Riley was full of questions. "Who is he?"

A pause. "I've never seen a face."

Riley thought back to the man in the car park who had been loading the van. He couldn't picture his face clearly. "How did he get you? … originally, I mean."

Will sounded confused. "He was waiting at home … he broke in."

"And?" Riley needed more, as much information as possible. "We can do this," he said. "We can get out of here." His voice was full of hope, but hope was something that Will lacked.

"What links us?" Riley said aloud. "What do you do for a living?"

"How will that help?"

"I'm just asking."

"I'm unemployed – I *was* unemployed."

Riley wondered about that.

"He's toying with us," said Will.

"I've got a camera in my room," said Riley, "near the ceiling."

"Wouldn't surprise me." Will paused, breathing heavily. "I think he likes to do that: I think he likes to watch. I need to rest … we can talk later."

Riley wanted to ask more, but the sound of Will's breathing made him stop. He thought about Will's injuries, and hoped they wouldn't be fatal. He didn't want to be left alone.

CHAPTER
35

On Wednesday morning, DCI Lane arrived at the incident room a little after 8 A.M. Perez was already there, along with a few civilian staff, including Malcolm Brown.

Lane looked at the framed photographs on Brown's desk. They had changed, and were now showing bridges across the River Thames. Lane recognized Tower Bridge as well as Waterloo Bridge, but couldn't be certain of the other two.

On the transparent screen, in the centre of the room, photographs had been added, showing the crime scenes from which bodies had been recovered. There was a photograph of the Acton site, one of James Stein's home, and several of the woods behind Stein's property. Lane was pleased that people were making use of the board.

He put down his things and picked up a marker pen, writing the name *Paulo Raymus* below a small picture. Perez watched as he wrote.

"Two victims accounted for," said Lane, "one M.I.A."

Lane looked at the question mark on the board. It represented the unidentified remains, found in Acton. "Croft said Raymus might still be alive."

"It's worth considering," said Perez, "though sometimes it's easier to get information from the dead rather than the living."

"True enough." There was a knowing tone in Lane's voice. He thought about taking it further, but was stopped as David Mear came into the room.

"Ah, my favourite marketing man," said Lane.

"It's *press liaison*," said Mear briskly. "Anyhow, Chief Superintendent Travers said I was to help you – help you establish good relations with the press, and use them to develop your leads."

That'll be a first, said Lane to himself. He should have chosen a career like Mear's: more money and less hassle.

Lane looked at the stiff mop of blond hair on Mear's head, wondering how much hairspray was required to keep it in place.

"I've had Channel 5 on the phone," said Mear. "They said one of their news crews filmed you the other day, at a crime scene. They said a grave had been discovered, with multiple bodies."

Lane remembered the trench behind James Stein's home. There had been a news crew outside. How did they know what had been discovered?

"Tell them they're barking up the wrong tree. It's not *multiple bodies*."

Mear scribbled down a note. "Just one then?"

"Absolutely," said Lane, with a straight face.

Mear left, double-checking what he had written.

"You shouldn't wind him up like that," said Perez quietly.

"He's Travers's man," said Lane. "He's probably reporting everything we say and do. *Press liaison* for God's sake. How much do they cost anyway?"

"I've received a couple of messages," said Perez. "Nolan said he examined the scene at St. Swithun's where you chased that suspect. He said he recovered no usable trace or prints. Ditto for the roof and the fire escape from which the man fell."

"He was wearing gloves," said Lane. "He was pretty much covered from head to toe. I wasn't expecting much. What else is there?"

"A complaint from Myles Appleferd. He said you harassed him."

"I hardly *harassed* him," said Lane, disgruntled. "Appleferd was unwilling to help, so I gave as good as I got."

"In any case, he had his secretary call to say he'd be making a complaint."

"He can join the queue. I'll just turn up at his place and harass him properly."

Perez wondered if Lane was joking. "Other than that there's nothing new."

"Not quite … we do have a lead." Lane held up Raymus's address. "Raymus lives in east London. We should have a look at his place."

· · ·

The Cole Estate, near Bethnal Green, was a desolate place. That was what Lane thought as Perez parked the car.

On either side were grey tower blocks, with white cladding. Most were fifteen-storeys high. Washing was hanging from many balconies, along with bikes, off cuts of carpet and mattresses.

Lane didn't know the area but Perez had some local knowledge. "Raymus's flat should be in that block up ahead." He gestured to a block on the right-hand side of the road. It wasn't as tall as the others. It was a long, low building, with walkways that ran along its length. They were tiered, one looking down on to the next.

"That place has more satellite dishes on it than NASA mission control," said Lane. He studied the building, looking for entry and exit points. Police training never went away.

At the entrance was a notice in white and green, explaining that the building was maintained by the borough of Tower Hamlets. There was a contact number, which had been sprayed over with graffiti.

The detectives took the stairs to the second floor. Ahead of them was a narrow landing. On the left-hand side were front doors, on the right a low wall and a railing. Below, further out, was another walkway.

Lane checked the address, thinking that this was somewhere that must be intimidating at night. "It should be up ahead."

Perez checked the door numbers, noting Lane's unease. "I think it's at the far end." He came to 210, and stopped in front of a dark-green door. There was a letterbox, but no window to look through. "I think it should be empty."

"According to the hospital he lives alone," said Lane.

Perez knocked on the door and waited. After several minutes Lane gestured to him to go ahead. Perez took a metal pick and tension wrench from his pocket, and set to work on the brass lock. He bent down and concentrated, listening as he worked.

"It would have been easier if there'd been a spare key," said Lane, looking under the mat.

"It would have been easier if he hadn't disappeared," said Perez.

There was a clicking sound. Perez turned the tension wrench through ninety degrees and the door opened.

"Good man," said Lane quietly.

Perez accepted the praise with a smile. Lock picking was a skill that Lane envied.

"Hey! What are you doing?" The voice came from behind them. The detectives turned to see a young man standing at the far end of the landing. He was seventeen or eighteen years old, with a round face and short, dark hair. His eyes narrowed.

"You lot should piss off. You know that?"

"We're conducting a –" Lane reached into his jacket to take out his warrant card.

"I don't want to see it!" The young man fixed Lane with a stare. Behind him appeared a second youth, wearing a red baseball cap. "They're Old Bill," he said.

"I know that!" the first replied. "They should just piss off!"

Lane felt angry but tried to suppress it. "We have reason to be here, sir, so calm down, and let us get on with our job." He turned away and opened the door of the flat. Perez stepped in and Lane followed, closing the door before the youth had a chance to reply.

• • •

"I've heard of being stupid, but he abuses the privilege," said Lane. He and Perez were walking around, inside the flat. It was a modest space in Lane's mind.

"That guy's just young and foolish," said Perez. "Don't let it get to you."

Paulo Raymus's flat was well kept. There was a narrow hallway, with rooms leading off. To the left was a bathroom, to the right a small bedroom.

"It's a starter home," said Lane, "compact and *bijou* – that's how estate agents would put it."

Perez didn't think much of estate agents, and had other things to focus on. He went into the bathroom and checked the sink. "One toothbrush, a razor and a towel – looks as if he lives by himself."

Lane walked into the living room and looked about. There was a small, threadbare sofa. Opposite was a large and dated TV.

"Our Mr Raymus lives a modest life," said Lane. He approved, and took out a pair of latex gloves and flicked through magazines on the table.

"Nothing of interest here." He looked through the living-room window. He could see the rest of the estate. There was a large, grey yard below, with two children riding on bikes. Beyond them was a playground that had been vandalized. Why did people always do that?

"I've got something," said Perez.

Lane walked into the kitchen, to see him flicking through the post. "A couple of utility bills, a payslip from the hospital, plus some letters."

"Who are they from?"

"Looks to be relatives," said Perez. He checked the address. "They're postmarked the Dominican Republic."

"Might as well open them," said Lane. "He can complain if and when he turns up."

Perez had a good working knowledge of Spanish, and spent several minutes reading the mail.

"One's from Raymus's sister, another from a friend. They don't seem to say anything of interest – they talk about family life – someone is sick – something about surgery."

"We'll take them with us." Lane had a lot to do, and didn't want to make a return journey if possible.

Perez unfolded an evidence bag from his jacket, putting the letters inside. "You know what's funny?" said Lane. "There's no sign of keys, a wallet or bank cards." He rechecked all the cupboards and drawers, and then checked the bedroom. "He must have taken them with him."

There were several metal tins in the kitchen. Perez opened them and peered in.

"There's some cash in here."

"How much?"

Perez removed an elastic band from a thick roll of notes. He counted out the money. "£780, all in twenties."

"A rainy-day fund perhaps," said Lane. "Best bag it." Lane sat at the kitchen table. "Why would someone want to kill Paulo Raymus? What does he have in common with Stein and Warner?"

"Nothing," said Perez. He considered the flat Raymus lived in. "They led very different lives."

"Yet someone may well have targeted all of them. There's a link that we have to find." Lane had been there before, but wasn't about to become complacent. Patience and detective work were required.

"Time to get going." He made for the front door and opened it. He stopped on the landing as he saw a figure. Something was wrong. It was the young man who had confronted them earlier. He was standing at the far end of the landing, with a Staffordshire bull terrier. He bent down and released it from its lead.

It bolted towards the detectives.

CHAPTER
36

On Lane's encouragement, Perez leapt over the railings on the left-hand side. Lane saw him land on the balcony below. Lane didn't follow: the dog was less than ten feet away, and he stepped back into the flat and slammed the door.

He heard a thud, and the door shook in its frame. There was a scrabbling of paws and then barking. Lane looked around the flat. He saw the living room at the opposite end, and had an idea.

He opened the front door quickly and stepped behind it. The dog ran in and dashed towards the living room. Lane emerged from his hiding place. He stepped out and pulled the front door shut, and a moment later he could hear scuffling on the other side.

Lane looked down and saw that his trousers had torn. How had that happened? It didn't matter. There were other things to worry about – that young man, for instance. He saw the youth at the end of the walkway, and the youth seemed equally surprised to see him. He made for the stairwell, and Lane followed.

The teenager was fast, and Lane knew it would be difficult to catch up. He reached the stairs and peered down. He could see a head moving.

By the time Lane reached the bottom of the stairs, he was out of breath. He was at the entrance to the block, and looked about. He ran to the corner of the building and saw the youth in the distance. The young man glanced back.

Lane wasn't sure he could catch up. The youth was headed for a narrow road, which ran around the estate. As he moved from the pavement to the road, he slipped and lost his balance. Lane seized his chance.

The youth struggled to get up, pressing his hand against his right leg. Lane ran to him and stooped down, hitting him in the square of his back. The youth cried out, and Lane struck him again. Lane hauled him up and dragged him across the road, slamming him against a wall. He felt livid, and made to punch him.

"Don't! … Please … I give up!"

. . .

It was a little after 10.45 and Lane was at Homicide West. He saw Chief Superintendent Travers in the corridor, outside the incident room. Travers was holding a transparent blue folder under his arm. *Application for Borough Commander* was written on the document inside.

Lane felt a mixture of surprise and relief. Surprise, as he had never considered Travers borough-commander material, relief because it meant he could be leaving Homicide West. Travers glanced down at Lane's trouser leg and disappeared into his office.

In the incident room there was a quiet hum of activity. At Malcolm Brown's desk a young woman was working with him. Lane recognized her from the previous day – an admin. assistant who shared the same eccentric qualities as Brown. They were sitting side by side, poring over paperwork from an archive box.

"Are those the records from Myles Appleferd?"

Brown looked up. "Yes, sir."

"Good. Let us know if you find anything."

"Of course, sir."

Lane sat down. He felt tired and looked at his torn trousers. *Perhaps I can use gaffer tape.*

He took a roll of silver tape from his desk, noted the shiny colour, and felt disappointed. "Perhaps I can staple it …"

Perez, who was sitting opposite, raised an eyebrow.

"I saw the governor outside."

Lane's face soured. "That guy's about as useful as an Icelandic bank. They should ring-fence him for his own good. Anyway, how are things shaping up?"

"The youth we arrested is still in custody. He's refusing to give us his name or that of his friend."

Lane remembered the young man's accomplice. "I'll get some uniforms to go back and do a sweep. I've arranged a meeting with Paulo Raymus's supervisor, at the hospital where he worked. He said he can see us at 11.30." Lane checked the time and took a stapler from his desk drawer. "Let's get going."

．　　　．　　　．

Daniel Riley woke up. He looked about, feeling disorientated. He was still locked in the room. The light was dim, but something had changed. He took a few moments to realize what it was: the trays of food had gone.

The trays, which had been pushed through the hatch in the door, were nowhere to be seen. Riley felt a spike of fear. He checked himself, and quickly realized that he hadn't been hurt. He looked up at the camera near the ceiling, and felt wary.

Riley remembered Will in the next room, and moved to the grille.

"Are you there?"

There was silence.

"Still here," said a voice.

"I think he came in." Riley heard the anxiety in his own voice. "He came in while I was asleep."

"Of course," said Will. "He does that. Moves things around."

Riley was surprised.

"Haven't you worked it out?" said Will. "He's drugging you – drugging us both."

Riley felt confused. "What do you mean?"

"Every time we eat, we feel sleepy and nod off. That gives him time to come in." Will was breathing heavily.

Riley looked about. He was worried.

"How do you know this?"

"I worked it out."

"How long have you been here?"

"I can't be sure." Will paused. "You're not the first person who's been in that cell. There've been others."

Riley felt uncomfortable but wanted to know more.

"How many?"

"Three or four. I don't know how long it's been. I tried to keep track, but it's hard. There's no day or night in here."

Riley looked at the marks he'd made on the wall – futile attempts to keep track of time. Had Will done the same?

"We need to get out," said Riley. "We *need* a plan."

"Count yourself lucky you're alive," said Will. "He likes to watch. He likes to see our fear. He feeds off it."

"What happened to the others?"

"They vanished."

"All of them?" Riley was anxious. "We have to work out what we have in common. If we're going to get out, we have to think."

Will sounded as if he was considering it. "What do you do – in the real world, I mean?"

"I'm a businessman," said Riley.

"I'm unemployed … Do you have any family?"

"Yes."

"I don't …" Will coughed and sounded as if he was wheezing. "How old are you?"

"Forty-two."

"You're older than me. Face it: I don't think we have much in common."

There was silence.

"I'm not going to eat the food," said Riley.

There was a groan from Will's cell. "That's what I said. You'll change your mind … starvation does that to you."

CHAPTER
37

Alfred Pine was a late middle-aged man, with greying hair that was receding rapidly. He had, however, small patches of hair above his ears, which gave him a distinguished look.

Lane and Perez were sitting in his office, at the Central Middlesex Hospital. It was a quarter to twelve, and Pine was unhappy that they were late.

"I have a lot of work to do, Detectives. If you could keep this short and to the point, I'd be grateful."

Pine seemed out of place – too smart and composed to be a facilities manager, and that made Lane curious.

"It's Paulo Raymus we wish to speak to you about." Lane took out his notebook and turned to a fresh page. "We understand you were his supervisor?"

"Correct. I was the one who reported him missing. When he failed to show up for work, for more than a week, I suspected something was wrong."

"Has he ever been absent before?" said Perez.

Pine shook his head, looking sincere as he spoke. "He's a good employee – reliable, prompt – always willing to go the extra mile. I have to say though that he hasn't been here long. He came to us through a recruitment agency. We hired him on a temporary basis, but the position became permanent."

"And is that how you tend to recruit?"

"It varies." Pine shrugged and feigned indifference. "Some positions can be filled on a temporary basis. For more senior roles we tend to look for permanent hires."

"Did the recruitment agency tell you much about Raymus?" said Lane.

"Not really." Pine seemed to be thinking back. "They said he had only been in the country a short while. He was here legally. They'd seen a passport as well as a visa, so I had no concerns in that regard."

"Does Raymus have friends and family in the UK?"

"I don't know him particularly well." Pine looked awkward. "We chat from time to time. I get the impression most of his family are overseas – he never seems entirely happy about that."

"Did he seem lonely or depressed?" said Perez.

"I never thought to ask," said Pine. He looked as if mixing with his employees was something he preferred not to do. "He's a good worker – gets the job done, and that's what matters."

"And what exactly is the nature of the job?" said Lane.

"He helps with administration – doing routine inspections of sites, including those that are mothballed, and helps with repairs and maintenance."

"An odd-job man?" said Perez.

"At times, yes."

"What concerns us is a question of access," said Lane. "How could a perpetrator come on to the Acton site repeatedly, without being seen?"

"We only inspect the site every few weeks," Pine replied. "It's been mothballed and there is little of real value there. As long as the main entrance remains locked, people are happy."

"Does Raymus have access to all the buildings owned by the Trust?" said Perez.

"Yes."

"How about keys?" said Lane. He looked at Pine keenly, searching for a reaction. "Was he given keys for all the buildings?"

Pine hesitated. "We don't let our employees take keys home. Everything is held centrally, for security. It's a principle we adhere to." Pine gestured to several metal cabinets behind him. "After Paulo went missing, I noticed that one set of keys was unaccounted for. They were for the site in Acton." Pine was uncomfortable as he spoke, and Lane felt the balance of power shifting.

"So Raymus took the keys?"

"It would seem that way."

"We've been unable to find much of Raymus's personal effects," said Lane, "– house keys, bank cards – a wallet. Were any of these items left here?"

Pine shook his head. "When Paulo didn't show up, I opened his locker. I didn't find any of those things."

"What did you find?" said Perez.

"A spare coat, some books, some shoes … nothing of value."

In Lane's mind, Pine was most concerned about image. He was a man who only really cared about himself. "We were wondering if Mr Raymus has been in any sort of trouble. Did he tell you whether anyone had threatened him, or if he'd had a falling out with someone?"

"Paulo and I aren't close. He's a good employee – does what you tell him – even with a smile, but he didn't confide in me."

Lane noticed out of the corner of his eye the purple cufflinks Pine wore. They contrasted with his orange tie. "OK … Perhaps we could see that locker you mentioned."

"Sure." Pine stood up and led them out.

·　　·　　·

"So what did you make of him?" said Lane. He was walking with Perez back to their car.

"I think Pine's an interesting character," said Perez. "He seems out of place – too intelligent, too sophisticated for the job he's doing."

"Great minds think alike," said Lane. "Did you notice his purple cufflinks and orange tie? He reminds me of a Quality Street."

Perez smiled. He sometimes wondered about people who dressed distinctively. Was it a sign of confidence or insecurity?

"Where does Raymus fit in when it comes to Stein and Warner?"

"He's linked," said Lane. "His clothes were found on land behind Stein's property. His remains may well be among those of Stein."

"Could he have had a falling out with them?"

"And they died along with him?" Lane thought about it. "It doesn't compute, but something links them. Raymus had only been in the country a short while. He wouldn't have known many people. He seems to have had few friends, yet he may well have been targeted."

"And most of his personal effects are nowhere to be found," said Perez.

"Let's assume someone wanted those keys for the site in Acton. They befriend Raymus, gain his trust and then ask him for them. Perhaps they offer him money … perhaps they steal them."

"Either way it ends badly," said Perez.

Lane's phone rang and he took it out, and checked the display. "It's Croft." He pressed a button and put the phone to his ear. After a minute, he thanked Croft and hung up.

"Well that was interesting."

"What has he found?"

"He's been looking at the remains from Acton. He's found fragments of three bullets – .38s. He believes Stein and the other vic were shot before their bodies were disposed of."

Perez didn't look pleased. "We have a killer who's flexible – prepared to shoot Stein and the person he was buried with, and hang Nigel Warner. We're dealing with someone who can adapt."

Lane felt weary. He knew killers who planned ahead were among the hardest to catch.

•　　•　　•

The incident room at Homicide West was almost empty as Lane and Perez returned. Lane felt annoyed, even though it was lunchtime. Malcolm Brown was still at his desk. His female friend had gone, but he was still poring over the documents that had been handed in by Myles Appleferd.

"Found anything?" said Lane.

Brown looked up. He was always uncomfortable when questioned, and didn't like being the centre of attention.

"Nothing so far. Mr Appleferd and Mr Stein seem to have exchanged a lot of correspondence. It looks as if Stein wasn't happy with the work Appleferd was doing."

"Advising him on how to finance his company?"

"Yes. Both seem to have been short-tempered men, judging by their emails."

"Did Appleferd threaten Stein?"

"No sign of it so far. There's a lot of information – about the state of Stein's company and how it could be improved. Do you want the details?"

"I don't like maths," said Lane, "it's too inaccurate. Just give me the highlights."

Brown thought about that.

"Profit margins at Stein's business seem to have been under pressure. He took over other engineering companies, and it seems to have put a strain on his cash flow. He was profitable, but that wouldn't have been the case for much longer."

"How many companies did he take over?" said Perez.

"Six within the last two years." Brown was relieved to be answering someone else's questions. "The takeovers were financed through a mixture of cash and loans. That was where his problems began. The loans had to be renegotiated as interest rates rose."

"And Appleferd was providing advice?"

"Bad advice – at least if you believe Stein. Stein was trying to control costs by cutting overheads. He'd shut offices, mothballed one engineering facility, and laid off staff. Layoffs were quite considerable – over twenty percent of the workforce."

"Lots of unhappy people," Lane murmured to himself. "Let me know if you find anything more." He paused as a uniformed constable came in. The man handed a note to Perez and then left.

"I wasn't expecting that," said Perez.

Lane didn't like being left out of the loop and leant across. "What is it?"

"It seems as if I had a visitor this morning – Alex Grey. Remember her?"

"The good-looking one from the construction company?" Lane was grinning to himself.

"The very same."

"Well what did she want?"

"It seems she called in to see how our investigation is going. She said if there was anything she could do to help, we should let her know." Perez held up the note. "How many times do people say that to us?" He looked at Lane for a long moment.

"You know what I'm thinking, don't you?" said Lane.

"*Zodiac Killer*."

Brown, who was listening, seemed confused. Perez saw his look and decided to explain.

"The Zodiac Killer was an American serial killer who was never caught. The detective leading the investigation interviewed many people over the years. However he said only one interviewee ever offered to help him with his case …"

"And that interviewee turned out to be his strongest suspect," said Lane.

Brown thought. "So people who commit murders often want to be part of the investigation?"

"It has been known." Lane smiled in Perez's direction. "Don't look so worried. Still, I'm glad it's you she likes, and not me."

CHAPTER
38

Lane spent several minutes on the phone to Chris Nolan. He wanted to know if any forensic evidence had been found that might identify the stranger he had pursued at St. Swithun's.

"There's nothing," said Nolan, in a dispirited tone. "No fingerprints – but then your guy was wearing gloves – and nothing on the car he landed on."

"Did he cut or injure himself?"

"It doesn't appear so. We did find black fibres – probably from the jacket he was wearing. If you have a suspect, we could possibly use it to rule him in or out, but the fibres come from a mass-produced line. By themselves they're not conclusive."

"Understood," said Lane. He thought about collecting Kern's clothing and getting it checked. Perhaps it had not been a good idea to let him go. "Thanks." Lane hung up and saw a young constable walking in. He handed over a note.

"It's from the custody sergeant," said Lane, turning to Perez. "It turns out that youth who set his dog on us, wants to talk. He says he has information."

·   ·   ·

Lane left Terry Carter in interview-room two for some time. When the detectives finally entered, Carter looked cold.

Interview-room two was the most uncomfortable one. It was always too hot or too cold. The chairs and table were damaged, and there was a smell that no amount of cleaning appeared able to remove. Lane sensed Carter's unease.

He hadn't taken the time to study Carter before. He was eighteen, of slight build, with pale skin and dark hair. The grey clothes he wore were loose fitting, and only emphasized his lack of build.

Lane and Perez sat down.

"Are you going to record this?" said Carter, looking across the table.

Lane shook his head. He held Carter's eyes and noticed that they were dark. There were dark veins underneath, and he wondered if he used drugs. If he did, he was still clear-headed and focused.

"It turns out that you're not a juvenile."

"I know how the system works," said Carter. He spoke with a trace of an accent.

"So you know it determines the way we do things – whether we have to contact your parents and so on."

"Does that mean what I've been charged with will go away?"

Lane's mouth tensed and he tried to remain calm. He placed a slim folder in front of him. "You were reluctant to give us your name at first: I can see why. It turns out you've got form – threatening behaviour, assault, possession with intent to supply – you could qualify as a one-man crime wave."

Carter looked unfazed and sat back. "I don't answer to you."

Lane felt anger rising. Another young man with a sense of entitlement and no sense of responsibility. "You said you wanted to speak to us. What do you have to say?"

"What charges am I facing?"

"Threatening behaviour, obstructing an investigation, failing to control a dog in public place … I'm sure I can come up with a couple more."

"Can I get my dog back?"

Lane's eyes widened. He made to say something but stopped, and Perez realized what he was doing.

"What do you have to offer us?"

"The flat you were looking at," said Carter. "I know a bit about it – I know the guy who lives there."

Lane was interested, but didn't want to let it show. "What about him?"

"I see him coming and going. I haven't seen him for a while. I know he works in a hospital. He speaks English, but not well."

"Did you threaten him?" said Lane.

"He's not Filth, like you," said Carter.

Lane's cheeks reddened, and Perez decided to intervene.

"You're facing at least three charges. You could go to jail – not a young offender's institute. You can help us, and you can help yourself at the same time."

Carter thought. "You weren't the first people to come to that flat. The other guy who came – he had keys. He didn't have to break in."

"What other guy?"

"The guy who was there earlier. He took stuff out in boxes – small ones – had a van. He took his time."

"What did this guy look like?"

"I dunno." Carter shrugged and Lane was frustrated. In his mind, young people lacked common sense.

"He was about your age," said Carter, pointing to Perez. "A white guy, tall – well built."

Lane flicked through the folder in front of him. He came to a picture of Michael Kern and took it out. "Is this the man?"

"I dunno. He was some distance away."

Lane felt more frustrated. Young people were indeed mo-rons. "Think!" he said loudly. "Use your brain!"

Carter tensed, and the room was suddenly quiet.

"Study the picture," said Perez. "Is this the man you saw?"

Carter looked down and felt confused. "I don't think so. He was similar. Fair hair – similar eyes, but it wasn't him."

Lane took out another picture. "How about him?"

Carter studied the photo.

"He looks too old. Similar sort of face though."

"Great," said Lane, "so I'm looking for someone who's a cross between my two main suspects. Could you identify this man if you saw him again?"

"I don't know." Carter's tone wasn't helpful. Lane leant across the table and Carter shrank back.

"We've got a sketch artist. If we got them to work with you, do you think you could come up with an image of this man?"

"I can try," said Carter, "– if it means I get my dog back."

Lane looked stone-faced. He stood up and made to leave.

Once they were in the hall, Perez checked that the door was shut.

"Are you actually going to return his dog?"

Lane was trying to calm down. "He's hardly got his finger on the pulse of reality. But if he can give me a decent sketch, I'll think about it."

CHAPTER 39

Daniel Riley shivered in his cell. He pulled a dirty blanket about him, trying to feel grateful for the warmth it gave.

The lights in the cell were becoming dimmer, as if power to the building was fading. He wondered where he was. This place wasn't purpose built. It was disused: somewhere that needed a generator. He hadn't heard any sounds from a generator. Come to think of it, he hadn't heard any noise for a while. He looked up at the camera, in the corner of the room. The red light was still on but it was now blinking. Riley hated it. He hated everything about his situation, and longed for home.

Riley saw his wife's face in his mind, and those of his children. He'd never appreciated them – he realized that, and he vowed that if he got out things would be different.

There was a sound of footsteps. A metal door opened and closed, and the footsteps became louder. The panel at the base of the cell door slid back, and a tray of food shot through.

The noise startled Riley. He looked at the food and remembered what Will had told him about it being drugged.

The footsteps in the corridor faded and Riley went over to the wall.

"Will … Are you there?"

Nothing.

"Will … Can you hear me?"

"What is it?" said a hoarse voice.

Riley had an image in his mind of what Will looked like. Young, thin, covered in grime.

"He brought food," Riley said, "– another tray."

"Well good for you." Will sounded tired and irritated, and Riley felt bad for disturbing him. "He hasn't brought me anything," Will continued. "Perhaps that's his plan; perhaps he intends to starve one of us."

"I'm not going to eat it," said Riley. He studied the food, which appeared normal. "If he's drugged it, Lord knows what'll happen when I pass out."

"You should be grateful for what you get."

"We have to get out of here," said Riley. "We have to work *together* – come up with a plan."

"You aren't the first person to have said that." Will was annoyed.

"How many more have there been?"

"I have difficulty keeping track." Will's voice trailed off.

Riley wondered when Will had last eaten. He sounded weak, as if he was having difficulty staying awake – as if he was losing the will to go on.

"You have to *fight*," said Riley. "*We* have to fight." He looked around him. The room was a strange place, never intended to be a cell. Perhaps it was originally a washroom or a laundry. Nothing made sense any more.

"I think the power to the building is going."

Will didn't say anything for a moment.

"In that case you should look at the door."

Riley looked at it, and Will continued. "I saw it from the corridor when he brought me in. There's a keypad on it … it's electronic."

Riley looked towards the cell door and felt a flicker of excitement. "There's nothing on my side."

"Look for wires. They've got to run through the wall – that could be your ticket out."

"You have to come with me," said Riley. "I'm not leaving you."

Will's voice was fading. "I don't have any reason to leave. I don't have anything to live for."

Riley was struck by that, but didn't say anything. He knew he had to focus on escape.

·　　　·　　　·

At Homicide West, Lane was on the phone to his crime scene manager. "The flat belongs to a Paulo Raymus. He may be a victim in our enquiry. Someone saw a man at the flat who might be our suspect."

"And you want me to check for prints?"

"You're a mind reader."

There was a hint of agreement at the other end. "Email me the details. I'll see if I can get there later today." Nolan sounded busy.

"I appreciate it," said Lane. "I'll send the information over now."

He hung up and spent several minutes on his computer, typing slowly, before turning to Perez. "Who knows – this may actually lead us somewhere."

Perez had been staring at the transparent board in the centre of the room. "There's been no sign of any journalists for a few days."

Lane thought about the ones he knew. "Perhaps they have bigger fish to fry."

"Perhaps we shamed them into backing off."

"Unlikely – most have no shame." Lane thought about all the journalists he knew who had integrity. It didn't take long to reach the end of the list.

Perez could sense a restlessness coming from him. "Are we going somewhere?"

"I think I may have found a way to identify our other victim from the site in Acton." Lane pointed to the board. "Come on. Let's go."

.   .   .

The Final Fitness gym, on Charing Cross Road, looked new and well maintained. It had large glass windows and occupied the first floor of a renovated Victorian building.

Through the windows, Lane could see treadmills and weight-lifting equipment. It was fairly busy, which Lane found surprising given the time of day. Lane showed his warrant card to the man at reception. "It's just routine."

The bald man looked unconvinced.

Perez followed Lane through a turnstile and entered the main body of the gym.

Men were working out, most of them in their twenties or early thirties. Lane couldn't see anyone older, and he couldn't see any women. He wondered why that was.

The gym had an agreement with the Metropolitan Police, to allow officers to use it for free. In days gone by the Met had had many of its own facilities, but cutbacks had sealed their fate.

Lane had his own views on gyms. Certain kinds of people went there, and he wasn't one of them. When he had been in the army, his drill instructor had been fanatical about gyms. "Brings your mind and body together," he said. A lot had gone wrong when Lane was in the army, and he didn't talk about it often.

Norton Fisher was bench pressing weights. The young police technician was lying flat on a bench, about to lift a bar. Lane took note of the weight Fisher was going to press: ninety kilos.

"Mr Fisher …"

Fisher looked up, surprised. A minute later and he might have dropped the barbell. Sweat was dripping from his spiky, brown hair. He was a tall, thin character, not a natural candidate for weight lifting.

"What are you doing here?" He looked at Lane, his eyes wide.

"We're here to arrest you," said Lane calmly.

Fisher sat up.

"Just kidding," said Lane. "You manage the Missing Persons computer, don't you?"

"I help manage the database," said Fisher. He hadn't seen Lane for some time, as he wasn't based at Homicide West. He did know of Lane's reputation however. "The person in charge is our governor, Superintendent Dune. If you want to speak to him, you should really –"

Lane raised a hand. "Dune and me don't see eye to eye. As you might be able to guess, I'm conducting a murder enquiry." He told Fisher about the bodies he had found, mentioning the site in Acton, as well as James Stein's home. "Some of the deceased had families – people who would've reported them missing. I was wondering if you could do something for me. I need information from the database."

"This is not really the best place," said Fisher, looking about. "How did you know I'd be here, anyway?"

"Telepathy."

Fisher was unimpressed. "I'm not back in the office until tomorrow."

"But you *can* remotely access the database. You're issued with tablet PCs, aren't you?"

"How do you know about that?"

Lane wasn't about to divulge his sources. "If you get out that tablet, I can get the information I need and be on my way."

Fisher seemed to relax a little, and inside felt less tense. "Give me a minute." He went to his locker in the hallway and returned with a grey tablet. He mopped his forehead with a towel and looked over his shoulder, as he booted up the machine and entered a password. Lane and Perez looked on as he went through a menu. There were several passwords to be entered. Perez was glad that there were multiple layers of security.

Fisher turned around.

"The database is updated continually. Missing people can be reported by phone, or a visit to a police station, or through contact with a police officer. Once a report is taken, all information is entered on to the system and circulated as a missing persons file. People can contact us for more details."

Lane didn't appreciate the speech but tried to look patient. "I've been unable to identify one victim. For various reasons I can't do a visual ID. If I was to give you some parameters, could you do a specific search and produce a list of missing people, who might potentially be my victim?"

A tiny frown creased Fisher's forehead. "I can do that."

Lane sat down and looked at the screen. "One of the deceased was a businessman – James Stein – he ran his own engineering firm. He was successful and well off. I think the other vic, who was found with him, may have had a similar background."

Fisher nodded. "So you want me to do a search for … missing males who worked as businessmen?"

"Correct." Lane looked at the screen. "Set the age to between thirty and fifty-five – people based in London or the southeast, who went missing within the last six months."

Perez found himself nodding slowly.

Fisher entered the information, and waited as the computer completed its search. Results began appearing. Two, then three then four.

Lane was pleased.

"We've got some possibles," said Fisher. "Tim Mannak, who worked for a bank, Daniel Riley – some sort of financier, and two eastern-European businessmen, both Polish. I can use the drill-down function to get more information." Fisher looked at Lane.

"Do it."

CHAPTER 40

Lane and Perez walked out of the gym. On the opposite side of the road, Perez saw a man parking a car. He was in his late fifties, well built and dressed in a smart, grey suit. He had a scowl on his face.

"That's Superintendent Dune," said Lane. "Ignore him. He's a naturally bitter man."

The detectives walked to their car and Perez felt curious. "I wonder what brought him out here. No doubt he'll be asking Fisher what we've been up to." Perez glanced at the notes he'd made on his phone.

"We've got leads," said Lane, "but you should call it a day. Go home to your wife – show her that I'm not a slave driver."

Perez gave a melancholy smile. "She doesn't think highly of you as it is."

"Some things never change." Lane started the car and reversed out, as Superintendent Dune glanced across the road.

On the main road, traffic was becoming heavy, and Lane regretted his decision to drive.

"Actually, can you do me a favour? If I pull up by the tube station, can you take the car?"

"Where are you going?" said Perez.

"There's something I want to check out. Hold on to the car. You can hand it back tomorrow."

•   •   •

Lane took the tube, travelling up to Hendon, in north London. The journey took longer than he would have liked. Delays, and a large volume of commuters slowed his progress, and he was in a bad mood by the time he reached Hendon station. He hated travelling in the rush hour, and tried to avoid it whenever possible.

Coming out of the station, he felt a wave of relief pass over him. The air was cool, the sky was darkening, and he felt relaxed. He walked briskly along the high street, and took a turning to his left, heading towards a residential area. The roads became quieter, and he took another turning on to a residential road which appeared deserted.

The house he wanted was on the opposite side of the street. It was a two-storey building, built in the 1930s, with a garage to the right and an open, gravel drive. Lane felt envious, and wondered how Mike Rasmussen could afford such a place. Tabloid journalists were obviously better paid than he thought.

Lane stood on the opposite side of the street, a short distance away, and watched until the front door opened. A woman stepped out. She was in her early forties, dressed in a blue trouser suit, and leading a small child by the hand.

Rasmussen came to the front door and exchanged words with her. He was roughly the same age as her, and had a pointed face that made him look like an eagle.

The couple exchanged cross words, judging by their raised tones. Lane smiled to himself: perhaps Rasmussen's life wasn't as perfect as he had imagined.

"Yeah, well, we'll see about that!" the journalist said.

"You have to be more flexible," the woman replied. "You should stop thinking about yourself and think more about us. I'll speak to you next week." The woman marched away, and Lane noted the sound of her shoes on the road. She unlocked a car, secured the child in the rear and started the engine.

Lane knew Rasmussen was divorced, but didn't know that he had children. As he watched, Lane decided to call his own wife. He selected a number in his phone and looked across the street.

"Hello?"

"It's me," said Lane. He dipped his voice.

"How are things?" said Irene.

"Not bad … Could be worse, I guess."

Rasmussen stepped back inside and closed the door.

"I'm just ringing to let you know I'll be home soon," said Lane. "Perhaps we can go out for dinner: it'd make a change. There's someone I have to speak to, but it shouldn't take long."

"Where would you like to eat?"

"You decide. Any place that does decent food."

There was a brief laugh. "That sounds like the man I know. I'll see you later … Take care."

Lane put his phone away.

He crossed the road, and walked up to Rasmussen's front door.

CHAPTER
41

On Saturday morning DCI Lane arrived early at the incident room to find it almost empty. Things were often quieter on a Saturday, with fewer civilian staff working.

Malcolm Brown's desk had papers neatly stacked on it. The framed photographs in one corner hadn't changed however, and Lane felt disappointed. He sighed and sat down. He preferred it when the incident room was busy. When it was quiet, he felt his investigations lacked a certain urgency.

Lane turned on his computer and accessed his email. There was a message from Chris Nolan, explaining that he had checked Paulo Raymus's flat.

There was no sign of Michael Kern's prints. In fact there were very few prints, which makes it seem unusual. The only prints I found were Perez's and yours.

Give me a call if there is anything I can do. C.

Lane thought about that. Nolan was probably off for the weekend. There was no need to bother him unless it was urgent.

On impulse, Lane went down to the holding area in the basement. He found Michael Kern's cell, and looked through the hatch in the door. The cell was empty, Kern having been released, but Lane stood outside thinking. There was something familiar about

Kern, something that reminded him of Stoltz. Lane realized he shouldn't waste time idling when there was work to be done.

.   .   .

The phone rang and Lane leant across to pick it up. It was twenty minutes later, and he was at his desk. He was surprised to hear the voice at the other end. He put the thought aside and concentrated on the call.

By the time Perez arrived, Lane was making good progress. Lane had a confident look as he hung up and made another call. He gave Perez a nod, and after a few minutes put down the receiver.

Perez had a small box with him. From the picture on the side, Lane could see that it contained a mobile phone. Perez saw Lane's enquiring glance.

"A new smartphone," Perez explained. "I'm getting rid of the old one."

Lane wasn't impressed and looked at his notepad. "You should just use these. They're cheap, they're simple and they don't need an instruction manual to understand."

"Perhaps …"

"But you represent 21st Century policing," said Lane.

"I'm going to see if I can synchronize it with my computer."

Lane could see trouble ahead. "Anyway, I've made some progress while you've been busy."

"And?"

"Arnold Nowak and Florian Duma – our two missing Polish businessmen – they've turned up."

Perez was surprised. "Where?"

"In Warsaw. It turns out they were arrested for fraud. I wouldn't have found out so quickly without some help."

"From?"

"Mike Rasmussen."

Perez was surprised and opened his mouth as he stopped and thought.

"He used to be an Eastern-European correspondent, for one of the national papers. Didn't you threaten to arrest him once, for possession of drugs?"

"Right on both counts. I paid him a visit yesterday evening – asked for his help."

"I bet he was pleased to see you." Perez took out his new phone.

"Rasmussen has an ego that needs to be fed," said Lane. "Plus he owes me. Anyway, he came up with the goods this morning."

"So that leaves the banker and the other guy. What was his name – Daniel Riley?"

Lane tore a scrap of paper from his notepad. "Riley has a wife and children. I spoke to his wife and she's agreed to see us." Lane reached for his jacket. "Time for us to go."

•   •   •

Erin Riley lived in a large, detached house on the outskirts of Harrow. Lane and Perez arrived shortly after ten o'clock, and parked on the drive at the front. Perez was carrying his smartphone as they got out, and he looked at it as Lane pressed the doorbell.

"You're like a kid with a new toy." Lane couldn't understand people's obsession with technology. There were more important things in life to worry about.

The door was answered almost immediately. Erin Riley was tall, nearly five foot ten, with shoulder-length blonde hair. She had a round face and attractive features, but there was a sadness in her eyes.

A trophy-wife thought Lane, and then wondered if he was judging her too quickly. He introduced himself and Perez, and she gestured to them to come in.

The house was quiet. Lane saw a framed photograph of two young children – a boy and a girl, although there was no sign of them in the house.

"Thank you for getting in touch," said Erin. She ushered them towards the living room. It was a large space, which was well furnished, and had a view of the back garden. Lane looked at the cream sofas, noting their pristine condition. Erin gestured to them, and the detectives sat down.

"Thank you for coming to see me," she said. "Can I get you anything to drink?"

Lane shook his head. "We'll be fine, thank you." He reached for his notebook, and felt himself sinking back into the sofa. It didn't look as if price guaranteed comfort.

"As I mentioned earlier, we're looking into your husband's disappearance. I was wondering if you could provide me with some information, starting with when exactly he went missing."

Erin felt concerned, and there was an urgency in her eyes. She wished other people felt the same way that she did.

"It started on Monday. He went to work on Monday but never came back."

"And what time did he leave?" said Lane.

"It wasn't a normal day." Erin thought about how to put it. "He was selling the company – the company he had helped set up. He didn't go in early. There was a meeting scheduled for the afternoon – one o'clock. They were doing the handover then, and he and the other directors were due to meet."

"Your husband was disposing of his business?" said Perez.

Lane noticed that Perez was trying to take notes on his phone. He was having difficulty.

"That's right." Erin looked at the phone as well. "He'd built up the business over several years. It was a joint venture between him, John and Damien."

"They're his fellow directors?" said Lane.

Erin nodded. "The plan had always been to sell the business when the time came. They had a buyer. The buyer had looked at the books and was happy. The meeting was just a formality – the point at which contracts would be exchanged."

Lane made a note of that. "Were you ever involved in your husband's business?"

Erin shook her head. She wanted to let the detectives know how she felt – the tension – the fear. "I've never been much good with figures. That's Daniel's specialty."

Lane wondered what Erin did for a living. She seemed intelligent, and he suspected she had had some sort of career before marrying.

"What does your husband's company do?" said Perez.

"It operates in two parts. One part provides consultancy services, the other helps firms raise money."

"Venture capital?"

"Pretty much."

"Was your husband under any pressure at work?"

Erin thought and shook her head. "No more than usual." She wanted the detectives to realize that time was critical. "He works long hours, but his disappearance is out of character."

"Does he do much travelling?"

"Not really. He's UK based. His business partners – they went overseas to attract clients, but Daniel's always been here." Erin looked at several photographs on the mantelpiece. "I can give you pictures if you want – if that'll help."

"We can take them with us when we leave," said Lane.

"Daniel's been trying to reduce his hours," said Erin. "It's been a source of tension between us." She wanted to say more, but was cautious about talking openly in front of strangers.

"And this was why he was selling the business?" said Lane, "so that he could spend more time at home?"

"In part." Erin wanted to go further but stopped. Lane studied her. She came across as persuasive, but there was something about her that he didn't trust.

"Mrs Riley, has your husband been threatened in any way?"

"I don't think so."

"How about business acquaintances? Has he made any enemies through his work?"

"I don't know about his clients. My focus is on our home – the children. Daniel's the kind of person who keeps things to himself. I just wish people would realize that something is wrong."

Lane considered that. "There're a couple of names I want to run by you: *Michael Kern, James Stein* and *Nigel Warner*. Are any of these names familiar to you?"

Erin shook her head. "Could they have been people who threatened him?"

"It is possible. Does he keep an address book?"

"There's an electronic thing – a bit like that phone." Erin gestured to Perez, who seemed embarrassed at the attention his phone was receiving.

"Did he have it with him when he disappeared?" said Lane.

"Yes."

Lane felt disappointed. "You said your husband set up his company with other people. Could you give me their names and addresses?"

"Sure …" Erin stood up. "Bear with me."

CHAPTER 42

Margate, Kent, 1973

He would ultimately change his name, but Shawn James Tanner was born on the 6th February, 1973. His birth wasn't unexpected, but his mother, Dee Tanner, ended up going to the hospital alone.

Her partner, Ronnie Angel, had broken up with her several months earlier. At the time she'd felt bad about it, but she'd come to hope that he'd reconsider and that he'd be there for the birth. But it didn't happen.

Shawn was born at 1.16 P.M., in a delivery that the midwife described as *tricky*. Dee had been in labour for more than six hours, and the position of Shawn when he was born, meant that a forceps delivery was required. This had created complications, at least in the midwife's eyes. Dee was barely aware of what was happening. She was simply in pain.

After the delivery, her son was whisked away, as the consultant on duty wanted to have a closer look at him. The consultant's eyes were sharp and intelligent. Dee remembered looking up through the glass window in the room, to see a balding man in his early sixties studying the baby. He spoke to the midwife but Dee couldn't hear what was being said. She wasn't lucid. She was still in discomfort, and she remembered a nurse offering to get her an injection.

Dee was kept in for five days, so that Shawn could be observed. At first she wasn't told what was wrong. In the end, the consultant simply said that nothing was wrong and that he just wanted to be cautious. Dee didn't believe him.

Dee had hoped her mother would come to visit her at the hospital. Her mother, Violet, never showed up, or her father, and that was something she resented.

·   ·   ·

Coming home was not a pleasant experience for Dee Tanner. With her young son in tow, she returned to the small flat she had been renting in Margate, to find the place cold and inhospitable. Calls to Ronnie, her ex-partner, went unanswered, and in the end she resorted to calling her mother.

Violet had never been the most understanding of people. She was a short woman with a quick temper, and had never approved of her daughter's relationship. There was a strained pause on the phone. "I knew he wouldn't turn up," she said. "What did you expect? He's an unreliable man. This was always going to happen." Dee knew her mother would say that her daughter should have chosen better – how she should have read the signs. Deep down she knew her mother was right, but she didn't want to dwell on matters. She had a son now who needed to be cared for.

Shawn was an easy baby, quiet – but perhaps too quiet. He needed regular feeding and would whimper quietly if it was missed, and Dee felt that the cold flat in which she was living wasn't the best environment for him. She spoke to her mother and asked if her father, Cyril, would like to see his grandson.

Her mother and father had a tense relationship, which was characterised by them not speaking to one another for days at a time. This often made things difficult, as they ran a boarding house, a short way from the Margate seafront. It was a successful business, but Violet didn't like running it, and felt she was always being taken advantage of by her husband. "The sooner we can sell up and get out, the better," she would say.

Cyril Tanner kept his mouth shut and counted the money as it came in. His quiet, humdrum life was suddenly interrupted, however, when his daughter turned up one afternoon and insisted it was time he saw his grandson.

·   ·   ·

Ronnie Angel decided to see Shawn. Dee had told him in repeated phone calls that he should meet his son. Ronnie had displayed reluctance, so Dee was surprised when he turned up at her door.

The small flat was neglected, and he realized it needed improving. Shawn was sleeping in a small cot, in the spare room. He remained asleep as his mother picked him up and passed him to his father.

Ronnie was nervous. He wasn't good with children; he had limited experience, and hadn't wanted to become a father. Shawn's birth had been unexpected, and Ronnie's relationship with Dee had never been good. He didn't see a future with her, although he was reluctant to admit it.

Ronnie looked at Shawn: he was at peace, much quieter than Ronnie had been expecting. Shawn seemed like a content child, completely unaware of his surroundings, or the relationship between his parents. Ronnie soon began to feel a bond. He had never considered what it would be like to be a father. Now he had a son, he could see that he might want to spend time with him. There was Dee though – he felt that she would be a problem.

Ronnie spent several hours with Shawn, and come the evening he was reluctant to leave. Dee didn't want him to stay over, and eventually he took the hint and left. The following day he had to work. He was a mechanic, and had been for over ten years. Come the end of the day, he phoned Dee, asking if he could come over again. He did the same thing the next day, and the next. After a week, rather than feel pleased, Dee was exhausted. She felt an undercurrent of unease. Her former partner was becoming a problem.

·   ·   ·

When Shawn was nearly a year old, Dee Tanner moved into the Everdale Boarding House. She had dropped hints for some time that the flat she was staying in was inadequate. "It's just too cold – too small – not suitable for a young child." Dee's parents listened and eventually relented, giving her a room at the top of the building.

The boarding house had sixteen rooms, let out on a medium-term and long-term basis. Most residents were male, aged from their forties to early sixties, men seemingly forgotten by society. Dee's father had inherited the boarding house from his parents, and had run it profitably for a number of years. Violet supported him. She didn't enjoy the work. It was a job, and it provided an income: that was what kept her going.

Young Shawn loved the boarding house. Once he began to walk he explored the place, travelling all over the sixth floor, noting the residents who came and went. There was an array of smells and sounds, strange people, some of whom were more approachable than others.

Dee should have supervised him more keenly, however motherhood was not something that came to her naturally. She found it hard work, even with support from her parents.

"You should go back to work," said Violet. Dee didn't want to do hear that. She didn't have any career plans. She had worked several office jobs before Shawn was born, providing secretarial and admin. support, but Shawn had given her a reason to turn away from that. And then of course there was Ronnie. He liked Shawn. He visited Dee regularly at the boarding house, and was keen to take Shawn out.

"He's too young," Dee would say. "He should be at home. Another time, maybe."

Ronnie had the manner of someone used to getting his own way. On more than one occasion he argued with Dee about access to Shawn. Shawn was often there, and noted the hostility. By the age of four, he was aware that his parents hated one another.

CHAPTER
43

Daniel Riley woke up. His cell was silent and the light was poor. A tray of food had been pushed through the hatch near the base of the door, but Riley hadn't touched it. What Will had told him had made him cautious. He didn't want to be drugged. He intended to escape, and was determined to remain lucid.

Looking around the room, something caught his eye: it was the camera near the ceiling. The red light on it was no longer working.

Riley moved over and reached up. The camera, inside the plastic dome, didn't track his movement. He felt excited and wondered if it had been switched off.

He looked at the lights and realized that something was definitely wrong. The main light had cut out, and an emergency bulb was now on. It was weak, and didn't look as if it would last.

Riley felt he had privacy. With no one to watch over him, he could move freely. He went over to the cell wall and put his mouth to the grate.

"Will … are you there?"

He waited but there was no reply.

He whispered. "Will … can you hear me?"

Nothing.

He wondered if Will had been given food – if he'd eaten it and fallen asleep. It didn't matter. There was little Will could do to help, but Riley wasn't going to abandon him. He was going to help. He was determined that they should both escape.

Riley looked at the large door on the far side of the room. If it was electronic, there had to be wires running through the wall. He wondered if the failing power had affected the door.

He felt a surge of hope as he walked over. He grasped the metal handle and pulled.

Nothing. The door remained shut.

Disappointment rose up, and he glanced at the wall to the left. It was covered in sheet metal, riveted into place. Riley ran a finger over the rivets, realizing that each one was covered with a metal cap.

He removed one cap and looked at the screw head. It was large – cross-shaped. All he needed was something to turn it with.

He went to the basin in the corner. It had a metal strip, running around the edge, and Riley realized that by prising it away, he could use one end as a crude screwdriver. With that, he felt hope returning.

.   .   .

Lane and Perez left Erin Riley's home.

"So what did you make of her?" said Lane, getting into the passenger seat.

Perez thought for a moment. "I'm not sure …"

Lane was less generous. "I get the feeling we started out with nothing, and we've still got most of it left."

Perez sat in the driver's seat. "She's keeping something back – I got that impression."

"Not a good marriage?"

"You think Riley could have run off?"

"It is possible." Lane looked at the contact details Erin Riley had given them, details of her husband's business partners, John Rice and Damien Redding.

"Christ, who calls anyone Damien?" said Lane. "Didn't his parents see *The Omen*? According to Mrs Riley, these guys should be at their office. Let's see if we can catch them – see what they have to say."

"There is one other thing," said Perez. "If Daniel Riley is part of this case, he can't be one of the two men whose remains we found in Acton."

Lane nodded. "He only went missing on Monday. Those remains were there for some time."

"Which means he's a new victim," said Perez. He felt worried and Lane noticed. Lane was more experienced and less inclined to worry.

"One step at a time. Don't worry about what you can't control."

· · ·

The detectives arrived at the offices of 3R Capital a little after 11.30. The building was a wide, grey structure, that looked as if it had been built in the '50s or '60s. It was smart, without being imposing, and Lane imagined that the rent wasn't cheap.

The street in front of the building was deserted and Perez noticed an off-ramp going down to an underground garage. "That's where Daniel Riley left his car."

"Let's park in front the building," said Lane. "You check out the garage – see if there's any CCTV. I'll head upstairs and speak to Riley's partners."

There was an old man at the reception inside. Lane showed his warrant card and asked for the offices of 3R. The man calmly gestured towards a lift, and a sign that indicated the offices were on the fifth floor.

Lane studied the logo of 3R, which was holographic. Fancy nonsense, he thought to himself. At the base of the sign were the names of the company directors: Riley, Rice and Redding.

Lane took the lift up, and expected to find a reception with someone behind it. Instead, as the lift doors opened, he saw two men stacking boxes. They were casually dressed, but by their manner and the way in which they spoke he had a feeling that they were the men he was looking for.

"Mr Rice? Mr Redding?" Lane held up his warrant card. "I was told I could find you here."

Jonathan Rice held out a hand. "You must be here about Daniel. Erin said you might be calling." Rice looked out of breath. He was in his mid-forties, a tall man, balding, with a round pleasant face. There was something about him that Lane liked immediately, and he silently reprimanded himself for going on first impressions.

"This is my business partner, Damien Redding."

Redding held out a hand and Lane shook it. He was smaller than Rice, with dark hair and wire-framed glasses. He was of a similar age, but there was something about him which made Lane feel cautious.

"We're just doing the clear out," said Redding. "We sold the business – you probably know about that." He wiped his forehead. "We've yet to pack up Daniel's things." He gestured to Riley's office. Lane could see a mahogany desk and a leather chair. Books were still on the shelves, and the office looked untouched.

"We've been wondering what to do with his belongings," said the tall man. Rice pointed to a seat. Lane moved over but remained standing.

Rice leant against the water cooler, and filled a cup before drinking it.

"We *are* concerned about Daniel. We thought we would have heard from him by now."

Redding nodded. "We have to be out of here by Sunday. The new people – they want us gone. Daniel was supposed to be helping."

Lane wondered about Riley. Rice and Redding had urgent but tired faces.

"I'm investigating what happened to your colleague. Have you heard anything at all?"

The men glanced at one another. "Not since Monday," said Rice. "We signed a contract to sell the company. Daniel was there for the signing. He's a part owner of the business, and benefitted just as we did. Afterwards we were supposed to go for a drink. Daniel said he'd join us, but he never showed up."

"And you didn't think to raise the alarm?" said Lane. He studied their faces.

"We assumed Daniel had decided to go home," said Rice. "On Monday night I called him but he didn't answer."

"His mobile?" said Lane.

"That's right. It was turned off. I called him again on Tuesday, but couldn't get through. Then I called his home. His wife answered and she was anxious. She explained that he hadn't returned." Rice looked at Redding.

"Was it Mrs Riley who raised the alarm?" said Lane.

"Yes. She contacted the police on Tuesday afternoon. She was unable to reach Daniel on his phone."

Lane tried to sound calm. "Do you know of any reason why Mr Riley might have wanted to disappear?"

Both men shook their heads.

"He was pleased that the deal had gone through," said Rice. "We all were. We got good money. Our intention had always been to build up the company and sell it, but ..." Rice let the sentence hang.

"But you think there may have been something else?" said Lane.

Rice looked at Redding, as if searching for reassurance. "Daniel's a private person – keeps things to himself. We knew however that he wasn't happy at home. It did cross our minds that he might have left."

"His family?"

"Yes."

Rice looked down, as if embarrassed.

"What happened to the proceeds from his share of the sale?"

"Nothing," said Rice. "He was paid by wire transfer. We were all paid that way – it happened on Monday. We signed contracts and the transfer was made within the hour. Money was deposited in my account, as well as Damien's and Daniel's."

"And how much are we talking about?" said Lane. He was more than a little curious.

Rice hesitated. "We sold the business for nearly £15 million. After all costs and borrowings are deducted, each of us made a little over £3 million."

Lane raised his eyebrows. "A substantial amount."

Rice couldn't argue with that. He felt embarrassed but still looked concerned.

"Do you know if Mr Riley made any enemies?"

Rice and Redding paused to think. "None that we're aware of," said Redding. "He was determined – a go-getter – went the extra mile to get contracts, sometimes treading on other people's toes."

"And out of the three of you, who was in charge?"

The men looked at each other. "No one was in overall charge," said Rice. "We had different areas of responsibility. Daniel was responsible for acquiring UK business. Damien and I looked after the overseas work."

"Did Riley seem anxious or nervous on the day he disappeared?" said Lane.

"He didn't seem nervous at all," said Rice. He was his usual self: reserved – sober. He's the kind of man who doesn't confide in many people."

Lane had already got that impression, and nothing was changing it. "There're a couple of names I want to run by you. Tell me if they mean anything. *Michael Kern, Nigel Warner, James Stein …*"

There was immediate recognition on both men's faces.

"We know the third one," said Rice. "Stein was one of our clients. *The client from hell* we called him."

CHAPTER
44

Margate, 1977

Ronnie Angel took to drink. What exactly prompted it wasn't certain, but the garage where he worked fired him. He found another job, but it wasn't as well paid, and Dee was reluctant to let him see his son. Ronnie thought about hiring a solicitor in order to gain access. This concerned Dee, and on the occasions Ronnie came to visit, she argued with him.

Shawn, living at the top of the building, saw his parents on the pavement outside. On more than one occasion Ronnie raised a hand, ready to strike Dee. Shawn felt a tremor of anxiety. He knew something was wrong. He was nearly five years old, but he couldn't pinpoint exactly what it was, or what normal behaviour should be. He wasn't sure exactly how he felt about his father. Ronnie seemed nice on occasion, but Shawn could sense that something wasn't right. Dee didn't help matters.

"I'll get access to him!" Ronnie shouted. "I'll get a lawyer. I'll get it done."

Like hell you will, thought Dee. But underneath she felt fear.

With Shawn in school, she thought about going back to work. She found a secretarial job, working part time, and afterwards picked her son up from school.

Shawn seemed reasonably well adjusted. He was quiet around Dee, but reports from his teachers said that he was boisterous and outgoing. Dee spoke to him about this, explaining what acceptable behaviour was. She wondered whether she had any effect. She wished Ronnie was different, and that he was a more positive influence. By now he was very much her ex-partner. He had taken up with another woman – someone younger – and Dee felt resentment. There would be no going back.

Resentment changed when one afternoon she came home with her son, to find her mother looking worried.

"It's Ronnie," said Violet, "he had an accident. He was drunk; he was hit by a car and killed."

·   ·   ·

Shawn Tanner was five when he attended his father's funeral. He had vivid memories for someone so young. It rained, and the cemetery had problems with rainwater, forcing people to keep off the grass.

Shawn's mother was present, as were his grandparents, but few people came from his father's side of the family. At the time it didn't seem surprising. Years later he would find out that his father had been ostracised because of a crime he had committed as a teenager.

Shawn noticed that his mother was unhappy. The bones of her face were hard and sharp. His grandparents were solemn, but he knew that they hadn't liked Ronnie.

Shawn wasn't sure how he felt about the loss of his father. His mother said the drinking had done it. It had made him clumsy – and then she blamed Mitch Arring. He had been Ronnie's boss, at the garage where he worked. Arring had fired him – shoddy workmanship and poor time keeping.

"If Ronnie hadn't lost his job, he wouldn't have been sent on the path downwards." That was how Dee put it.

Shawn saw many stone-faced people at the funeral, and by the end of the day he felt unhappy. Mitch Arring was present. He was a well-built man, in his thirties. "A useless, uncouth man." That was what Dee said. She went up to him and confronted him.

She told him he had a hell of a nerve showing his face, that he was responsible for Ronnie's death. People tried to hold her back. Shawn saw everything: the look of surprise on Arring's face, the denials, the attempt by Dee to strike him.

Shawn began disliking Arring, and years later, prompted by stories from his mother, he would get his revenge.

•   •   •

When Shawn was nine years old, his grandfather died. Cyril Tanner collapsed one morning, in the kitchen of the boarding house. Violet called an ambulance, but there was little that could be done, and he was pronounced dead on arrival. Cyril was seventy-two years old. "He should have lived longer," said Dee said, after remaining silent for a long time.

She gave up her part-time job to help her mother run the boarding house. Shawn got his own room, and he had to admit that he liked living there. The other rooms were almost always occupied. There were a number of long-term residents – men who didn't seem to work, or who were too ill to work – although in Shawn's mind they seemed fit enough to lead normal lives.

Violet began to slow down, and her daughter did most of the work. Shawn helped out on occasion. He disliked laundry or cleaning, or assisting with meals, but he kept quiet and did as his mother asked. He was different when he was at home. He was more contained. When he was with friends, or at school, he could be his true self. A teacher once described him as *calculating*. His mother hated that. She reported the teacher, who was given a verbal warning. Shawn didn't say anything, but he was aware of what had been said and in later life he realized the description had been right.

One long-term resident of the boarding house was a retired soldier, by the name of Harold Benning. He had served as a sergeant in the army, and had done tours of duty overseas. Shawn liked listening to him. Harold told him about the people he had met, the training he had received, and how cultures varied. "It's a hell of a mixed bag out there," Harold would say.

He told Shawn about the skills he had acquired, while training as an explosives technician, and there was a quiet pride in his voice. The story fascinated Shawn. He decided that that was what he wanted to do, and at the age of sixteen he announced he was joining the army.

CHAPTER
45

Jonathan Rice walked towards his office, as if retreating to a point of safety. Lane and Redding followed.

"What do you mean he was *the client from hell*?" said Lane.

"James Stein runs a company called Stein Engineering."

Ran, thought Lane. But decided not to inform him that Stein was dead.

"Stein expanded his company rapidly," said Rice. "There's a lot to be said for growing a business slowly and steadily, but he didn't follow the rules. I think he over-extended himself financially."

"And he came to you for help?"

Rice nodded. "Riley told him he had to slash costs – cut overheads and reduce the size of the workforce. Riley told him his company could survive by narrowing its focus."

"And how did the news go down?"

"Not well." Rice looked at Redding who was uneasy.

"Stein was angry and aggressive," Redding explained. "I think his ego had a lot to do with it. He didn't want cutbacks. He sought advice from another consultant, Myles Appleferd."

Lane was surprised to hear the name but tried not to let it show.

"In the end Stein decided to follow our suggestions," said Rice. "He cut costs and did restructuring, but he was reluctant to pay us for the advice."

"What did you do?"

"We pointed out the facts – that we'd helped him – that we'd improved his chances. He said that we'd given him bad advice, that he'd lost staff, and that several were now bringing claims against him."

"We couldn't see how that had anything to do with us," said Redding.

Lane thought about the remark. Redding seemed to care more about himself than anyone else. Rice cut in.

"Stein threatened to sue us. We didn't get paid and he threatened to sue: it doesn't get much worse than that."

Lane took out his notebook. "When did you last hear from James Stein?"

"A while ago – several months at least. I'm hoping he may have given up on his plans. Perhaps he may be seeing sense now."

He won't be suing you, thought Lane, *that's for sure.* "Have you got any correspondence from Stein – anything recent?"

Rice thought. "There may be something on Daniel's computer. If you want to wait, I'll check … we *need* to find out where Daniel is."

Lane waited as Rice went next door.

·   ·   ·

Lane met Perez in the garage, in the basement of the building. It was a large, open-plan space. There were columns at regular intervals, supporting the ceiling, while neon signs in green and white directed bystanders to emergency exits.

The air was cool, and there was something foreboding about the place. In the distance, Lane could see a ramp leading up to the exit. Overhead lighting flickered, and there was a faint hum of electricity. Lane sniffed the air. He could smell diesel, although at that moment the garage contained few vehicles.

Perez was examining a sign on the wall. "How did it go upstairs?"

"Jekyll and Hyde seem interesting enough," said Lane. His face hardened.

"That good, eh?"

"It was useful, I suppose." Lane explained to Perez that Rice and Redding had known Stein. "He was a client, and by all accounts he had a temper."

"That's something we didn't know," said Perez. "His junior at Stein Engineering said he was a good boss. Easy to get on with."

"Yeah, well, someone is being economical with the truth." Lane frowned, and wondered why people were reluctant to speak ill of others. "The men upstairs also know Myles Appleferd. It turns out he was some sort of competitor, offering consultancy services to Stein."

Perez looked into the distance, as he tried to piece things together.

"It all fits," said Lane, "but it's just beyond our grasp … What did you find out down here?"

Perez looked to the back of the garage. "This parking bay – number twenty-three – it was used by Daniel Riley. His car was found here by security. All the bays are allocated apart from those four, in the corner. They're used by visitors or contractors. There're no cameras here, but there are two at the entrance. One covers the left-hand approach, the other the right."

"Between them they should catch all the vehicles coming and going."

"Exactly." Perez sounded confident. "This sign on the wall shows that the cameras are maintained by a company called Datax."

Lane's eyes narrowed. "There's a contact number. Get in touch with them – see if they have footage from Monday, at the time Riley went missing."

"Already on to it," said Perez. "Someone said they'd call me back."

"Good work." Lane turned and walked up the exit ramp. He felt cold air brushing his face, and saw daylight creeping in. His phone began vibrating. He looked at it but didn't recognize the number.

"Hello?"

"Chief Inspector?" It was a shrill voice. "This is David Mear."

Lane pictured his press-liaison officer, and felt disappointed.

"I'm in the incident room," said Mear. "We had a call come through regarding someone you're interested in: Michael Kern."

Lane concentrated. "What's happened?"

"It seems there's been a fight." Mear was taking his time as he spoke. "A uniformed officer saw an incident near Charing Cross Road."

Lane felt the hairs on the back of his neck rising.

"When was this?"

"About a quarter of an hour ago. I've been trying to reach you –"

"I'm underground … in a car park." Lane was impatient. "Just give me the details."

Mear recited what he had. "There is one other thing. A picture came in from a sketch artist. Something based on information from Terry Carter?"

"He's a yob, who I asked to work with the sketch artist."

"I'm looking at the sketch right now," said Mear. "The thing is, it does bear a resemblance to Kern."

CHAPTER 46

Charing Cross Road was busy. Lane and Perez arrived a little after 12.30 and parked on a side street. Lane got out and was dismayed to see the number of shoppers.

"These people are living in a teapot and looking out of the spout."

Opposite the Garrick Theatre Lane saw a uniformed sergeant. He was in his mid-fifties, with grey hair and a clean-shaven face. He looked capable and determined.

"Sergeant Vaughan?" said Lane, walking across.

Vaughan nodded and held out a hand. "Chief Inspector? I understand I may have met one of your murder suspects."

"Quite possibly." Lane studied the crowd. "What exactly happened here?"

"I was following my usual beat from the square," said Vaughan, "when I spotted your man going into that bank." He pointed to the branch. "The man came out and got into an altercation with a passer-by. I stopped to ask what was going on, and your man said it was nothing to do with me. He said he was the kind of person who could get away with murder, and that got my attention. I wasn't sure if he was joking, so I asked for a name and ID. While I radioed it in, he turned and slipped away."

"He *is* a person of interest in our enquiry." Lane was thinking about Kern. There was no sign of him on the near side of the street. Lane crossed the road, and Perez and the sergeant followed.

Where could he be? Lane's eye passed the window of a pub. Inside he could see crowds. Something stood out: a tall figure. Could it be him?

"My inspector and I will go in," said Lane. "You cover the front. If that's him, and he should get past us, you know what to do."

Vaughan nodded, and they made their way towards the entrance.

•　　　•　　　•

The Pint & Picture was a large pub, which had recently been refurbished. There were wooden chairs and tables outside, and a number of tourists relaxing and drinking.

Lane looked through the window once again. He could see the bar on the right-hand side. There were high tables dotted around, and the place was crowded – too crowded.

Christ. This doesn't make the job any easier.

He pushed open the door and stepped in. He was hit by the sound of chatter. There was a strong smell of beer, and a member of staff pushed past, balancing several pints on a tray. She moved deftly, placing the pints on a table then disappearing towards the rear.

Lane scanned the crowds and Perez sensed his agitation.

"There're too many *bloody* people." Lane's eyes reached the bar and he looked towards the left-hand side. The hair, the height, the build: it was definitely Kern. Lane felt a needle of excitement, and tapped Perez on the shoulder. "Over there."

Perez studied Kern. He seemed to be leaning against the bar, facing the wall. There was no one with him. Perez checked the figure's profile. He was at ease.

"You take the right," said Lane, "I'll take the left."

They separated, threading through drinkers, and Lane felt tense. The drinkers were oblivious to his presence, and several didn't move as he asked them to. He raised his voice and made eye contact, which seemed to have the desired effect.

In a little over a minute he was behind Kern. He took in the tanned jacket.

"Michael Kern?"

Kern turned. There was surprise in his eyes, and he lunged to the bar and tried to throw something at Lane.

Lane swerved to the left and Kern leapt over the counter. A young member of staff was startled, and Kern pushed him away, heading for the exit at the rear.

Lane opened the bar door and moved past the barman. He went through the staff door at the end and saw a corridor.

There was a door in the distance and Lane made for it. Pushing open the door, he was surprised to see daylight. He was on the main road behind the pub. He looked to his right and saw Kern.

Lane thought about backup but decided he didn't have time. He sprinted down the street. Tourists moved out of the way, but a few stopped and stared. Lane focused on his quarry. Kern was running across the road. Traffic was heavy, and a car came to a halt too late, causing Kern to pitch forward on to the bonnet. Momentarily Lane paused.

Kern slid off the bonnet. He remained on his feet, and after a second carried on, picking up his pace.

Lane raised his hand, persuading a van to stop, and shouted at a car, which was trying to overtake. The driver braked and Lane dashed forward. A horn sounded, but Lane ignored it and focused on Kern.

Kern was heading down a narrow street lined with shops. The number of tourists was increasing, and Lane noticed he was nearing Covent Garden.

He dodged crowds, and could make out Kern ahead. He was taller than those around him, with well-defined shoulders and fair hair.

Lane was becoming tired. Kern was nearly twenty years younger, and it was beginning to show. Kern reached a zebra crossing. Less than a minute later Lane reached it too. A car stopped, a horn sounded and Lane swore.

The streets were too crowded. Lane could make out Covent Garden market. Kern was heading for it.

"STOP!"

Kern flinched but continued. Lane tried to increase his pace, but realized he was running out of energy.

Kern reached the market, which was overflowing. Lane saw him disappear into a tight group of people and felt worried. He made for the group, but realized that there was no way to cut through. He looked left and right, trying to work his way around.

He managed to do so, and saw another group of tourists. There was no sign of Kern.

Had he made a mistake?

Lane had a spinning feeling that gave way to anger. *Why run? Why would an innocent man run?* Lane checked again and again, and realized he had lost him.

CHAPTER
47

Daniel Riley fought fear and exhaustion.

The room in which he was locked was almost silent. He hadn't heard anything from Will, in the next cell, for some time and was concerned. From somewhere in the distance there was the sound of a motor. The lights in the room became dimmer and then flickered.

Riley wondered when his captor would return. There was no sound from the corridor, and there hadn't been for a while. Perhaps the man was dealing with Will. Perhaps he'd taken him away … and the thought made Riley shiver. He tried to push it aside and focused on the task in hand.

The metal door was locked, but to the left were several panels, and Riley was trying to remove the screws which held them in place. If Will was correct, there were wires behind – circuits, which controlled the door.

Riley paused for breath. He knew he had to keep going, but it was difficult work. The screws were turning, but it was taking time. Even with a proper screwdriver it would have been a slow task.

Riley took care not to cut his fingers on the strip of metal he was using. He had to look after himself, if he was to stand any chance of escape.

·　　　·　　　·

Lane, Perez and Sergeant Vaughan spent nearly an hour searching Covent Garden. They were unable to find Kern, and by the time Lane returned to Homicide West it was after three o'clock. He was frustrated.

David Mear was sitting at a desk, looking relaxed. Lane's face became a mask of anger.

"Haven't you got *anything* to do?"

"It's been a quiet afternoon," said Mear. "How did the hunt for your suspect go?"

"Not well." Lane sat down and turned on his computer, punching the button on the monitor. "We were that close – that close to getting him."

Perez tried to be the voice of reason. "We don't actually know that Kern is guilty. We have evidence that he worked at one crime scene, but that's it."

"Then why run?" said Lane. "And why talk about murder?" Lane thought about his commanding officer, who had pressured him into releasing Kern. "If that guy was half as sharp as his suit, we might actually get somewhere."

The incident room was quiet, with only three civilian staff present. They were listening to Lane but were trying to be discrete.

"Kern'll resurface," said Perez. "He'll come again."

Lane rubbed his eyes. "He's hiding something …" Lane looked at his computer and tried to open his email. "Damn … this thing has crashed." He studied the monitor closely and squinted. There was an error message and he looked at it with surprise. "I don't believe it: there's a spelling mistake in that error message."

Perez walked around, and Lane decided to work on something else while Perez fixed the machine. Lane reached to his tray and picked out an internal envelope. He recognized the sender's name.

"That's from the sketch artist," said Mear.

Lane took out the sketch and studied it.

"Is that the guy who Terry Carter saw?" said Perez.

Lane thought about Carter and the dog that had chased them.

"Apparently so." Lane read the note attached. "It's supposed to be a good likeness."

He studied the sketch. The man was in his late thirties or early forties, with short, fair hair. He had a long face, and eyes which were set close together.

"It doesn't look like Kern."

"Yes, it does." Mear pointed to the large board in the centre of the room, on which Kern's picture was displayed.

Lane stared for a long moment. "Perhaps the eyes are similar, but that's as far as it goes." He studied the sketch. The man's face was long, but Kern's was round, and the difference troubled him.

"Let's take it with us. Come on."

"Where are we going?" said Perez, with surprise.

"To check the remaining name on the list from Missing Persons – that banker. We got some good background information on Riley. Perhaps we'll get some information on him too."

CHAPTER
48

Things with Mitch Arring and me didn't end well. I want to tell you about it, and I want to be honest. The man was an arrogant prick. I went to see him – I was twenty-three, nearly twenty-four at the time, and I'd been putting it off for a while. He still worked as a mechanic, and had a garage in Ramsgate, moderately successful by all accounts. That didn't bother me though.

I remember vividly the day I went there. It was a Friday. I deliberately chose that day, as I knew he'd be working on his own. I found him behind a hydraulic ramp. He was cleaning tools, laid out on a wooden bench, and he didn't recognize me.

Arring was a big man, in his early fifties. He had cheeks that puffed out, making him look fatter than he was, and spiky grey hair with dark eyes. He was tough and capable, and that made me relish the challenge.

"What can I do for you?" he said, slowly.

I didn't answer. I merely studied him. His dark blue overalls were smeared with dirt. He didn't have standards. I remember thinking that.

"You don't remember me, do you?"

"Did I do a job for you?" Arring was curious.

"I don't own a car. I steal them though …"

That made him pause, and I savoured the moment.

"What can I do for you?" he said again. There was anxiety this time.

"How long have you been working here?"

"More than twelve years now. I moved from somewhere else."

"I know," I replied. "You were in Margate."

"Did I do work for you?" Arring was worried.

There were so many things I wanted to say. I wanted to tell him about my family – about my lack of a family – how I missed my father, even though he might have been inadequate. All I simply said was, "Ronnie."

Arring thought and made the connection. Fear crept into his eyes. "You're his –"

I walked in a semi-circle towards him. The workshop was very quiet, but I still glanced left and right.

"Ronnie was a good man." What I wanted to say was he tried to be. *I'm not sure I believed that, but I like to think that I'm a good actor.*

"Look," said Arring, "any beef I had with Ronnie – I regret that, but that's in the past now, and I hope you'll accept it –"

Arring's size wasn't protecting him. He raised both hands, palms towards me, and that was when I made my move. I used a tyre iron by the wall. I moved his body afterwards, using one of his own cars. They never found him, and that's something I'm proud of.

·   ·   ·

Tim Mannak had been missing for six weeks and Lane felt that that wasn't a good sign. He was sitting in the living room of Mannak's house, in Arnos Grove, north London. Mrs Mannak was there, and she seemed pleased that he and Perez had taken an interest.

"It's been over a month," she explained. "I've heard very little from the police." She was a small woman of slender build, in her early fifties. She was of Lithuanian descent, and seemed meek in Lane's mind. He looked around the living room. There were family pictures, some in black and white, but no photographs of children.

"And your husband is a bank manger?" said Lane.

"That's right. He used to work at the Aldgate branch, but then we moved here. It's been easier for him to work locally, in terms of travelling and so on."

"On the day your husband went missing," said Perez, "can you describe what happened?"

Mrs Mannak felt relief as she spoke. She was glad she could voice her feelings.

"It was Tuesday when he went missing. It was a normal day. He left early – about eight o'clock – and took the underground. He usually travels by the underground, but he never made it there. They called from the branch a little after 9.30, to ask if he was coming in."

"How did your husband seem on the day he disappeared?" said Lane.

Lillian Mannak paused and looked confused. "He seemed normal."

"Was he tense or nervous at all?" said Perez. "Had anything been preying on his mind?"

"Nothing more than usual. His work is stressful. He manages the branch but he also supervises another one. They work him hard, but he's paid a bonus. We've always been grateful for that."

"Had he had any quarrels or disagreements?" said Lane.

"Not that I'm aware of." Mrs Mannak looked doubtful. Lane thought about the way she spoke.

"His work isn't always easy," she continued. "He has to deal with all manner of people. While he says most of them are good – the minority, well …"

"Are difficult to deal with?"

"You could put it like that." Mrs Mannak sounded embarrassed. "My husband has to deal with everything from large businesses to individuals with mortgages and loans. He has to make tough decisions, sometimes calling in loans or repossessing properties."

"Leaving people in a bad place," said Lane to himself.

"Quite …" Mrs Mannak looked down. She looked old. "Tim sometimes brings his work home with him. He tells me things, perhaps things that he shouldn't."

Lane felt interest flickering. "What are we talking about here?"

"About his customers … the ones who are difficult. He has … he's been threatened on several occasions."

"What was the nature of these threats?"

"People would threaten to come back – *sort him out*." Mrs Mannak was uncomfortable. "I could never do such a job. I could never deal with the public. It's the difficult ones I would worry about …"

"Does the name James Stein mean anything to you?" said Perez.

Mrs Mannak shook her head.

"How about Nigel Warner or Paulo Raymus?"

Again she shook her head. "Are those other missing people?"

"Sort of," said Lane. He took a small polythene bag from his jacket. "There're a couple of pictures that I'd like to show you. Could you tell me if you've seen any of these people before?" He handed over a photograph of Kern, and she studied it.

"I'm not sure I'd trust him."

"A good judge of character," said Lane wryly. "Have you ever seen him though?"

"No …"

"How about this one?"

Lane unfolded the artist's impression of the man Carter had seen at Paulo Raymus's.

"I don't know him." Mrs Mannak's eyes strayed to Perez. She trusted him. "You will find my husband, won't you? He's never done this before."

Perez searched for the right thing to say. "We'll do our best. Can you give us details of the other people your husband works with?"

Mrs Mannak thought. "I know his deputy, Joe. I'll give you his address."

"That would be helpful." Perez waited while she went to a sideboard, and took an address book from the drawer.

•   •   •

The air was cold and uninviting as Lane and Perez left the house. It was after five o'clock but it was still bright. Lane inhaled the cold air and it made him feel alert.

Perez spoke quietly. "You think he's dead, don't you?"

"There's a lot of land behind James Stein's house that we haven't yet examined. I've got a feeling Mannak's tied into this. I'm not sure exactly how. This all has to do with money and business."

"And now we have a bank manager who's missing."

"We'll speak to his colleagues," said Lane. He checked his notebook. "This guy Joe – we'll start with him. If Mannak had difficult clients to deal with, it's something we need to look at." Lane checked his watch. "You might as well head home. We can make an early start tomorrow."

Perez was grateful. He liked spending weekends with his wife whenever possible.

They reached the car and Perez unlocked it. Lane turned back and looked at the house. Mrs Mannak was standing by the living-room window. A solitary figure, maintaining a vigil. Sooner or later she'd have to face bad news. Lane suspected that.

CHAPTER 49

On Sunday morning, Lane arrived early at the incident room. He was used to working on Sundays. He had done it regularly throughout his career, although it was not something that his wife appreciated.

Three civilian staff were present. They nodded *morning* to Lane and carried on with what they were doing.

The large transparent board, in the centre of the room, was still there. Lane added the pictures of Daniel Riley and Tim Mannak, and stepped back to look at the information that had been collated.

All five victims were male, aged from their late twenties to early fifties. They had all lived in London, but that was where the similarities ended.

An assistant, whose name Lane couldn't remember, walked over. It occurred to him that he had to try harder with names.

"Chief Superintendent Travers was in earlier," the young woman said.

Lane was surprised. Travers didn't usually work on Sundays.

"Up to no good, no doubt."

"He was checking your board," said the woman. There was a smile in her voice. "He's not that bad, you know. He didn't rise to the rank of chief superintendent by being inept."

Lane wasn't sure he believed that. "Even a blind squirrel finds a nut once in a while." He didn't want to discuss Travers, and sat down at his computer. It seemed to be working, unlike the previous day, and that was something to be grateful for. There was a note attached to the monitor from the IT department.

You really need to take better care of our equipment.

Lane screwed up the note and sighed: not a good start. When Perez arrived, he was carrying a padded envelope.

"I got this from the front desk." He checked the sender's address. "It's from Datax."

Lane looked up, hoping for good news. "The security company at Riley's office?"

"The very same. I asked them to send footage of the car park, from the day Riley went missing. It looks as if someone over there's fairly efficient."

Lane made to say something but stopped as Travers appeared by the door.

"Tony?" Travers was looking pleased with himself – never a good sign. "A quick word, if I could?"

Lane felt tension rising. "Certainly, sir." He rose from his desk.

·   ·   ·

Travers's office had potential. Lane thought that. But at the same time the potential was wasted. What should have been an elegant space was filled with badly arranged furniture. There were too many piles of paper, poor lighting and an overall sense of waste. There was no invitation to sit down either.

"Tony, we have to talk about overtime."

No we don't, thought Lane. *We have to talk about results.*

"I have budgets to think about. Now this man, Kern, why do we need the surveillance on him?" A ghost of a smile appeared on Travers's face.

"Kern worked at the house belonging to one victim – hell, two victims."

Travers didn't like swearing. A black mark for sure, and Lane made a mental note. "Aside from working there, he has convictions for violence – we have to think about patterns of escalating behaviour."

"Hmm …" I have to think about other things. How many suspects do you have?"

"Not enough," Lane murmured.

"What do you hope to gain from the surveillance?"

"I hope he'll slip up"

"How exactly?"

"I'm not sure yet." Lane regretted saying that, but the words were out.

"Precisely: this is a fishing exercise."

"No it's not!"

Travers didn't like the tone. "It's unnecessary, Tony, OK?"

"Sir?"

"I'm cancelling the surveillance. I wish officers would think about all the things I have to do." Travers paused for a long moment. "You don't do yourself any favours. You should be more like Inspector McKay … be a team player, and understand what I want …"

"Kern is a viable suspect." Lane wanted to tell Travers to search his common sense, but decided it would be better just to leave.

"Sir …" he simply said with a nod, and made for the door.

•   •   •

Lane decided to head out without speaking to Perez. He took his car from the car park and drove into central London, arriving near Tottenham Court Road shortly after ten o'clock. He found the side street he wanted and parked in one of the empty bays.

The road was quiet, with few people about. Up ahead he could see the Victorian building, which housed Stein Engineering. A man was coming down the steps at the front. He was in his mid-forties, with a round, boyish face. He wore wire-framed glasses: he was Stein's former assistant, Stan O'Mara, who Lane had interviewed several days earlier.

O'Mara was supervising two workmen, as they brought a large wooden packing case out of the building. They loaded it into a van, and O'Mara climbed in to check that it was secure.

Lane walked to the rear.

"Mr O'Mara?"

A head appeared and O'Mara looked startled.

"Jesus Christ."

"I don't think he's got anything to do with it."

O'Mara took a moment to process what Lane had said.

"Chief Inspector … what can I do for you?"

"I'm glad I caught you." Lane looked at the inside of the van. Several packing cases were already strapped in place, using leather restraints tethered to the floor.

"It's for a presentation we're doing," said O'Mara in an irritated tone. "We're getting everything shipped off today. It's for a new oil and gas installation." He tried to look amenable.

"Could I have a word?" said Lane.

O'Mara hesitated. He grabbed hold of one side of the van and jumped out. "Let's use my office." He gave some instructions to the men who were loading, and escorted Lane into the building. Few people were around. Lane looked at the empty offices and saw O'Mara's, where he had interviewed him before.

O'Mara pushed open the glass door and gestured to Lane. "Can I get you anything to drink?"

"I'm fine … thank you."

O'Mara was different to when Lane had last met him. He was more confident and self-assured. It looked as if he was successfully filling his boss's shoes.

"Sometimes we work seven-day weeks," said O'Mara, noting Lane's interest. "Have you made any progress?"

"A little." Lane took out his notebook and flicked through. *It's about the money*, he reminded himself. *Just follow that.*

"I've spoken to several people, in particular Myles Appleferd, John Rice and Damien Redding."

O'Mara recognized the names. "They're consultants. Appleferd runs his own consultancy, and Rice and Redding run another."

Lane was pleased that O'Mara had admitted that. "It seems as if both companies provided advice to your firm."

O'Mara nodded. "They were hired by James. He grew Stein Engineering by taking over other companies. He moved quickly – aggressively, but as a result the business became unwieldy. He spoke to the consultants with a view to improving things."

"And there were disagreements, weren't there?"

"There were," said O'Mara, looking down. "James received conflicting advice. Appleferd told him not to reduce headcount, while Rice and Redding told him to cut staff."

"In the end what happened?"

O'Mara looked ill at ease. "To be honest, Chief Inspector, you haven't caught me at a good time."

Lane wasn't about to be diverted. "The art of pleasing everyone is something that no one's yet mastered … There were redundancies, weren't there?"

"A few."

"And the image you painted for me earlier, of Stein being a benevolent, caring boss, that isn't entirely true, is it?"

"Perhaps …" O'Mara wasn't sure what to say. "Look, James could be difficult. He was capable – ruthless – that's why he was successful. That's why this company is still here."

"Were you aware that your boss took 3R's advice, but decided not to pay them?"

O'Mara felt embarrassed. "I did know something about that."

"We haven't talked about your company's banking arrangements," said Lane. "Do you know a bank manager by the name of Tim Mannak?"

"I don't believe so. Our bank manager is woman – Mrs Hallow. We have a good relationship with our bank."

Lane took out two pictures and handed then over. "Do you recognize either of these people?"

O'Mara looked at the picture of Kern. "I don't know him." He stared at the artist's impression of the man who'd been seen at Paulo Raymus's.

"He seems familiar." O'Mara studied the man's eyes.

"I may have seen him somewhere before."

CHAPTER
50

Daniel Riley looked at the mechanism for the door. He saw a series of circuit boards and wires behind the panel. He didn't know much about electronics, and felt a stab of confusion. What was he to do?

There was no sound from the corridor, and worryingly, no sound from Will's cell. Riley had called out several times. The fact that there'd been no reply, made him wonder.

He focused on the circuits but confusion blurred his thoughts. Picking up the piece of metal he'd used as a screwdriver, he began undoing the screws holding the board in place. Why be delicate? He had to get out, and he let himself get angry. He grabbed the circuit board and pulled. There was a snapping sound, as plastic broke. Wires came away and a red light went off. There was a clicking, and the noise hit him like a punch.

Riley glanced at the door and wondered if it was unlocked. Tentatively he reached for the handle. He held his breath and pulled.

The door began to slide, and Riley felt a bolt of excitement.

.   .   .

DCI Lane drove towards Brentwood. By the time he arrived, it was after eleven a.m. The street he pulled up on was a residential one.

There were detached houses at regular intervals, most with double garages and good-sized plots.

Lane was unimpressed. *The rich get richer and the poor buy another smartphone and a 50-inch TV.*

He found number twenty-six and noted the people-carrier parked on the drive. There was a child's bike nearby, which had fallen over. It was bright pink and sprayed with glitter.

From inside the house he could hear noise: a child's voice and then a raised one, deeper – a man's. Lane pressed the doorbell and waited. After a moment there was a shuffling of feet and the door opened.

The man standing in front of him was in his late thirties. He was tall and razor thin, with dark, curly hair. He had a pale face, with a shaving rash, and Lane could see a red line where he had cut himself.

"Mr Dawson?" said Lane.

"That's right."

Lane reached for his warrant card and held it up.

There was noise from a child in the background, as something fell over. Joe Dawson looked down the hall. A man appeared behind Dawson who stepped aside, allowing him out. The man had a round, pleasant face, and nodded to Lane before leaving.

"Speak to you next week," Dawson said.

"My new handyman," Dawson explained to Lane. "Trying to negotiate the best price. You better come in. I got your message, but to be honest weekends are usually pretty hectic around here." He closed the door and pointed down the hall, to a window at the far end. "We can talk in the conservatory." Dawson sounded harassed.

He led the way, and a small child, in pink, looked at Lane as he walked by. She was no more than three or four, and looked at him with wide eyes. Lane towered over her, and she seemed daunted by his size.

"That's Emily," said Dawson. He sounded as if he wished he was somewhere else.

The conservatory at the back offered a good view of the garden. A sofa and two chairs were set up around a coffee table.

"Can I get you something to drink?"

"I'm fine … thank you."

Lane sat down. Dawson pulled the conservatory door shut, and Lane wondered if his wife was around.

"I guess you're here about my boss," said Dawson. He seemed melancholy as he spoke.

"Tim Mannak is a person of interest. We're looking into his disappearance, and I'd be grateful if you could tell me anything you know."

Dawson gave an odd little smile. "Well, I know a lot."

.　　　.　　　.

At Homicide West, Perez was looking at CCTV footage from Datax. He had borrowed two DVD players from downstairs. The usual technician, who was a friend of his, wasn't there, and the man who had loaned him the equipment had viewed him suspiciously.

Perez watched footage from the two security cameras. One camera showed vehicles coming into the building, where Riley had worked, the other showed vehicles leaving.

Perez knew the task could be time consuming and frustrating. Work such as this often was. However, he knew the time Daniel Riley had arrived at the office – a little after one o'clock.

He checked the time code on the cameras and fast-forwarded to 1.00 P.M. There was nothing. He fast-forwarded again to 1.05 and then 1.10, and saw Riley's car arriving.

The light-grey Audi approached the car-park entrance and waited while the barrier went up. Riley drove down the ramp at speed and disappeared from view.

Perez leant forward. He waited and watched to see if any other vehicles arrived. After a delay of some thirty seconds, a transit van appeared. It was black, judging by the faded image on the screen. He couldn't make out the driver. The resolution wasn't good enough, and the angle of the camera made the windscreen of the van seem opaque.

The van waited patiently as the barrier rose. It drove in, following the same path Riley had taken.

Perez continued to watch the footage, feeling increasingly tense. There were no other vehicles. He looked at the other camera, showing footage of the exit.

Nothing.

He checked the time code and waited.

Still nothing.

Then he saw a maintenance man walk past, carrying a bucket and mop. Perez considered when Daniel Riley's meeting had finished. According to his colleagues, it had been just after 3.00 P.M. It was a pity the cameras didn't revolve. Perez watched the footage on fast-forward, and slowed down as the time code reached 3.00 P.M.

At 3.21 he saw a black van leaving. It was the same van that had followed Riley in.

Perez paused the footage and sat back, thinking. He pressed rewind, to watch it all again.

•   •   •

At his home, Joe Dawson tried to be honest.

"I know about his job. Tim and I have worked together for nearly four years. I'm his deputy."

"At the local bank?" Lane took out his notebook.

"That's right. I'm acting manager now – ever since Tim, well, since he disappeared."

"And how was Mr Mannak in the run up to his disappearance?" Lane wanted to sound casual, and hoped he was coming across in that way.

"He was fine, the same as ever really. He's an easy-going man. He didn't seem anxious or nervous about anything."

"Had he confided in you about any problems he might have had?"

Dawson paused. "Tim and I aren't close. I don't know much about his home life. I know he's married – that he doesn't have children – but beyond that I don't know a great deal.

"As for work, it's the same as ever. There've been cutbacks, and that's been preying on people's minds, but … but these things happen." Dawson wasn't sure how happy he was talking to a complete stranger. He studied Lane closely.

"Mrs Mannak suggested her husband might have had difficult clients to deal with. Could you tell me about that?"

Dawson gave a knowing look. "We *all* have difficult clients, or *customers* as we now have to call them. We deal with money, and people are always wanting more, or worse still, avoiding us when repayments are due."

"And that causes friction?"

"Most definitely. Tim deals with a whole mix of people, from private individuals to corporate clients. He often makes the final decision as to whether loans are extended or called in. It can be difficult."

"I guess no one likes their bank manager," said Lane.

Dawson didn't appreciate the comment, and he let it show. "People think we lend money to anyone who can fog a mirror, but that's simply not the case."

Lane liked the way he had put it.

"There're checks and balances. We have to be accountable – we have to be professional. And the people we deal with – the general public – they don't always see that."

"Are there any customers that stand out?"

Dawson thought. "There have been a few. There was this one guy who actually visited Tim at his home. His loan had been called in – he ran a small business. Apparently it meant he'd go under."

"And he confronted Mannak about this?"

"Words were exchanged. Tim said he was threatened, but he wasn't actually hurt."

"Was it reported to the police?"

Dawson shook his head. "Tim doesn't work like that. It isn't something he'd want to do. He always tries to see the best in people. I guess I'm different." Dawson paused, as if deliberating whether to say more.

"All of us have been worried about him. To be honest, the police haven't taken his disappearance very seriously."

Lane thought of Sergeant Haimes, at the Missing Persons Unit.

"I've kept a list over the years," said Dawson, "of customers who've been difficult. I haven't told head office, and I'm not sure if they'd appreciate it. If it helps you … if it helps you find out what happened, I'd be willing to pass it over."

Lane was beginning to like Dawson. "That's definitely something I'd be interested in."

CHAPTER
51

Daniel Riley was free. The metal door of his cell slid back. He moved the door slowly, fearful of making noise, and once the gap was a foot wide he stepped out.

The corridor was unfamiliar. The floor was made of cement, and the walls were light grey. There were puddles of water on the ground, and he looked up to see pipes running along the ceiling. There were lights, in small metal cages, at regular intervals, but the light they gave out was weak. The whole place had an uncomfortable feel to it.

Riley crept quietly to the door of the next cell and tapped on it.

There was no reply.

"Will? Can you hear me?"

He waited, listening for movement. Was Will still there?

Riley looked towards the base of the door and saw a small hatch, through which food could be put. He crouched down and tried to slide it open, but it wouldn't move. He felt frustrated. He tried the handle of the door, putting his should against it and gently pressing. He applied more force.

Nothing.

I'll get help, Riley thought. *Once I'm out of here, I'll get help.*

He looked along the corridor. It was at least twenty yards. The basement appeared to be rectangular. On one side was the corridor itself, and to the left several doors, behind each of which was a cell. Riley listened at each door but there was no sound.

Time to get out. There was a door at the far end corridor, and he walked towards it with a sense of trepidation. As he reached it, he held his breath and grasped the handle. It turned and the door swung open.

In front of him he could see stairs, leading up. They were steep and narrow, and there was little light.

Riley climbed. A stair creaked, and then another, but he continued slowly, pausing to listen. As he reached the top he came to a door. Through the keyhole he could see light. Riley felt hope and his heart skipped a beat. He turned the handle and the door opened.

He was on the ground floor of a house. He was in a corridor, and at either end was a room, giving the ground floor the shape of an H. The whole place had a dated feel, except for the ceiling where there were lights in alcoves. They looked new. He moved towards the larger room and was dismayed to see no windows. Instead there were planks of wood, nailed into place where windows should be.

He looked into the other room, but could see no way out. There were more boarded-up windows, but no door. This didn't make sense. There had to be a door somewhere. He took in the furnishings – a chair, a table – something covered with a dustsheet. He ignored the details: he only cared about escape.

The ground floor was a similar size to the basement, but it was in better condition. The light-coloured walls made it feel almost like a home.

Riley moved towards the largest boarded-up window. He could see that care had been taken, with more than a dozen planks nailed into place. He thought about prising one away but needed something to work with. There was no sign of tools or equipment.

He looked through a gap between the planks, and thought he could see gravel.

He heard an engine, and the sound of tyres, and saw a vehicle pulling up. Its outline was dark and a shiver ran up Riley's spine: he'd seen it before.

·   ·   ·

When Lane returned to Homicide West, he found the incident room quiet.

"This place is like a cemetery for the living." He looked at the two monitors Perez had set up. "What's going on here?"

Perez felt pleased with himself. "I was checking CCTV footage from Datax, from the afternoon Daniel Riley went missing."

Lane could sense that Perez had found something.

"There *is* something that may be of interest." Perez pressed a button on the DVD player.

"This is when Daniel Riley first came in – after lunch, on Monday afternoon. A couple of minutes later a van followed."

Lane looked at the footage. He saw a dark van, coming down the ramp after Riley's car.

"Riley's meeting finished just after three o'clock," said Perez. "He came down and put his things away in his car. He was meant to go back up to his colleagues, but he never made it … Now look at this."

Lane checked the time code and saw the dark van leaving just after three o'clock. He caught a glimpse of the number plate.

"I've spoken to maintenance," said Perez. "The van doesn't belong to any of its contractors. Now this is where it gets interesting." Perez smiled with his eyes. "I spoke to Tim Mannak's wife. The week he went missing, she said she saw a van parked in her street. She thought it was a delivery van, but it was there on a number of occasions, sometimes for twenty or thirty minutes."

Lane opened his mouth. "Did she see a driver?"

"No, but she remembers the make and model, and it matches this."

Lane was pleased. "Good work."

•   •   •

"So who is this guy?" It was half an hour later and they were in Lane's car.

"His name's Asif Khan." Perez looked at the PNC printout. "He has no criminal record. According to the DVLA, he owns the van we want – a VW Transporter. According to their records, he owns several vehicles: he runs a courier company. That could have been what he was doing at Riley's office – delivering parcels or post."

"And the same thing at Tim Mannak's place?" Lane was sceptical. "He's in the vicinity of two men when they both go missing. This needs a closer look." Lane's resolve stiffened as he gripped the steering wheel.

"The DVLA have a Wandsworth address for Khan," said Perez. "It's a business address, but it looks as if he lives on site." Perez thought. "If this is the guy we want, what is his link to Stein, Mannak and the others?"

"One thing at a time," said Lane. He felt experience guiding him. "Let's hear what he has to say."

The detectives drove through Bermondsey, towards Elephant and Castle, before heading towards Wandsworth.

"They're regenerating the area," said Lane, glancing left and right. "It's about bloody time too. Elephant and Castle is rougher than the back of a bricklayer's arse."

Perez smiled to himself.

Several minutes later they came to a residential road of small, post-war houses, on the edge of Wandsworth. Lane was about to say that it must be the wrong place, when he saw a large open yard in between the houses. There was a warehouse, with a wide door, set back from the road. Above it was a residential unit. Lane could see several vans parked outside, but no sign of the black transit.

A man was loading a van. He was tall and slim, with a black beard and a cap on his head.

"Could be him," said Lane. He pulled up on to the forecourt and glanced over. "Let's have a chat."

CHAPTER
52

The man loading the van watched Lane and Perez as they approached. Lane took out his warrant card and held it up.

"DCI Lane – I'm from Homicide West. I was wondering if I could have a word with Asif Khan."

"He's not here at the moment." The man smiled, as if taking the sting out of his words. "I'm his brother. Is there anything that I can do?" He wiped a hand across his forehead and stepped away from the van.

Lane wondered if the man was naturally calm, or if he was trying hard to conceal something. "We're interested in speaking to your brother regarding an ongoing enquiry." Lane looked around the yard which had recently been swept. He was looking for signs of a VW Transporter but could see nothing, and wondered if there was more space behind the warehouse.

"Asif'll be back shortly," said his brother. "He has some deliveries to do."

Lane stepped away and walked towards the side of the warehouse, leaving Perez to take up the questioning.

"Does he often work on Sundays?"

"We work most Sundays – not a full day, but we're self-employed. When you run your own business it can be hard. I'm Naveen, by the way." He held out his hand and Perez shook it.

Perez studied Naveen Khan, and took in his laid-back nature. Few people he met when conducting enquiries were so laid back.

"You don't seem surprised to see us."

"We get visits from the police from time to time."

Perez was surprised but Naveen continued. "No point worrying about what you can't control." Perez saw the inside of the van which was being loaded. There were white boxes, sealed with brown tape.

"Office supplies," said Naveen, in response to the look. The van was three-quarters full, and Perez was surprised at how much had been fitted inside.

"You courier all sorts of things?"

"As long as it fits in the van, we'll move it." Naveen picked up another box. It was heavy, and the lines across his forehead deepened as he put it in. The presence of a police officer didn't bother him, and he gestured to the warehouse. "If you and your colleague want to wait, Asif'll be back soon."

Perez turned towards the warehouse and paused. "Out of interest, what does your brother look like?"

Naveen gave a smile. "He's quite fat and covered in tattoos."

Perez raised an eyebrow.

"Just kidding," said Naveen. "If you wait, you can see for yourself. He won't be long."

.   .   .

Asif Khan arrived a little after four o'clock. He was driving a black VW Transporter, and pulled up in front of the warehouse, in the middle of the yard. He saw Lane and Perez, but walked over to his brother, speaking to him for a moment. He was tall and slim, in his mid-forties, and bore more than a passing resemblance to Naveen.

He walked towards the detectives and Lane took out his warrant card. Khan accepted it. He studied the card and then Lane.

"I guess you better come into the office." He walked into the warehouse, which was dimly lit. There was a smell of engine oil.

Lane and Perez noted boxes stacked up, and tools hanging on the walls.

Khan's office was at the rear. There was a large glass window, and through it the detectives could see a desk and filing cabinets. Khan walked in and sat down, gesturing to Lane and Perez to join him. Khan turned on a desk lamp, and reached down to a small fridge underneath. He took out a can of coke and offered two cans to the detectives.

"We'll be fine … thanks." Lane sat down and could see that Khan was older than his brother. There were lines around his eyes, and flecks of grey in his hair. He was softly spoken, but looked as if he was a man who wasn't easily intimidated.

"I guess your brother explained why we're here."

Khan gave a half-smile. "Apparently you're interested in one of my vans." He looked out to the forecourt, and Lane followed his gaze.

"We're interested in a vehicle that matches the description of yours. It was seen in the vicinity of several crimes we're investigating."

"Since you're from Homicide West, I'm guessing it must be serious." Khan took a sip of coke. Something was wrong – Lane was rapidly realizing that.

"Could you tell us where you've been over the last couple of weeks?"

"I've been here, doing my job." He gestured around. "Between us, my brother and I do everything. We do deliveries throughout London, for a variety of businesses. We use the VW, and we have two other vans – Toyotas. Look, I have to be straight with you. This isn't the first time I've been visited by you guys. My VW has been involved in all sorts of crimes. I've had five tickets for parking, three for speeding, and a summons for threatening behaviour towards a woman."

"And you didn't do any of these?" said Perez.

"Darn right I didn't." Khan put down the drink and felt indignant. "I've been in contact with an inspector in Traffic – a guy by the name of Quinn.

"When I got the first ticket for speeding, I wasn't best pleased. Then four more followed. I protested my innocence, explaining that I wasn't there. There was camera footage, and the person who was driving the van wasn't me."

Perez was confused. "The vehicle was displaying your number plate?"

Khan nodded.

"And it wasn't stolen?" said Lane.

"No. I'm the only person who uses it. The vehicle has been cloned. There's another vehicle out there, similar to mine, with identical plates. The matter's being investigated by Quinn. He told me to refer all incidents to him. You can reach him at the Road Policing Unit."

Lane felt disappointed as well as surprised. "So someone, at some point in time, has seen your vehicle and copied the plate?"

"That would appear to be the case." Khan felt he had better things to do. He reached behind him and opened a cabinet, removing a thin folder. "This is all my correspondence with Traffic. Give Quinn a call. He can bring you up to speed."

Lane flicked through the file and saw letters on police-headed paper.

"And when was the last time this happened?"

"About four weeks ago. It was the incident involving threatening behaviour. Apparently the guy driving my van threatened a woman. I don't know the details – I wasn't there – but I can assure you that it wasn't me."

"Do you have a description of the man?" said Perez.

Khan looked blank. He felt it wasn't his place to answer the question. "It's best you ask Quinn. He has more information than I do."

Lane made some notes. "I suppose this puts a different light on things."

"Believe me, I'm not best pleased." Khan felt annoyed. "But what can I do?"

"Do you have any idea who might have done this?" said Perez, "– anyone with a grudge?"

"I don't think that's the case. I've had the van for more than a year … These incidents started happening five or six months ago."

Lane was thinking. "You said you deliver for businesses around London. Does that include businesses in the city centre?"

Khan nodded. "We do deliveries to many companies. We work in the public and private sectors."

Something snagged in Lane's mind. "Do you do any work for the NHS?"

"I've done work for several trusts. The Lewisham Trust, the Richmond one, as well as the Acton Hospital Trust."

There was immediate reaction in Lane's eyes.

"Small world," he said quietly.

CHAPTER
53

Daniel Riley returned to his cell, knowing deep down that he was not brave enough to confront his attacker. He closed the door and listened to the sound of footsteps, as his kidnapper moved about. The man came down the stairs and walked along the corridor. There was a sigh, the sound of something being dragged, and then keys going into a lock.

Riley realized that the cell next to him was being opened. Was Will being brought back, or was someone being brought in to replace him?

Riley felt a mixture of hope and confusion. The hairs on his arms stood on end, and he took short breaths. He had to think about escape but there were too many obstacles. The man he was facing was stronger than him. Riley had never been brave. He had always pretended to be things that he wasn't, and deep down he knew he was weak.

He looked at his cell door and the lock on the inside. When would his abductor notice the damage, and what would he do?

There was noise from Will's cell – dragging, and then a muted thud.

Riley concentrated, straining to listen. He believed he could hear whispering. Then the cell door slammed.

Riley heard footsteps: the man was leaving. The door at the end of the corridor slammed and all sound faded.

For a moment, Riley felt an eerie silence. He could feel his heart beating. Then his cell door slid back. The sound startled him and he jumped. His abductor was standing outside. His face was covered, and all Riley could see were eyes.

"What have you been up to?"

Riley thought he recognized the voice, but it was gone in an instant.

The man stepped in, hauled Riley up and punched him. He let Riley fall and picked him up again, grabbing him by the neck.

The man pulled Riley's head to one side and looked into his eyes.

He knows what's happened. He knows I got out.

Riley felt pain, as his abductor punched him again.

.   .   .

Lane and Perez were driving back to Homicide West. Perez was driving as Lane sat in the passenger seat, staring ahead. His face was stiff and expressionless.

"We need to get in touch with Traffic," said Perez. He touched the brake, as they approached a junction. "Do you know Quinn?"

"His name rings a bell. To be honest, I don't have much to do with them." There was a hint of contempt in Lane's voice. "You know what people call them? – black rats. They'll happily turn on their own. If Quinn's looking into this van, we need to get the information he has."

"I know they aren't always forthcoming," said Perez. He had met obstructive police officers before. It didn't happen every day, but when it did it disappointed him.

Lane felt anger. "We need that van. Find it, and we'll find the man we're after."

"We need to check Khan's background too."

Lane nodded. "I have a feeling his story will check out though." Lane reached into his jacket. "I got this earlier today." He took out the list that he had been given by Joe Dawson. "I got it from the deputy at the bank, where Mannak worked."

Perez glanced at the names and felt worried. "What is it?"

"It's a list of people who caused the bank problems. Dawson compiled it. He's either anally retentive or forward thinking – I'm not sure which." Lane considered Dawson as Perez quickly glanced at the list.

"There must be over fifty names there."

"Fifty-eight," said Lane. "I think it's fair to say that banks aren't popular." He struggled to remember a time when they were. "We'll run these names through the PNC. I also want to cross-check it against employees at Stein Engineering, and people who worked for the Acton Hospital Trust. Something links Mannak to the others."

Perez felt things were coming together. "Once we establish what our vics had in common, we should be there."

"When we get back to the station you might as well head home," said Lane, "– let your wife know that I'm a reasonable man."

Perez managed a smile. "*Reasonable* isn't the word she uses."

Lane could live with that. "A lot of people can't wait for my funeral. We'll make an early start tomorrow."

CHAPTER
54

On Monday morning, Lane drove straight to the headquarters of Traffic. He thought about waiting for Perez, but in the end decided to go alone. He didn't intend to be subtle. He didn't intend to be diplomatic or polite. Quinn was going to give him what he needed, and obstruction wouldn't be tolerated.

Lane pulled up in the car park a little before 8.45. He noted Quinn's space, and saw that an old Peugeot was already there.

Lane got out, locked his car and walked towards the front of the building. He showed his warrant card to the young woman at reception. "Inspector Quinn? Is he about?"

The woman was caught off-guard. "Yes …" She tried to catch another glimpse of Lane's warrant card. "Do you have an appointment? It's really –"

"I'm sure he'll be pleased to see me." Lane headed upstairs, passing shields and plaques on the walls. There were several framed photographs of previous heads of Traffic. "Pretentious nonsense," Lane muttered to himself. Chief Superintendent Grant, who headed up the division, was someone he had clashed with before. He hoped he wouldn't run into him before he got what he wanted.

On the first floor, Lane looked along the corridor. He saw several doors with silver nameplates. There was one for Grant, and Lane thought he could hear noise on the other side.

He continued down the corridor and came to an open-plan incident room. The walls were painted light green, and there were several young officers at desks. On the far side of the room were civilian workers, with lots of paperwork piled around them, all surrounded by a strong smell of coffee.

A few officers glanced at Lane. He searched for Quinn, and his eyes came to rest on a small man, with dark hair and an aging face.

"Can I help you?" Quinn said. He picked up his glasses, trying to place Lane's face as he walked towards him.

"I hope so."

Lane explained who he was and what he wanted. Quinn listened, but Lane could see that he was reluctant to help.

"I know this Mr Khan," said Quinn eventually. He didn't offer Lane a seat. The seat at his desk was stacked with papers, and he wasn't keen to move them. "I've looked into his case."

"And?"

"And I think he has a point." Quinn lowered his gaze. "It looks as if the vehicle in question has been cloned. It isn't uncommon, particularly for high-end commercial vehicles."

"The reason being financial?"

"Invariably. Vehicles are stolen, their identities changed and then they're sold on. Often it's just a fraudulent sale, but sometimes they're used in the commission of crime."

To Lane it sounded as if Quinn was delivering a much-practiced speech. Lane felt Quinn was the kind of police officer who did the minimum. Going the extra mile was most likely a foreign concept to him.

"I think the cloned van may have been involved in other crimes," said Lane.

"Perhaps …" Quinn appeared disinterested.

"I'm looking into multiple homicides," said Lane. He was hoping to provoke a reaction but it wasn't happening. "This van is a credible lead."

Quinn looked doubtful. "What do you want of me?"

"I was hoping you could give me your intelligence reports. Khan told me the vehicle attracted parking and speeding fines – that the driver was involved in a dispute with someone."

Quinn was unhappy. Lane could see the shutters going down.

"I just can't give out that information."

"Can't or *won't*?" Lane's face darkened. "We're on the same side here … at least that's what people think."

"That doesn't extend to giving away intelligence reports."

Lane tensed. "Do you want me to take this to the chief super?"

"You know him?"

"He and I go way back." Lane neglected to mention the animosity between them. "Where is he – his office?"

"He's busy," said Quinn sharply.

"Which is French for hoisting a couple." Lane mimed someone drinking. "I know of his reputation. Believe me, he's a man who's been promoted beyond his pay grade." Lane took a step towards the door and Quinn spoke up.

"Give me a minute … I'll see what I can do."

.   .   .

I can see everything now. All the mistakes I have made, and all the possible things that could trap me. And it's frustrating. There are too many observant people, too many databases and too many cameras. It makes life hard and increases your workload.

I do feel rage and I do try to control it. I want you to know that. I didn't want my life to be like this. Others are responsible. People simply don't care. I have skills and people need to know that. I'm not just anger, and when it's all over those who deserve it will have been punished.

.   .   .

Lane returned to Homicide West. It was a little before 10 A.M. and he was pleased that the incident room was buzzing. Uniformed officers were busy, assisted by civilian staff.

Perez was at his desk, as was Malcolm Brown. Lane glanced at the photographs on Brown's desk. They had changed, and were now showing scenes of London in winter. Lane continued to glance at them as he spoke to Perez.

"How're things going?"

"Swings and roundabouts." Perez looked more confident than he sounded however, and that gave Lane hope. "We've been going through the list you got from Joe Dawson."

"And?"

"We've got a couple of possibles. We divided up the list of names. Of the fifty-eight, fourteen have criminal convictions. Five of those are for minor offences, but the other nine is where it gets interesting."

Lane wanted to hear more and looked at the list of names Perez had produced. All were male. Several were foreign sounding, but nothing stood out.

"These nine people have done time for offences ranging from threatening behaviour, to assault and grievous-bodily harm. There's also one convicted sex offender." Perez circled a name near the bottom of the list.

Lane studied it. "*Ivan Blake*." It wasn't a name he recognized. "Who were the offences committed against?"

"Young girls, aged between ten and fourteen. He was sentenced to twelve years, and has been on release for two. He lives in east London."

"I don't think he's our man," said Lane. Experience was guiding him. "A paedophile doesn't fit the profile. Concentrate on the other eight. These people all had grievances with Mannak and the bank, but we need to make connections with Riley, Stein and Warner." Lane felt something dawning on him.

"Cross-check the names against a list of employees at Stein Engineering. Stein employs how many people – over a thousand? Get a list from their HR. If someone who worked at Stein also had dealings with Mannak, that's someone we need to look at." Lane sat down, reassured by their progress.

"How did your visit to Traffic go?" said Perez.

"*Road Crime Intelligence* – I think that's what they're calling themselves these days." Lane hated ridiculous naming but tried to dismiss it. "Inspector Quinn was reluctant to share what he had. In the end he relented though – my natural charm saw to that."

Perez raised an eyebrow, and Lane pretended he hadn't noticed.

"He gave me these reports regarding the cloned vehicle." Lane raised a blue file.

"And?"

"The van's received parking and speeding fines." Lane flicked through the list. "All the offences were committed in the Greater London area – more in north London than the south."

"Whoever is using the van is most likely London based."

"Agreed. What is of interest is this: whoever is driving that van had an altercation with a woman in a car. She reported him."

"Did she give a description of the man?"

Lane pointed to a sentence near the bottom of a page. "*White male, height six foot two, light-coloured hair, blue eyes, late thirties to early forties.*"

Lane knew eyewitness reports could be unreliable. "I'm going to see this woman – Gloria Gwyneth – see exactly what she has to say. You continue with the list."

Lane made to leave and Perez stopped him. There was a subject that he was reluctant to bring up. "There is one other thing … you've made the local press." He unfolded the newspaper and Lane looked at a small article on the front.

POLICE CHIEF WITHHOLDS INFORMATION IN MAJOR ENQUIRY

Lane saw a picture of himself, standing outside Homicide West. His cheeks reddened, as he tried to recall when the picture had been taken.

"*Damn.* I didn't think many people had taken an interest."

"Top brass won't be pleased," said Perez.

Lane considered his options. "If Travers wants to know where I am, you haven't seen me."

Perez smiled inwardly. Malcolm Brown was listening.

"You haven't seen me either," said Lane.

Brown nodded, wondering how good he would be at lying.

Lane took the paper. "Best bin this."

Lane arrived at Mitre Square, in central London, a little after eleven o'clock. He had arranged to meet Gloria Gwyneth at her place of work, and as he looked around the square he saw a number of office buildings.

There was something depressing about the area. In Lane's mind, the square had a distinctive '90s feel. He remembered Mitre Square when it had been different, and knew all about its history.

He went into a building called Challingdon House, and asked at the reception for Mrs Gwyneth. The receptionist told him to take a seat, and presently a middle-aged woman came down from the first floor.

Gloria Gwyneth was a small woman, in her mid-forties. She had blonde hair tied into a bun, and had a severe look on her face. She was smartly dressed, in a dark-blue jacket and skirt, and wore high heels that clattered on the floor.

"Mr Lane?"

Lane held out his hand. "Mrs Gwyneth? Thank you for taking the time to see me."

"Not at all." Gloria reached into her handbag and took something out as she headed towards the entrance. "Thank you for meeting me at work. When I got your call, I was surprised to hear from you, but I'm glad someone is looking into what happened."

"I'm actually with Homicide West," said Lane. He didn't want to be mistaken for someone from Traffic. He followed Gloria as she stepped outside and lit a cigarette. She offered him one but he declined.

"I'm pretty sure I haven't been involved in any homicides, Chief Inspector." Gloria was amused. Her make-up made her skin look pale, and contrasted with her bright-red lipstick.

"I don't want any of my work colleagues knowing what happened. That's why we're out here … I hope you don't mind."

"I understand," said Lane. He looked around the square. There were several men in suits, sitting under trees, smoking as they talked. Lane looked at the watches on their wrists, and a thought ran through his mind: *that's God's way of saying you've got too much money.*

"So you deal with homicides?" said Gloria. "I'm not sure how that fits in with me."

"I'm interested in the motorist you had a disagreement with," said Lane. "You gave a description to Inspector Quinn."

Gloria nodded. "This happened a while ago, at least a month and a half. I was driving through Tottenham Hale, when I was cut up by a van. He pulled out from a side street and I had to swerve. I honked and swore at him, but he didn't seem to care." Gloria drew on her cigarette and looked at Lane.

"We both continued driving, and passed Tottenham Hale station. I had to stop at a set of lights, and the van was in front of me. We were in a line of traffic, when I saw the van door opening. The driver got out and walked towards me. The look on his face – he was livid. I couldn't understand why, but I could see that he meant to hit me."

"Were you alone?"

"Yes. The road was busy, and it was during the day, but I still felt afraid."

"What did the van driver do?"

"He began shouting. He stood by my window and kept shouting at me to wind it down. He tried the door handle and then hit the glass."

"How did you respond?"

"I was terrified. There was nowhere to go." Gloria was recalling the event and there was fear in her eyes. "I couldn't back up as there were cars behind."

"How long did he stay there?"

"I'm not sure." Gloria looked at her cigarette. "It could only have been a matter of minutes. The lights changed and the traffic started moving. Cars honked and the man had to move. He didn't really have a choice."

Lane took out a photograph. "Did he look anything like this?"

Gloria studied the photograph of Michael Kern. "No ... he was similar though. Similar hair – light coloured – and blue eyes too. He was in his late thirties or early forties. I gave all of this information to the police officer."

Lane imagined Quinn filing the information away. "I just wanted to hear it from you. How about the van? Can you tell me anything about that?"

"I don't know much about vans. It was big, new – sprayed black."

"Was there anyone with him?"

"I'm not sure. No passengers got out."

"And the back of the van?"

Gloria shook her head, as she didn't fully understand what Lane was getting at. "It didn't have windows. It was sealed – metal doors at the back and panels on the sides."

"So if there had been anyone inside, you wouldn't have been able to see?"

"Yes. I have to say that the man seemed crazy. He didn't have to do what he did."

Lane was thinking. "Did you notice the direction he went in after he drove off?"

"I was focused on escape. I changed my route and headed towards Arnos Grove."

"And that was the last time you saw him?"

"Absolutely." Gloria looked relieved. "He was big. At least six foot. Well built, especially across the shoulders. I'll tell you something else, Inspector." Gloria looked emphatic. "He had problems. People who have lots of problems try and take things out on others. They overreact."

Lane considered that as Gloria looked around the square. She disliked it. "You know about the history of this place? Jack the Ripper is supposed to have murdered one of his victims here."

Lane was familiar with the area. "Catherine Eddowes ... I know the story." He seemed reticent. "I wasn't going to bring it up ... some people are easily spooked."

"Don't worry," said Gloria, her face softening. "Everyone who works here knows the story."

·   ·   ·

When Lane retuned to Homicide West he found the incident room busy. "How's it going?" he said, looking at Perez.

"We've made some progress. Stan O'Mara – the guy at Stein Engineering – he faxed over a list of all the company's employees."

"And?"

"We're currently checking it against the list of bank customers, who displayed threatening behaviour."

"Good." Lane sat down and looked at Malcolm Brown. He was cross-checking the names.

"Another thing," said Perez. "Travers wants to speak to you. He's seen the paper."

Lane swore to himself. He debated going to see Travers, but in the end decided not to. "That idiot will just go postal on me." He watched Perez and Brown as they worked. He decided to help, but after a while it became apparent that no name appeared on both lists.

"It doesn't look as if there's a match," said Perez eventually.

Lane studied the lists. "Stein Engineering employs over a thousand people. Is this a list of current employees?"

"Yes."

"Common sense isn't going out of fashion. Let's look at *former* employees. The company made people redundant. Let's look at disgruntled, *former* employees."

CHAPTER 56

Daniel Riley rolled on to his side, trying to get away from the cold floor. His kidnapper had left the cell. There was noise from the other side of the door, as the man tethered it with a rope.

Riley was losing hope. His attacker hadn't said anything. He'd simply struck him repeatedly. Riley wondered who he had wronged – what he had done to deserve this. He wasn't going to see his family again, and he suspected everything would soon be over. He felt like crying.

He pushed himself up but fell down, pain in his chest. Blood was coming from his nose. He wiped it away, and tried to stem the flow with the sleeve of his shirt.

From the cell next door, he could hear noise. There was movement – a scuffing of feet.

"Are you there?" The voice was tentative. "… are you still there?"

Riley stopped.

Will?

He moved to the grille. "Is that you?"

"Yes." Will's voice was tinged with pain. Riley suspected he'd been beaten too.

"Are you OK?"

"I've been better. He took me away … attacked me."

Riley considered that.

Will's voice picked up. He had news, and wasn't sure how to put it.

"I can get us out of here. There was a key – I took it. I can get out."

·   ·   ·

Stan O'Mara did what Lane wanted, albeit grudgingly. He sent over several faxes, containing the names of employees who had left Stein Engineering over the last four years.

"Will that do?" he said, after the final fax had gone through.

"It'll do for now," said Lane. "If I need more help, I'll get back to you."

O'Mara hung up.

"We need to get these checked out." Lane divided up the faxes among the staff in the incident room. They began checking names against the list of bank customers who had threatened Mannak.

After several minutes Brown said, "I've got it." He looked up and pushed his glasses back into place. "This guy – Tanner – he left Stein about a year ago. He was made redundant."

"And he appears on Mannak's list?"

Brown pointed. "According to the list from Mannak, Shawn Tanner visited him several times. The last time was roughly eight months ago. He was angry. It looks as if there were problems with a loan."

Lane felt a flicker of excitement, but it was tempered by experience. "We need more to go on. Get on to the bank. I want to know everything there is to know about Mr Tanner, and why exactly it was he was angry."

Lane turned to Perez. "Check the PNC – see if he's on it." Lane leant forward and picked up the phone to call Stan O'Mara. He wanted to see what he knew.

·   ·   ·

It took a while to get through, and the female receptionist sounded embarrassed and taken aback.

"What do you mean he isn't there?" said Lane angrily. "I just spoke to him."

"He had to step out. I know he was dealing with you. He asked for faxes to be sent over."

"I got them," said Lane tersely. "Tell him to call me when he gets back." He hung up and let his anger subside. He watched as Perez checked Tanner's details on the PNC. Lane's trail of thought was interrupted by Brown.

"Sir?" Brown was nervous as always. "I just spoke to the bank."

"And?"

"They have a record of Mr Tanner. Apparently he held a mortgage with them, but he had repayment problems."

"He fell behind?"

"Some time ago." Brown consulted his illegible handwriting. "That was why Tanner went to see Mannak. He tried to get the re-payments suspended. Mannak didn't agree to it."

"What happened next?"

"It looks as if his home was repossessed."

Lane tried to put it in context. Tanner had worked for Stein Engineering. He'd been made redundant and he had lost his home.

"We do have a Shawn Tanner on the PNC," said Perez. "He was born Shawn James Tanner, in Kent, in 1973. His last address matches that of the repossessed property." Perez pointed to the screen and Lane walked around. "He has convictions for assault and grievous-bodily harm."

"Who did he attack?" Lane scanned the screen and saw a picture of a man who looked similar to Kern. There was something else though, but it vanished as Perez spoke.

"He assaulted a friend." Perez scanned the details. "This was several years ago, when they were on holiday. There's a parole officer's report … hold on.

"Tanner broke a friend's jaw. After a brief prison sentence, he found work. He held a job at Stein Engineering for several years … he was some sort of technician. This is our man: it seems to fit."

Lane looked at the face, and a feeling of familiarity came back. He realized he had seen him before, at Joe Dawson's house.

"This man was at the home of the deputy bank manager," said Lane. "He was a handyman. He was leaving as I arrived." Lane checked the time. Dawson would be at work right now. "Call the bank and tell them I'm sending over two uniformed officers. We need to make sure Dawson is safe. Is there a current address for Tanner?"

"Hold on," said Perez, scrolling down. "There is a mail forwarding address. It's also in London."

"Well let's see who's there."

• • •

Lane dashed down the stairs, putting on his jacket as he moved. Perez followed a few metres behind, moving quickly but quietly. There was an urgency in the air, and the officers that they passed could feel it.

Once outside, Lane looked behind him.

"People are not happy with the bad press you've being generating," said Perez.

Lane felt philosophical. "We better hope our lead pans out then." They made for Lane's car. He drove, reversing out of the car park, forcing an unmarked police car to stop. Perez began leafing through the printouts.

"What's the postcode?" said Lane.

"West Norwood – SE27."

"I know the area. That's near Streatham Common."

They drove in silence, Perez carefully reading the notes on his lap.

"He's forty-two years old. It looks as if he was once married. Tanner had grievances against James Stein *and* Daniel Riley. The decisions they took led to him being made redundant."

"And then he lost his home," said Lane, "something he would blame on Mannak."

"How about Stein's partner?" said Perez. "Where does he fit in?"

"Nigel Warner may have been in the wrong place, at the wrong time. As for Paulo Raymus, I'm not sure." Lane showed hesitation. "Raymus worked for the Acton Hospital Trust, and perhaps the access he had made him useful. When he stopped being useful, he was disposed of …"

Perez considered that. His phone bleeped and he studied it.

"It's from the unit we sent over to check on Dawson. He's been at the branch where he works all day. So far nothing out of the ordinary has happened."

"Good. Tell the officers to stay put," said Lane. "Get two officers sent over to his home, in case Tanner turns up there."

Perez nodded and made the call.

Lane eventually slowed down as they reached a residential street, in West Norwood. Perez reeled off the address and Lane made several turns.

"This is it," said Perez, "Wilberforce Road. It's number twenty-five we need." Perez looked at the pre-war, semi-detached houses, which lined both sides of the street. "This is not what I was expecting." There were wheelie bins on the pavement, and the road looked as if it had been recently swept. "It doesn't feel right."

Lane was thinking the same thing, and was feeling wary.

CHAPTER 57

Daniel Riley listened to the sound of movement in the cell next door. Will put a key in the lock and turned it. The bolt went back and the door opened.

Riley waited, his heart floating in his chest. There was movement in the corridor – it had to be Will.

"I'm going to get you out of there," said Will. He spoke in a hushed tone. "*Damn.*"

"What's happened?" said Riley.

"Your cell door – he's tethered it with rope. I don't know if I can cut it."

Riley felt hope fading. "Look around. There's rubbish in the corridor. Look for something you can use."

There was a sound of footsteps as Will moved away. Finally, after what seemed like too long, he returned.

"I've got something. Hang on."

·   ·   ·

DCI Lane stood on the pavement and looked at the house. There was no sign of movement at any of the windows. There was netting across all of them, and that annoyed him.

"There's a car on the drive," said Perez.

Lane took note of the blue saloon.

"We should call for backup." Perez reached for his mobile. "If Shawn Tanner is in there, there's no reason to expect he'll come quietly." Perez looked across to Lane. He could see the look of re-solve building on Lane's face, and realized what he was about to do.

"You call it in. I'm going to find out if he's there." Lane strode towards the house.

"*Bull in a china shop*," said Perez. He put through the call, watching as Lane reached the front door.

The door of number twenty-five was bright red. It was in good condition, and looked as if it had recently been painted. Lane made to rap on it, but stopped. He paused, and with the tips of his fingers pushed the door. It swung open smoothly.

There was a hallway beyond, with beige-coloured walls. Lane took note of the wooden floor. He looked down the length of the hall and stepped forward. He felt tense.

He knew what Tanner looked like. How would he react when confronted? Lane realized he was holding his breath, and looked through the first door he came to – a living room. There was a strong smell of paint, and the room was deserted, with furniture covered in dustsheets. It looked barely used.

Lane moved along the corridor and saw the kitchen at the end. There was noise from above – creaking. Lane tensed and lis-tened carefully. There was more creaking: someone was moving.

Lane tried to ascertain the pattern of movement. He tried to visualize the direction of the footsteps.

He walked towards the stairs and mounted them in double strides. At the top there was a small landing, with several doors which were open.

There was shadow and movement coming from one room, and Lane walked towards it. Inside was a man in white overalls. He was in his sixties, with a grey moustache and bags under his eyes: it wasn't Tanner.

"Who are you?" said Lane.

The man stared back. "I'm the landlord. Who *the bloody hell* are you?"

**CHAPTER
58**

Twenty minutes later Wilberforce Road was busy. An armed response unit had arrived and Perez had taken them to one side, explaining what had happened. Lane was in the living room of the house, and sitting opposite was Gerard Griffiths.

Griffiths explained that Tanner had rented the property. He had fallen behind with the rent, and had posted the keys through the letterbox, before leaving.

"How long ago was this?" said Lane.

"About five weeks?" Griffiths sounded vague, and that was something Lane didn't appreciate it.

"We are keen to talk to Mr Tanner. Do you have any idea where he might be?"

"He did speak about a friend – boasted about it really. Said he knew someone with money – that the man had a place he could use. He laughed about it – that was odd."

"And you didn't find it funny?" said Lane.

"No." Griffiths thought for a moment. "To be honest he made me uncomfortable."

·　　·　　·

Daniel Riley waited in his cell. Outside, Will was working on the ropes that secured the door. There was the sound of breathing, and Riley could sense Will's frustration.

"How's it going?"

"Not sure," said Will. "These ropes … he's done them up tightly. They're not coming away."

Riley was conscious of time. What would happen if the man returned? If he caught them, they'd both be dead.

"Hold on," said Will. There was the sound of footsteps fading away. Riley waited, but there was nothing. He could feel his heart beating fast. Had Will gone? Had he abandoned him?

Riley called out. Eventually there was noise – scuffling. Will had returned, and Riley felt relief pass over him.

"I've got something."

There was sound from the other side, as Will started cutting the ropes. "I found it upstairs. There's loads of stuff up there."

"I know," said Riley quietly.

The ropes gave a little and the door slid back. Riley looked through the gap and could see Will's face. It was round. He had bright eyes, and smiled a little as he glanced in. "Don't worry. I'll get you out."

·   ·   ·

At Wilberforce Road, Lane looked at the faces of the armed response officers. They had formed a small doughnut, as they huddled and talked. The officer in charge, Paul McBain, was a friend of Lane's. McBain was in his fifties, a stocky man, who bore a passing resemblance to Lane. He had on body armour that made him look even bulkier, and was carrying an assault rifle.

"Wrong house?" said McBain.

"It looks that way," said Lane. "Could have been a lot worse though."

McBain read Lane's expression, and knew him well enough to know that there was more. "You have a hunch?"

"Give me a minute." Lane walked away and noticed a brown saloon, pulling up in the distance. A journalist he knew was getting out.

"Christ on a bike."

Lane tore his eyes away and punched a number into his mobile. Perez joined him.

"When I was speaking to the landlord," said Lane, "he said something which got my attention. He said Shawn Tanner spoke of a friend – a wealthy one. How many wealthy people do we know in this investigation?"

"Just the one," said Perez. "Stein."

Lane smiled inwardly. At the other end of the phone, Malcolm Brown answered.

"Malcolm, it's me. There's something I want you to do. James Stein – I want you to find out how much property he owned. We know about the place in Epping, but I want to know if there's anything else."

From where he was standing, Perez couldn't make out what Malcolm was saying.

"Good. Call me back." Lane hung up and glanced across.

"Now we just wait."

•   •   •

Ten minutes later Malcolm Brown returned the call. Lane could tell by his tone that he had found something.

"You're right, sir. James Stein did own more than one property. He was left a property by his parents when they died. It's in Kingston upon Thames – a Victorian place – a listed building."

Lane put his phone between his neck and shoulder, and took out a notebook.

"The address?"

Brown reeled it off.

"Good work, Malcolm."

"There're a couple of other things," said Brown. "According to the council, the property has been empty for some time. Stein wanted to convert it into a testing facility, for his work. The council wouldn't let him proceed. They said that the street wasn't suitable for commercial premises."

Lane looked into the distance and saw a journalist. He was inspecting the marked police cars.

"*Crap.*"

"Sorry, sir?"

"Not you, Malcolm. We'll head over there." Lane ended the call and flashed the address at Perez. "Let's go with this."

CHAPTER 59

Curzon Street, in Kingston upon Thames, was quiet. There were large Victorian houses on either side of the road, most with gated drives.

On one plot, at the end of the street, a house had been demolished and replaced with a newer building. It had a steel frame, with large glass panels in place of walls.

Bloody trendy architecture, thought Lane. "The place we want is number thirty-eight." He pulled up on the left-hand side and looked at a driveway. There were wooden gates at the front, which were closed. They looked past their best, and the black paint on them was peeling.

Perez got out and moved towards the gates. Behind him two cars, containing the armed response teams, came to a halt.

"The gates are unlocked," said Perez. He spoke quietly. Lane followed him and pushed open one gate, peering in. There was a long drive, with narrow strips of lawn on either side. The driveway was gravelled and weeds were growing through it.

"The drive bends around," said Lane turning back. "The property is at the far end."

Paul McBain had joined them. He looked at his armed officers. "You four go to the end of the street and see if you can access the rear. There's a park nearby. The house looks as if it backs on to it."

"Bushy Park," said Lane. McBain remained with Lane and Perez, as Lane made a decision. "Let's take the front."

McBain didn't argue. They passed through the main gate, closing it behind them. The gravel crunched as they walked, and McBain moved ahead, a rifle across his body, at waist height.

Perez didn't like the noise they were making. Every step they took could be heard. Lane realized what Perez was thinking, and with a shot of confidence increased his pace.

After twenty yards, the drive began curving to the left. Grass had spread on to it, narrowing it in places. Lane could see a large, Victorian house, partially obscured by fir trees. Parked in front was a black van.

Lane felt both excited and tense. He scanned the tinted windows of the van but could see nothing. McBain checked the van, one window at a time. He looked towards the windows of the house, but could see no one.

A hundred and fifty years ago the house would have looked modern. Today it looked tired, with faded arches and stained brickwork. Most stark however was the number of windows that had been boarded up.

Then Lane saw something: movement on the ground floor. He began running.

"Where're you going?" McBain hissed, and followed at speed.

• • •

Daniel Riley waited as the last of the ropes securing the door was cut. The door of his cell slid back and he saw Will. He was smiling.

"I used this," Will said, holding up the small knife. "The place is deserted. Come on."

The pair moved along the damp corridor. They took the stairs at the end, and as they approached the door at the top Riley urged Will to stop.

"He isn't there," said Will. "No one is." He was keen to go.

Riley strained, listening for sound. Will pushed the door open. They were looking into the hall Riley had seen before. He noted a kitchen at the back, and light coming from a room at the front. Things had changed, and he felt nervous and confused. Will saw his reaction and beamed. "Let's chance it."

Riley made for the door to the left of the living room.

A window on the right-hand side of the room was open. Riley barely noticed it, but Will did.

Riley reached for the door. There were several locks and a chain. *Had this been here before?* Something was wrong. He took off the chain, and turned the locks at the top and bottom.

"Come on." He turned back to see Will, who was looking on intently.

"This is what I look forward to," said Will. "… the look of excitement. They're nearly there – almost free – and then I take it all away."

Riley felt confused.

"I've enjoyed watching," said Will. "They call me Tanner."

"What?"

"I took you."

Tanner raised his knife.

Riley felt an unreal feeling. He frantically tried to open the door. He turned back, expecting to be stabbed, and saw a large man approaching Tanner from behind. The man put an arm around Tanner's neck, and had a look of determination as he pulled him down.

Tanner swung out, attempting to stab Lane, but it didn't work. Instead he used an elbow to strike Lane in the stomach. Lane let out a breath and was forced to let go.

Tanner lunged, anger flowing from him like heat. There was a sharp cracking sound, as a window shattered, and Tanner looked up to see an armed officer.

Tanner turned and made for the kitchen.

·   ·   ·

Lane felt pain in his stomach. He staggered up and looked in the direction Tanner had gone. The hallway was narrow. He made his way along, steadying himself as he picked up speed. He came to the end and saw boarded-up windows.

Where was he?

Lane looked left and right. There seemed to be no way out. He touched the planks of wood across one window, and realized that they were joined together. They were hinged, and could be opened like a door. He pulled them back.

He saw an open window and the garden beyond. In the distance there was blood on the ground. Lane reached for his radio, climbed through the window and ran. There was crackling and interference, and Lane glanced at the radio screen.

"Damn."

Droplets of blood on the concrete formed a trail. Lane looked ahead and saw movement by the line of trees in the distance. He ran faster and noted the length of the garden. Something registered in his mind, something about its state.

He made it to the end and climbed through a break in the fence, cursing as his arms caught on branches. There was a road beyond – a narrow one with light traffic. Lane looked anxiously for Tanner. Had he taken a car?

On the opposite side of the road was a wall nearly six feet high, with trees growing over – Bushy Park.

Lane scanned the wall and saw a metal gate. Tanner was going through.

"Stop!"

Tanner flinched but continued. Lane ran into the road and a car was forced to stop. He made it through the gate, into the park. He was breathing heavily and felt pain in his chest. One or two people were walking past. They turned and stared.

Where are you? Lane looked further along and saw him. Tanner had increased his pace, running down the path which traced the edge of the park. There was heavy tree cover, and Lane looked left and right, trying to anticipate where Tanner would go. He failed to notice the young woman, by the pond. Tanner passed her, caught hold of her, and turned her round, so that she became a shield.

Lane came to a halt a few feet away. Tanner brought up his knife. His eyes were manic. His face was red, and all composure had gone.

"*I'll kill her! Let me go, or I'll kill her!*"

He angled the knife, pointing the tip to the side of the woman's neck.

Lane could feel pressure building in his head.

"It doesn't have to end this way. You *have* choices …"

Tanner wasn't listening. He began backing up, pulling the woman with him.

She suddenly seemed younger than she was. She looked at Lane, wanting to scream but not quite managing it. Tanner spun her around and pushed her into the pond. Lane looked on as Tanner fled.

CHAPTER
60

He reached forward and tried to help the woman. She was light, and Lane managed to pull her from the water. He didn't stop any longer. He looked up to see where Tanner was going.

"To the left," she said. "The path bends round – you can get out that way."

Lane straightened up and ran. How far ahead could he be? No more than fifty yards, surely?

Lane followed the path and tree cover gave way to a large, wide exit. He ran through and realized he was on the B-road again. There were residential houses ahead, pre-war, detached, with cars parked on the drives. The road was straight, and Lane was thankful for that. In the distance he could see Tanner. He shouted. Tanner heard and glanced back, reducing his pace. Lane sprinted and realized that the road wasn't coming to an end but bent sharply to the left.

Lane saw lines of parked cars, a grass verge with trees, and a steep embankment on the left that rose up. He began to slow down.

Tanner was no longer on the road but Lane could hear rustling, and looked up the embankment to see Tanner climbing. He was near the top. *Christ.* Lane looked at the slope. He began making his way up, holding on to tufts of grass and low-hanging branches. Tanner was younger and fitter, and it was beginning to show.

Lane looked to his right and saw a railway bridge, spanning the road. Was Tanner making for it? Tanner suddenly seemed to be in difficulty.

At the top of the embankment was fencing made out of wire, strung between concrete posts. Tanner was climbing through, but his size meant he had become stuck.

Lane managed to grab hold of Tanner's shirt and pulled. He felt heat and sweat, and Tanner kicked out, knocking Lane back.

Lane fell down the embankment and frantically reached out, grabbing hold of a tree root. Tanner made it through the gap. Lane groaned in pain, and his face darkened. He regained his balance and made his way back up. He forced himself through the gap Tanner had created.

Lane could hear the sound of gravel. Ahead of him, stretching in either direction, were railway tracks. He saw several sets of rails, and a live rail, and watched as Tanner made his way across. Where was he going? Was he headed for the other side, and the embankment down to the road?

Tanner stopped in the middle of the tracks. He had his back to Lane, and paused for a long moment before turning round. He was breathing heavily and his hair was a mess. Perspiration was running down one side of his face. The chase had taken more out of him than Lane though.

"You shouldn't have stopped me," said Tanner. "Stein and the others – they deserved it. They had it all … I had nothing." Tanner wondered if his life could have been different – if he could have made different choices. Family … stability … could he have had those things?

Lane watched the swift play of emotions on his face.

"You're not taking me," Tanner whispered, and stepped on to the live rail.

CHAPTER
61

Lane was sitting by the road below the railway bridge. He felt exhausted but his breathing was slowing, and he checked himself over. He saw Perez approaching, followed by an armed response officer.

"They're trying to shut the power off now," Perez explained. "How're you holding up?"

Lane gestured up to the railway track. "Better than him, I guess." He tapped his jacket pockets. "… times like this I wish I still smoked."

Lane was aware of forensic officers arriving, as well as paramedics. They were filling the residential road that he had pursued Tanner down.

"There's a railway station about 150 yards that way." Lane pointed to his right.

Perez nodded. "I've sent a couple of officers up. They've already stopped all trains."

"The public'll appreciate that." Lane felt past his best. "Give me a hand up, will you?" He reached out and Perez slowly pulled him up, straining under his weight.

"You don't look too bad" said Perez. In his mind, Lane had moved faster than many younger officers.

"I wouldn't pass the police physical. I didn't anticipate having to run this far." He wanted to sit down somewhere more comfortable. "The man back at the house, is it Riley?"

"It is. I've got paramedics checking him over. He doesn't seem to be in bad shape. A bit dehydrated, and it looks as if he's been beaten, but I think he'll pull through. Do you want to speak to him?"

"All in good time." Lane made to walk and realized that he was limping. *How had that happened?* He put an arm around Perez's shoulder and leaned in.

"Something else," said Perez. Crime scene officers had moved behind them, setting up a cordon around the embankment. "Your least-favourite journalist is here, and Travers is on his way."

Lane felt philosophical.

"Such is life …"

"A pair of well-oiled weasels," said Perez, under his breath.

Lane was surprised and glanced at his junior. "You're turning into me: I'm impressed. Come on. We've got work to do."